BLOOD AND TEARS

By Jamie Zakian

BLOOD AND TEARS

Limitless Publishing, LLC
Kailua, HI 96734
www.limitlesspublishing.com

Formatting: Limitless Publishing

ISBN-13: 978-1-68058-949-8
ISBN-10: 1-68058-949-0

Dedication

For the dreamers, the thinkers, the lovers, the
fighters, and all the freaks like me.

Chapter One

"God damn, motherfucker," Sasha grumbled to herself over the thump of her boots on concrete steps. After a year and a half of trolling around Queens, she should be used to the stench of ass crack and exhaust, except she wasn't. That's when the invisible vice around her heart tightened, again. Every afternoon, when Sasha stumbled from Rosalie's apartment, a pout snuck onto her lips. The idea of leaving her beautiful girl to stroll along dirty streets didn't bring the frown. It was the scenery. Birds didn't chirp in the city, leaves never rustled, and frosty blue eyes weren't leering at her. No, not the eyes. It was the mockingbird's call she missed, totally.

Sasha popped a cigarette in her mouth as she walked down the sidewalk. Before she could reach for her zippo, a hand landed on her shoulder. She gripped onto a thick wrist, leaned back, and flipped a solid body over her shoulder. The chump landed on his back with a thud, and Sasha pressed down on his neck with her boot. A gust of wind blew her hair. Her brown waves blocked her view of the asshole's shock, but that didn't stop her from twisting the guy's arm.

"Sasha," a low voice rang out.

That soft roll of a smooth southern tongue, even muffled under Sasha's foot, sent a spike to her chest. Her fingers trembled, and the arm in her clutch slipped away.

"Vinny?" Sasha scurried back, gawking as Vinny peeled himself off the dirty sidewalk. The look on his face was unreadable but Jesus Christ, she forgot how the sun shined a bit brighter when he was near. It took all she had to keep from diving into his arms. "I—"

Vinny rushed forward, and Sasha shrank down. He wrapped his arms around her, holding tight, pulling her into a warmth she thought had extinguished long ago.

"You fucking bitch."

She couldn't tell if anger or sarcasm trembled Vinny's voice, and she didn't care. Her head had found a piece of home once Sasha laid it against the familiar ridges of Vinny's chest. All the things she'd convinced herself were gone came flooding back, and she didn't want to let go.

Vinny wrenched back from the tight embrace then shoved Sasha. She bumped into some dude with a briefcase who had the nerve to call *her* a dumb bitch. "Hey, fuck you too, buddy!" she yelled at the guy's back. Her middle finger went up, spanning the sidewalk of rude-ass people flowing around her.

"Guess my postcard got lost in the mail," Vinny sneered, and Sasha turned back to face him.

"I don't—"

"Look at you!" Vinny said, swatting at Sasha's feathered hair. "I almost didn't recognize you."

Sasha rolled her head to the side. Streaks of blonde cut through her brown hair, spilling down the sleeve of her flannel shirt. "My girl's a hairdresser."

"Your girl?"

There it was, the reason Sasha left her holler. The mockery those she loved most made of her life had begun. Pretty surprising, that it took Vinny five whole minutes to ridicule her. She'd tag his ass with a left hook and storm off, except he looked so tired, so beat down already.

"You wanna grab a beer?" She gestured to the bar behind her, and Vinny rolled his eyes.

***

Sasha picked at the label of her bottle, stealing glances at Vinny. He didn't fidget like her or shift his gaze. A hardness lingered in his eyes, one that hadn't dwelled there before, and the hardness was fixed on her.

"So," Sasha took a swig off her beer, looking into the corner, "how you been?"

Vinny's elbows hit the table, rattling a little bowl of pretzels. "Really? How the fuck do you think I've been? I thought you were dead."

3

He looked pissed. This would require some hardcore explaining, which called for a big fat joint. In one swift move, Sasha pulled a joint from her front pocket and lit her zippo. For the first time since they'd sat at that tiny table in the back of this dive bar, Vinny tore his eyes from Sasha to glance around.

"It's cool," Sasha said through a puff of smoke. "They don't fuck with me here." She held out the joint, and Vinny looked away. "Whatever." And back into her mouth the doobie went, doing its magic to hide the guilt in her stare.

"Dez knew you split but I fought for you, actually fought him for you. I had them all convinced Dante took you." Vinny's eyes glossed over for just a second before fury rushed in to cloud their shine with rage. "How could you do this to me, to your kid?"

"My kid died in the cellar, with everything else."

"No!" Vinny jumped up, sending his chair to the floor in a crash. "Your soul's the only thing that died in the cellar." He slammed his palm down on the table, rocking it on its legs. "Tyler asks about you all the time."

Sasha looked at the bar and the man who was already on the phone.

"Sit down, Vinny."

"Fuck you, Sasha."

Vinny turned and walked out the front door, leaving a picture on the table. A cute child's deep brown eyes lured her stare, much like a train wreck.

"Damn kid," Sasha said, gliding her finger along the glossy photo. "You got big." The kid still had the same goofy smile as that baby she saw in the last picture, the one that was seared into her eyelids, the one that haunted her every night once her head hit the pillows.

Sasha rose from her chair, butting the joint out in the ashtray. This time, she took the picture with her when she left.

***

Laughter flowed in waves as the doors to Fat Tonys swung open. Sasha strolled through the restaurant, not one head turning her way. The glitz no longer held a sense of awe. In fact, it kind of sickened her. There were people struggling to survive this city's wrath everywhere she looked and these assholes just sat at their hand-carved tables, chuckling like clowns while nibbling on their sixty-dollar-a-piece plates.

Sasha walked up the small stairs across from the bar, nodding to the boys around the long table before taking her seat.

"Where you been, Sasha?" Enzo, the Don's right-hand man, asked, which meant Antonio wanted to know.

Sasha steered her gaze to the head of the table, which wasn't easy with the waitress leaning over her shoulder to set down a glass of wine. "I ran into an old friend, from back home."

"Really?" Antonio said. He sounded surprised, but the hard stare hinted otherwise.

"Yeah. The dude must've used his spidey senses to track me down, 'cause I was real careful."

"Huh." Antonio tapped his cigarette in a crystal ashtray, holding an icy stare. "Maybe the boys should hang around with you for a while."

Heads nodded around the table, except for Sasha's. "That's not necessary."

"But still. I'd feel better if Marco and Ricci tailed you 'til this all blows over."

The chair squeaked as Sasha settled back. These people, her new crew, had never made her feel like an object, until now. There must be something about her that made people assume they could own her. Hell, a neon sign could be flashing *Vulnerable Girl for Rent* above her head and she wouldn't see it beyond the cloud of smoke, which wafted from the freshly lit joint in her mouth.

Antonio cocked his head, and the made men at the table quickly made their way to the bar. Antonio's shifty eyes, the tap, tap, tap on the ashtray's edge, spread ice beneath Sasha's skin. The Don was nervous. People who strummed the Don's nerves usually disappeared, and they were the only two people at the table. Antonio waved Sasha over, and despite her body's strong reluctance she slid down the row of chairs to his side.

"I got the medical report back this morning," Antonio said, turning to face Sasha. "There's no doubt about it, you're a Lazzari."

This wasn't news to Sasha. One step inside Antonio's house and she saw what could've been her pictures lining the walls. Except it wasn't her dark stare in those photos, it was Dante's.

"The test was just a formality," Antonio said with only sincerity. "I didn't need it. I could see my

6

brother the moment I laid eyes on you." He took Sasha's hand, his chubby fingers squeezing lightly. "I know what it was like for you, growing up. That's not the kind of family you'll find here. You're not bound to this place, to me. If you miss your people, you're free to go home. And if you wanted to come back, you'd be welcomed with open arms."

Antonio's words, and the affection behind them, felt foreign. There had to be an angle; Sasha just couldn't see it yet.

"Would you like to know where your trucker friend is staying?" Antonio asked, leaning back in his padded chair.

"You know?"

"Of course. An eighteen-wheeler can't roll through my city without me knowing."

Sasha didn't want to know where Vinny was staying. One more glimpse of Vinny and she'd hightail it back to the hills, begging to be punished for crimes she hadn't committed. Her gaze fell. Her blonde waves shrouded her view, blocked out the bobble-headed grins of the fools dining below their private section and the sexy waitress who was weaving between tables. Behind her golden streaks, she could be a different person. Sasha Lazzari, a woman to be feared, respected.

The picture peeked out from her breast pocket and she jolted back, sitting up straight.

Antonio's hand landed atop Sasha's, rubbing gently. "What is it?"

Of all the people Sasha had met in her entire life, the man beside her was the only one she'd ever really trusted. Slowly, and without looking, she pulled the picture from her pocket and handed it to him.

"Is this your son?"

Since a massive lump took up residence in Sasha's throat, she nodded.

"My great-nephew. He's one handsome little man. Has your eyes."

"Let's hope that's the only thing he has of mine."

Antonio chuckled, passing the photo back. Sasha didn't look at the picture, didn't have to. That kid's face had properly etched itself into her brain.

"What's his name?"

"Tyler, I think." Sasha squirmed in her seat, in her own skin. "I just left him. I never…I didn't…"

"You know," Antonio slid a pack of cigarettes in front of Sasha, "I had a brother who walked away from his kid to give her a better shot at life, and it worked out for the best in my opinion. But in your situation, I wonder. Is it best for that child to grow up without his mother?"

Boots thumped up the small steps, interrupting Sasha's whirling thoughts. She turned in her chair and AJ, the only person who could walk up to this table at this moment and not get whacked, sat beside her. AJ had no respect for tradition, which was a problem, as he was the Don's only son.

"You were attacked?" AJ asked. His question could easily be mistaken as a declaration of war.

"No!" Sasha said, her glare much harder than her bark.

"It's all over the street that one of our guys was threatened in the middle of Joey's pub. I wanna know who this jackoff is and make an example of him."

"Calm down," Antonio said, lifting his hand.

"No, pop! We can't let shit like this stand, or people will think we're getting soft."

"No one's moving on our territory!" Antonio yelled, stopping the clink of glasses and mindless chatter in the entire restaurant. The tone of Antonio's voice, the curl of his large fist, shriveled Sasha's spine. Judging by the sudden hush in the room, it affected everyone else as well.

Antonio's wide, tense body loosened, and as if on cue the background noise kicked on. "Some of Sasha's family is in town, for a visit."

"Great," AJ muttered. "More hillbilly fucks littering the streets."

"Hey!" Antonio's fist hit the table, quaking everything in the area, including Sasha. "You need to show your cousin more respect."

"She's not my cousin."

AJ's finger wagged in Sasha's face, and she leaned back. It was either that or grab the butter knife and start slicing.

"Yes, she is. I got the final test results this morning. That makes her an underboss of this family, your equal."

"That's bullshit!" In a fit of stomping feet, AJ scampered off, followed by his trio of thugs.

Once the spoiled brat, and future leader of the Lazzari family, stomped from sight, Sasha turned to face Antonio. "I'm sorry. I didn't mean to cause trouble. You can tell him I don't want to be an underboss."

9

"I'm afraid that's not how it works. Your father controls half this city. It's your responsibility to look after his interests until he gets back. AJ will just have to find something else to do from now on."

Sasha couldn't orchestrate a more fucked day if she tried. She just stole her brand new cousin's turf, which was a little more serious than melting his G.I. Joes, though it left the same foul stench. If ever there was a reason to split…she glanced at Antonio, catching a light smirk.

"You did this on purpose," she said, leaning onto the table.

Antonio's face cleared, but his gaze still held a glimmer of amusement.

"You knew if you laid down the weight, I'd bolt."

A chuckle heaved Antonio's belly. "You might not have the jacket on anymore, but the patch said it all. You are a runner."

That shook Sasha to the core, made her want to prove him wrong. She crossed her arms, held herself tight, but couldn't replicate the embrace that clutched her body only an hour ago.

"Where's my crew staying at?"

Antonio nodded, sliding a folded piece of paper in front of Sasha.

Chapter Two

Since Sasha couldn't shake Marco and Ricci, she made them drive her to the Travelers Motel. Unfortunately, she'd only had time to smoke one joint before they got there. She needed at least three more. Her gaze locked on Vinny's door, and a little bit of vomit crept up the back of her throat.

"You want us to go knock for you?" Marco snickered from the front seat.

A slew of obscene-laced grumbles trickled from Sasha's mouth as she opened her door. Once outside and surrounded by the twinkle of city lights, her muscles uncoiled just a tad. It was enough for her sorry ass legs to function, so she pushed them forward.

She stood in front of Vinny's door like an idiot, her arm rising and dropping. The boys in the car were probably getting a kick out of this one. "Fuck this. I'm out."

The door flew open, and Vinny's grumpy face filled Sasha's view. Her smile spread wide, even though his glare deepened. She'd wrap her arms around him, feel his body against hers, if she didn't think he'd toss her ass to the filthy pavement.

"How'd you find me?" Vinny asked, eyeing the men in the car behind Sasha.

"This is my city."

"Your city," Vinny snorted, hurling a spiteful glare.

The flare in Vinny's gaze was too cute. Sasha had to look away and force back her rising grin. "How'd you find me?"

Vinny leaned against the doorway, shrugging. "What do you want?"

"World peace, equality for all."

"I'm serious."

"So am I." Sasha reached for Vinny's hand and he pulled away, so she snatched his arm. "What I really want is for you not to hate me."

"You took off, started a fancy new life with city clothes, forgot all about me."

"I never forgot you." Sasha glided her hands to Vinny's neck, twisted her fingers into his hair. "I picked up the phone every night to call you, but I couldn't dial."

"Why?"

Vinny's breath flowed over Sasha's lips, drawing her closer. Their chests rubbed together, sending sparks that finally kick-started her defunct heart.

"If I heard your voice, I would've came running back and I can't go there. Everywhere I'd look, I'd see her." The her could have been her mother, Candy, or the teenage girl she could never be again. There were too many ghosts lingering in her holler, too many reasons to stay away to pick just one.

A tear snuck loose, rolling along Sasha's cheek. Vinny pulled her close, and their lips connected. His entire body trembled, unless it was the quake of her own muscles ricocheting into him. She ran her fingertips along the ripples of his chest. The tongue probing her mouth, rough hands gripping her waist, pushed her limits of self-control to the brink of nonexistent.

Sasha grabbed onto Vinny's belt, and he shoved her away.

"No!" he yelled, the pain in his voice a sliver of the pain warping his face. "You can't do that. Not even the great Sasha Ashby can fuck her way out of this one."

"That's…" *rude, right, a stab to the confidence*, "not who I am anymore."

"You changed your name, to what?" Vinny didn't look surprised, more like he was calling her out.

"It doesn't matter."

"Why don't you wanna tell me? Embarrassed?" Vinny pulled Sasha forward, patting her down. "Where's your wallet?"

"Stop!" She elbowed him in the gut, and a gun cocked behind her. "Guys, it's cool." She turned, staring down the barrel of AJ's revolver.

"Step aside, Sasha. This punk's getting a lesson on how to treat the Lazzari family."

The pathetic goons who probably followed AJ to the bathroom chuckled and cracked their knuckles. These guys didn't know Sasha very well, ain't seen her mad yet. Vinny stepped back. Smart guy. He could tell she was about two throat slashes away from a huge mistake.

Sasha walked forward until the gun pressed into her ribcage. "No."

A shotgun cocked, and one of Vinny's doppelganger prospects crept into the light, aiming double barrels at them all.

"Let's go," Sasha said, pushing AJ into his lackeys.

The prospect backed away, keeping his gun on them as Sasha shuffled the men toward the parking lot. Once AJ holstered his revolver, she looked back at Vinny. "You need to get the fuck out of this city, right now." Her eyes begged for him to listen and pleaded for forgiveness. "Please."

Vinny grabbed a backpack off the bed and pushed his prospect, who still held the shotgun tight, toward the semi across the lot. "We're gone."

Sasha watched Vinny climb into the driver's seat of her father's old International, waiting for him to look back. He didn't. That old motor whistled to life, sending chills down her spine, and Vinny didn't look her way once. Sasha turned from the whoosh of airbrakes, the gleam of a trailer-less semi rolling by. Those things would only cloud her mind, land her at the bottom of the Hudson.

"Look, AJ—"

"You might have my father fooled, but you're no Lazzari."

"Dante is my father. I don't like it any more than you do, trust me."

AJ inched forward, bumping up against Sasha's chest. "I'd kill you in a heartbeat if I could."

14

"That's sweet." Sasha patted AJ on the shoulder, savoring the frenzy spread across his face. "I appreciate you handling Dante's interests while he's away. I'd appreciate it more if you'd continue to do that."

"Fucking hilarious," AJ opened the door to his black sedan, hurling a sharp glare, "how you think I need your permission."

"What the fuck is your problem?" Sasha grabbed onto AJ's door, stopping him from slinking into the car. "Are you ornery because your father prefers my company, or just disgusted with yourself because you wanna fuck your cousin?"

AJ rocked in place, his cheeks shuffling through every shade of red. "Nasty, inbred, hillbilly fuck."

Sasha blew a kiss, backing away. A smirk lingered on her lips as AJ dropped into the passenger seat. An engine revved, and she stumbled back from the peel of wheels taking off. AJ was one lucky asshole. If she didn't have shit to do, he would have been the one getting a lesson on what happened to a person who pissed off a nasty inbred hillbilly fuck. Sasha walked to her own awaiting sedan and slid into the backseat.

"That was some premium looking out guys," she said, her stare shifting between the two men in the front.

Marco shrugged, starting the car. "Boss told me to look out for you. Boss told me to look out for AJ. What am I supposed to do?"

Smart guy. Must be how he'd survived this life for so long. Sasha should take a page from Marco's book, lay low, see how it all played out, except she was a fucking idiot.

"Take me to Tony's house."

"It's late," Marco said, the way one would dismiss a child.

Leather crinkled as Sasha leaned back, crossing her arms. One glimpse in the rearview mirror and Marco hit the brakes, busting a U-turn.

***

It must have been the lack of weed because here Sasha stood, at the boss' home, unannounced, past eight. Like a fool who wanted to eat a bullet, she pressed the doorbell. Before the last chime could sound, the door flew open.

"I've been expecting you," Antonio said, holding out his arm to invite Sasha in.

"Really?" Sasha kept her stare low, hurrying past the pictures of dark eyes that lined the hall.

"Yeah. You're here to say goodbye."

Sasha turned, catching a set of those dark eyes in real life. Letting people down had become the norm in her life, but that didn't take away the sting of the act. "I'm sorry. I disappointed you."

"No." Antonio smiled, traipsing toward Sasha with his arms out. "I'm proud of you. Family is what matters."

A soft hug wrapped around Sasha's body, holding tight. It was a different kind of embrace, warm and inviting, unlike any she'd experienced before.

"Come back soon." Antonio drew back, rubbing the sides of Sasha's arms before drifting away.

"Even if it's just to visit."

"I will. Thanks, Tony."

"There's going to be a lot of heartbroken women in Queens," he said, opening the front door. "This is yours." He grabbed a briefcase from the small table beside the door, holding it out.

"What's this?"

"Fifty G's. Your earnings, for the work you've done the last seventeen months."

"I can't." Sasha waved her hands, backing into the doorway. "You've already done too much, getting me out here, setting up my physical therapy."

"It's yours." Antonio shoved the case into Sasha's hand. "Besides, I have a lot of spoiling to make up for."

After another hug, Sasha left the closest thing to family she'd ever grasped. To put distance between herself and Antonio could only be for the best, since the things she cherished always ended bloody.

***

Vinny

"That was...intense," Cash said, sparking a joint.

Vinny gripped the steering wheel, barreling down on the gas. He could strangle Otis right now for making him bring backup. If Cash wasn't sitting in the passenger seat, he would've pretended this jumblefuck never happened. He'd go back home and admit Dez was right, that Sasha was dead. Then he'd drink 'til that bitch was washed from his memories.

"Yeah," Vinny mumbled, easing off the gas just a tad. "Good thing you didn't have to use the shotgun. The spray would've hit me."

"I got slugs in there." Cash leaned against his armrest, holding out the joint. "But I was talking about that kiss."

A groan burst from Vinny's mouth as he snatched the joint. This was fucking great. Fucking Otis was a dick and a half.

"Don't tell Dez about that shit," Vinny said in a harsher tone than he intended. "I got enough problems with him." He hit the joint twice before he decided he wasn't passing it back. "In fact, don't tell anybody. Not your brother, cousin, Otis, not even your fucking priest."

"I won't." Cash squirmed in his seat, must've figured out he wasn't getting the joint back. "It's just…" More fidgets, followed by the tap of boots, erupted from the passenger seat. "I didn't know Sasha was crazy in love with you."

That brought a snicker to Vinny's lips. For providing him seconds of comical relief, Cash earned the joint back. "She's not in love with me. Sasha can only love Sasha."

"Uh, no. The way she looked at you, it was movie-type shit."

Dumb bastard didn't get it. They'd never see Sasha again. Well, maybe at her funeral, which would be soon judging by her new friends.

"At least we got to see the big city," Cash muttered, handing Vinny a stub of a joint.

Vinny peeked in the rearview mirror, glimpsing

the twinkle of city lights. Sure, it looked nice, from the outside. Inside, it was cold, dirty, ugly. The perfect place for Sasha.

***

Sasha

It only took five minutes in a stairwell and an entire joint for Sasha to work up the nerve to open Rosalie's door. She walked into the apartment, stopped short by the scent of garlic bread and weed, her favorite combination.

Rosalie popped her head out from the kitchen, a smile on her cherry-red lips. "You're home late. Bad day?" Teased hair flowed as Rosalie rushed forward, peeling the flannel shirt from Sasha's shoulders.

"Yeah, it's been…different. Listen, babe—"

"Oh, no." Rosalie pushed Sasha onto the couch, climbing atop her lap. "You think I'm letting you out the door to play gangster with them boys all night?" Soft skin glided along Sasha's cheek, a tongue grazing her bottom lip. "Not until you play with me first."

"Rosy—"

"Don't Rosy me."

Rosalie unbuttoned her tight leather top, letting loose the luscious breasts trapped within, and Sasha's mind went blank. Luckily, her hands and mouth knew what to do. She gripped onto the ass riding her lap, running her lips over Rosalie's hard nipples. The sweetest gasp flowed from the woman in her arms. It drove Sasha's teeth to bite down on soft flesh, bringing much louder moans forth to tickle her ears. There was something, something she came here to do besides make a woman cum. Whatever the fuck it was, it would have to wait. Tan skin shuddered under her touch, tight pants peeled off to reveal lacy panties, and those long legs opened up to her.

Sasha licked a path from knee to thigh, biting every time Rosalie squirmed. A light punishment, for not taking it. She clutched onto Rosalie's hips, pulling her to the edge of the couch. A thin strip of lace panties stood between the tip of her tongue and the heat just beyond it. Stupid fabric, thinking it could hold her back. Sasha pushed the panties aside, sinking deep between Rosalie's thighs.

Chapter Three

About halfway through a cigarette, Sasha's brain clicked back on. On a scale of one to asshole, she was a triple dick. The most uncool thing to do was fuck a chick then leave town, and that's exactly what was about to go down. At this point, the only option was to get the hell out of this apartment as quick as possible.

Sasha scooted away from Rosalie's wandering hands, pulling on her pants. "Look, Rosy." She kept her back turned, dressing at lightning speeds. "I gotta leave the city for a while. There's no point in you waiting around for me, since I don't know when or if I'll be back."

A peek over the shoulder revealed one furious woman, and Sasha darted her eyes away.

"No, you didn't. You did not just fuck me then break up with me."

Rosalie jumped up off the couch, and Sasha scurried back. It was a goddamn stroke of luck she'd already loaded her gun in its holster, because that feisty Italian broad was the shooting type.

When Rosalie hurried into the bedroom, Sasha headed for the front door. Knives, bullets, pot and pans could start flying at any moment, and she was smack-dab in the danger zone. She didn't even get a chance to grip the door's knob before Rosalie stormed back into the room. The woman held no weapons, just an armful of cargo pants and flannel shirts.

"Here's your shit, bitch." Rosalie opened the window and tossed the clothes out. "You can take all the crap you bought me too!" Out went the stereo receiver, then the VCR. Rosalie struggled to lug the TV to the window, and Sasha ran in front of her.

"Come on, babe." Sasha took the TV. Big mistake, because Rosalie used her now free hands to toss slaps.

"Babe! I'm not your babe."

Sasha dropped the TV back on the stand, looking out the window just in time to catch some dude rifling through her stuff. "Hey!" She lifted the end of her shirt, flashing the butt of her gun. "Don't touch that shit." The douchebag scampered off, and Sasha turned back to face Rosalie, just in time to duck out of the path of an ashtray that sailed toward her head. Glass shattered, which was Sasha's cue to make a swift exit.

Rosalie latched onto her arm before she could get one foot across the threshold.

"Don't go. I love you, Sasha. Please, don't leave."

Rosalie's arms circled Sasha's waist as she skated her lips on Sasha's neck, but the desperation beneath her kisses soured their sweetness. She pried Rosalie's hands from her body, heading for the stairs. "Goodbye, Rosy."

"Fuck you! Whatever redneck skank you're running to, I hope she's worth it."

The woman's whiny city screech echoed down the stairwell, flowing over the random shouts to shut the fuck up. Sasha stepped onto the sidewalk, taking a deep breath. One whiff of fresh air was all she wanted, but a piss-scented breeze was what she got. An endless supply of assholes and an unending reek of funk. The spirit of this city was strong enough to creep inside a person, taint their soul with its dirtiness.

"Not me," Sasha yelled to herself, like all the other crazy people on the streets of Queens. She grabbed her clothes off the sidewalk, throwing them in the bed of an old pickup she'd bought for three-hundred bucks. The picture tapped her chest as she climbed into the truck. This time, aside from the standard scraping of her heart, the photo stirred a frenzy of excitement in her stomach. Sasha pulled the picture from her pocket, wedging it into the dashboard. That kid's silly smile was infectious, sticking to her own lips as she drove from the concrete jungle.

***

Dez

A semi's rumble shook the clubhouse floor, and Dez jumped up from the desk. His hip bumped a chair, knocking it to the floor as he dashed to the window. He hated that thump in his chest. Hope swelled every time his brother took that rig out, crashing down in an unbreathable wave of sorrow when he returned without Sasha. Maybe this time, it would be different.

Wood creaked as Dez dug his nails into the windowsill. A small chance existed. Sasha could've been taken, held against her will this entire time. The larger odds that she ran off and Vinny lured her back were just as good. At this point, he didn't give a fuck. Seventeen months, twenty-two days, and five hours had passed since he'd gotten the call that she'd woken up. He might finally be able to look into her eyes again.

Vinny's boots hit the gravel, and Dez saw that look. The look didn't reflect the usual mix of hope and disappointment. His brother held a broken gaze. There wouldn't be any more searches. Sasha wasn't with him, and she wouldn't be coming back.

A sharp ache pierced Dez's chest. His tight shoulders dropped into a slump, his body crashing against the wall. Tears clouded the backroom from sight, blurred the glossy table that had been long abandoned.

"What's wrong, Daddy?"

Dez stood up straight, wiping his eyes. "Nothing, buddy." Looking down at his boy almost broke his shit to pieces. All he saw was Sasha in that cute little face. It didn't stop him from scooping Tyler into his arms and holding tight. "Uncle Vinny's back. Let's go say, s'up."

***

Special Agent Philip Daniels

"It worked." Agent Daniels hung up the phone, grinning at the director. "She left the city."

"It was smart, to tip the Archer kid off to her location."

A compliment from the director of the Federal Bureau of Investigations himself, and a glass of scotch to boot. Daniels reeled in his glee, keeping it professional. This case would make his career, change his life, earn him back the respect of his wife and children. A RICO case, the biggest he'd ever seen, spanning almost every criminal organization in America. It had already claimed the life of one agent. He'd be famous for closing the Ashby case. They'd make movies about him, casting Mel Gibson. It wasn't a far stretch, in his opinion.

"Now what? Should I pick her up?" Daniels asked, straining to keep the eagerness from his voice.

"No." Smoke wafted around the director's face as he puffed on a stogie. "Wait until she gets on the compound. That way, we'll have an excuse to comb through the entire wretched place, look for our missing agent."

"Don't worry, sir. If there's any trace of agent Prescott, a tooth, a speck of blood, I'll find it."

***

Vinny

After a truck ride from hell and a visit to a place that might have actually been Hell, all Vinny wanted was a pile of joints and a fresh bottle of whiskey. He wasn't gonna get it. Before his ass even left the semi's seat, Otis and Kev were on the clubhouse porch.

Vinny jumped from the truck, eyeing his room above the garage. Otis and Kev closed in, and he almost bolted for the stairs.

"Uncle Vinny!"

Tyler ran across the lot, pushing past Otis. That little guy's bright smile, his stubby legs peddling across the lot, wiped the pain from Vinny's mind. He knelt down, and Tyler nearly mowed him over. Tyler clinging to his neck was much better than a pile of joints, by far.

"You made it back in time!" Tyler said, squirming out of Vinny's probably too tight hug.

"You didn't think I'd miss your birthday, did ya?"

Dez pushed his way to the front of the small crowd that now surrounded Vinny. "What happened?"

Vinny stood, but he couldn't lift his gaze. They were all staring at him, he could feel it. What an idiot he'd been, convincing them to hold hope, convincing himself. Now they all were waiting for good news, and he didn't have anything but shit to say.

On the first attempt at speech, Vinny almost told them Sasha was dead except that lie would only benefit Sasha and destroy everyone else. Well fuck that, and fuck Sasha.

Cash took Tyler by the hand, tugging lightly. "Come on, little man. Show me the cake the girls made for you."

The second Tyler slipped into the clubhouse, Dez grabbed onto Vinny's arm. "Sasha's dead, isn't she?"

"Nah. She's great, living it up in the city." Vinny's words came out in a sneer. It would feel like shit to trash the woman he'd wasted most of his life chasing, except he'd lost the ability to feel a long time ago.

Without a word, Otis turned and walked toward the clubhouse.

"Are you sure?" Kev asked, managing to look more confused than he sounded.

"No. I'm making shit up, asshole. Yeah, I'm sure! I talked to her myself, right before she had her new friends toss me out the city at gunpoint."

For the first time since coming home, Vinny looked at Dez. He expected sadness, maybe even a bit of agony, but didn't anticipate to find a face full of rage, aimed at him.

"You..." Dez said through clenched teeth. He balled his big fist, again and again, before aiming it Vinny's way.

Vinny stumbled back as Dez slammed his knuckles into the semi's door. "I wanted to let her the fuck go." He drew his fist back from the dented metal. A stream of blood flew from his now busted skin as he pointed at Vinny. "Not you. You had to keep chasing whispers of her name, spreading hope, making me believe she'd be back. You had no right."

This would be the point where Vinny started hurling insults then punches. It should be, but the fire never ignited in his veins.

"Sorry," Vinny muttered, brushing past Dez and heading for the garage. He'd shout, swing, defend himself, if he had a leg to stand on. Dez was right. He'd wasted his time, his life. Four years of waiting for Sasha to wake up, damn near two more tracking her coward-ass down, and all the nights before that they'd spent together, just to have her spit in his face. Sasha was her mother's daughter all right. A user, abuser, an intoxicating drug that cloaked its destruction under guises of love. He should've seen it sooner. Now that he did, blue skies seemed gray and the gentle breeze stung his skin.

Vinny opened the door to his room, grumbling at the sight of bare skin. Usually, a buck naked bleached bimbo was the ideal end to a long road trip. Usually. Today was an alone-time kind of day. One of those smash everything that reflected his image days, and company would distract from that fun.

"Not now." Vinny left his door open to make it easier for Crystal to leave.

"Bad trip?"

Instead of reaching for her clothes, Crystal groped at Vinny. She ran her hands through his hair, and he cringed. All he could feel was Sasha's fingers tickling his flesh, Sasha's lips teasing his mouth.

"Stop!" Vinny grabbed Crystal by the wrists,

pushing her away.

"Okay." Crystal's grabby hands came back, groping his chest. She pushed Vinny onto the bed. "Just sit down for a sec." She plucked a joint from the ashtray, lit it up, and slid it between Vinny's lips. "Let me help you unwind real quick, then I'll split." Her knees hit the ground, and she fumbled with his belt. "You don't have to do anything. Just sit back and relax, baby."

What the hell? A blowjob would be pretty fucking awesome right now. He did deserve it, after such a stressful trip.

A chill took his body by surprise when lips wrapped around his cock. Vinny leaned back, scooting closer. It was gentleman-like, his way of helping out. Smoke flowed into his lungs as her tongue slithered up and down his flesh. His gaze drifted to the window, and a hint of blue seeped back into the gray sky.

Chapter Four

Sasha

Rusty springs squeaked as Sasha wiggled on her bench seat. For three hundred bucks, she didn't think this old Ford would make it past West Virginia, but here she was driving up the curvy road into her mountains. Rough stone sparkled in the headlights, the truck's old motor chugging up the steep incline. The strangest sensation spawned in her chest, one she didn't recognize. It wasn't fear, excitement, or dread. More like all that shit rolled up into one giant ball of what-the-fuck.

As the truck rounded a bend, its headlights shined off a newer section of guardrail. Sasha hit the brakes, staring at the gleam that didn't belong. It was too clean, didn't have enough dents to match the gray metal on either side of it. This was the spot, the place where her heart had permanently shattered, the dark hole of death that took her ability to love away.

Sasha opened the door, taking a deep breath of

crisp night air. The gentle breeze, which flowed so freely here, gave her the strength to walk to the edge of the road. Part of her actually expected to find a mangled Mack truck in the valley far below, spilling out bloody clumps of her beautiful girl.

"Candy," Sasha uttered, choking on the lump that hatched even bigger lumps inside her throat. If this lonely stretch of road wasn't made of rock and pavement, she'd torch the fuck out of it.

Her legs carried her back to the truck, thankfully, 'cause her mind was running a bit slow. It was the lack of weed. Only roaches littered the ashtray of her pickup, none big enough to smoke. Fuck, she was about to eat them little bastards. Her surprise homecoming would have to be executed semi-straight, which was only half-bad.

A slight tremble quaked Sasha's hands as she steered her pickup onto the compound. The same dented front gate sat wide-open, right beside the same faded sign rising above the chain-link fence. Ashby Trucking, also known as home sweet hell.

Halfway up the gravely hill, the thump of speakers tickled Sasha's ears and pushed a smile onto her lips. "Hasn't changed a lick," she muttered, driving through a maze of cars and rowdy people.

After finding a place to park and taking a few deep breaths, Sasha climbed from her truck. Chills spread through her body with every step she took. How strange to walk this property and feel as though she were treading where she didn't belong. Voices screamed in her head over the cheers wafting from the clubhouse. They told her to run, to leave this place if she loved the people in it. She

31

froze mid-step, just a few feet away from the clubhouse. Her crazy person voice could be right. She didn't even know why the fuck she came to this holler. It wasn't too late. She could hop in her truck, roll out, and nobody would be the wiser.

"Sasha?" Vinny said, his deep voice drowning out all other sounds.

A thickness clung to the air, suffocating Sasha for the briefest of seconds. She must be getting rusty, because she used to be able to sense Vinny's electric vibe before he snuck up behind her.

Sasha turned and looked into Vinny's shocked eyes. "You're not the only one who can make surprise visits, motherfucker."

"What are you doing here?" Vinny asked, pulling Sasha away from the clubhouse.

Sasha yanked her arm free, which earned her a hard glare. It would've been great if she could've started this off without fucking it up, but doing things proper wasn't her strong suit. "I, uh…didn't like the way things left off, between us."

Vinny didn't say a word, his brain might've conked out on him, which only added to the awkward vibe that surrounded them.

"So, big party," Sasha said, glancing at the clubhouse. "Is it a special occasion?" Based on Vinny's face, she didn't want to hear the answer. With her luck, she probably stumbled into the middle of his engagement party. Or worse, this could be Dez's wedding.

"It's Tyler's birthday," Vinny said, a tinge of spite trembling his voice.

"Oh shit! I didn't know. Fuck!" Sasha slapped

her forehead twice, but couldn't whack the feel of scumbag from her brain. A real mother would know their child's birthdate. Then again, the majority of *real mothers* weren't in a coma during their child's birth.

"I don't have a present." Sasha looked at her truck. She'd give the little dude that, but it was kind of shitty.

"I think seeing you would be enough of a present." Vinny scanned the crowd, looked at his feet, then up to the actual stars in the sky, pretty much anywhere else that wasn't her direction.

"Would the kid even know who I am? I don't want to confuse him on his birthday and everything."

"Tyler knows you. There's pictures of you everywhere, all over the clubhouse."

Vinny glanced at Sasha. It was only for a second, but she caught the affection in his stare.

"I tell him about you all the time," he said, so low his voice barely flowed over the music, "about the old shit we used to do."

"Oh God." Sasha chuckled, even though the thought scared the shit out of her. "The kid probably thinks I'm a psychopath. Where did you tell him I was?"

"He thinks you're sleeping, like a princess in a fairytale."

Sasha stepped in front of Vinny, taking his hand. "And I needed a prince to kiss me and wake me up?"

It was a tiny one, but Vinny smirked and Sasha savored every bit of warmth it radiated.

"Sasha!" Kev yelled, pushing his way down the clubhouse steps. "Holy fucking mother of shit. It is you!" He damn near tackled Sasha, scooping her up in a bear-hug. "I knew you'd be back. These guys are fucking stupid."

The moment Sasha's feet hit the ground, a light tug pulled at the end of her flannel. She looked down and big brown eyes stared up at her, shimmering in the moonlight.

"Mommy?"

The one word, spoken in a meek voice, took Sasha's quaking knees to the ground. "Hey, little dude," she choked out. The kid's goofy smile flashed, so much brighter in real life, and she chuckled. It was either laugh or burst into tears.

Tyler crashed against Sasha's chest, holding as tightly as tiny arms could, and the air burnt from her lungs.

"You woke up for my birthday," he said, his breath rustling her hair.

Sasha drew back, studying the kid's face. Dez would come along any second and literally toss her ass off the compound. She wanted to memorize every curve of Tyler's chubby cheeks, every sparkle in his deep eyes, before the child was gone from her life forever.

"What the fuck!"

Too late. The new prez caught her scent. Sasha rose with every intention to stand tall, but shrank down under Dez's stare.

"Look Daddy, Mommy woke up for my birthday," Tyler said, pulling Sasha closer to Dez.

"That's..." Dez scanned the crowd moving in

around them, stopping his glare on Vinny, "amazing, buddy."

"Best present ever!" Tyler tugged on Sasha's arm, yanking her toward the clubhouse. "Come on, I gotta show you my cake."

"No." Dez reached for Sasha, and Otis held him back.

"Let the kid have this." Otis turned to leer at Sasha. "It might be his only chance to meet his mother."

Sasha cringed. These fuckers did welcomes just like she remembered. She took Tyler by the hand, letting him pull her into the clubhouse.

***

Dez

Dez leaned against the bar, hawking every one of Sasha's moves. The smiles she slung at *his* son, her fingers running through *his* child's hair, it made him want to ram his fist into everything. That bitch had a lot of nerve. After what she put him through, to waltz back in here, without a hint of remorse on her face. If it wasn't Tyler's birthday, he'd wrap his fingers around her neck and squeeze.

Vinny stepped beside Dez, gawking at Sasha as she played all the people around her. They thought it was a miracle. Stupid assholes also thought she'd been transferred to a private facility, instead of running out on her family like a spineless coward.

"What the fuck?" Dez practically shouted without tearing his gaze from the heartless demon

35

of a woman who held tight to his son.

"I don't know," Vinny said, grabbing a bottle of whiskey. "I didn't think she'd come back, ever."

"What happened in New York, really?"

"I didn't fuck her."

"That's a surprise." Dez snatched the bottle from Vinny's hand, taking a long swig. He needed to get good and loaded to keep from wrecking shit, to keep from grabbing Sasha and holding her close, to keep from forgiving her for trampling his heart.

"She told me she thought about us," Vinny said, with more sadness than anger. "That she picked up the phone to call every night, but she was scared."

"Scared." Dez took another gulp just as long as the first, maybe longer. "Of what?"

"Probably your fist, shattering her face." Vinny snatched the bottle and walked into the crowd.

That's when it happened. Sasha's eyes cut through the sea of faces, shined beyond the clouds of smoke, and locked onto Dez's glare. A firestorm whirled inside his chest. The love he felt for her, which only grew deeper the harder he'd clung to her ghost, flared into overdrive. Her stare was like acid, ripping at the lining of his gut, tearing open old scars of abandonment. And the ache. His entire body ached for her touch, yearned to wrap itself in her feel, scent, taste. It all crashed down on him in waves. Love, hate, need. His mind spun faster than the room. He didn't know what to do. Hug her, hit her? God how he wanted to pull her into his arms, just as much as he wanted to toss her ass over the side of the mountain.

Dez balled his fingers so tight he feared his fists

would never unclench again. He needed to go, get some air, but there was no way in hell he was letting Tyler out of his sight.

A hand landed on Dez's shoulder, and his arm cocked back.

"Whoa!" Otis said, his grip on Dez's shoulder tightening. "You good?"

Otis's smooth voice sent a layer of ice to cool Dez's fiery mind. Sasha may have cast a spell on everybody else, but Otis would still ride with him on the fuck-Sasha bandwagon.

"No. I'm not fucking good." Dez turned to face Otis, resisting the urge to latch onto the guy in search of comfort. "What do I do?"

"What do you wanna do?"

"Man, not you too. Fuck." Dez dropped his stare to the faded wooden floor. Sasha had gotten to Otis, and she hadn't even talked to the man yet. He'd be next. Another sheep, in line for the con-man's slaughter.

Otis leaned against the bar, staring up at the ceiling. "I wanna take Sasha out back, beat the shit out of her," he said in a near growl. "I also wanna hug her and never let go."

"Yeah." Dez knew that feeling, times ten. "Can we do both?"

Otis chuckled, but Dez was eighty-five percent serious, maybe sixty-five percent. Dez stared across the room. Panic drove his heart to pound. His eyes found Tyler amid a group of children, and of course Sasha was gone. For a second, Dez thought it was a dream. Then he caught the look on Otis's face, broken, lost, tortured. It was like looking in a mirror.

"Guess we don't have to worry about it," Otis said in a grumble. "Bitch took off again."

Dez headed for the door. This time, if Sasha was going to leave him, she'd have to look him in the face before she did it.

***

Sasha

Sasha tried to keep up with that kid. One minute it was Hot Wheels, the next *The Dukes of Hazzard*, and a whole bunch of shit she didn't understand in-between. It didn't take Tyler a long time to find somebody else to ramble at, leaving her alone with Otis's and Dez's leers. By the looks of it, she was in for one hell of a beating. Those assholes better have fists wrapped in luck. She didn't roll with the punches anymore. She shot back.

Except she felt inclined to let them whoop her ass. It was this property. Something about this holler, and the people slithering on it, brought the little bitch out in her.

Sasha stepped onto the porch, eyeing her truck. Misery lingered on this mountain. It would consume her if she stayed. She thumped down the steps, stopping once she felt gravel under her boots. Tiny pebbles crunched under her fidgety foot, her gaze stuck on that old Ford.

"You just gonna split?" Dez called out, his voice sending both spikes and sparks into Sasha's chest. She'd replayed memories of him over a thousand times in her mind, but she got the smooth drawl of his voice all wrong. It was so much deeper, stronger, in real life.

"No, I—" Sasha turned to face Dez, struck by the gleam in his frosty-blue eyes. Even in the dark, hidden in shadows and soaked in hate, his gaze ran through her soul. "I was just gonna rummage through my truck for a joint."

Dez pulled a freshly rolled joint from his inside pocket, sat on the bench, and lit it up. Sasha crept back up the steps, making sure to keep far from Dez's reach. After about three hits and twenty glares, it became apparent he was going to smoke that joint to his head. The first punishment, with many more to come, most likely.

"What the fuck do you want, Sasha?"

Besides a hit of that joint, she had no goddamn clue. "I tried really hard to forget about this place, all the shit that happened. Then fucking Vinny showed up." She walked in front of Dez and leaned back against the porch's rail. "Vinny put a picture of that kid on the table. He'd gotten so big. To me it's only been like a year, but really over five have passed and...I don't know." Her knees quaked, wanting to buckle for optimal begging position. She didn't dare. Forgiveness was too good for her, and she wouldn't burden Dez to grant it.

"I can leave," Sasha said, pointing at her truck. "If you want."

"Holy fuck, I get a choice this time. We can go get *the kid*. Maybe he can pitch in on it too."

"Cute." Sasha dropped her gaze. This whole best behavior shit really sucked and could only last so long. "I didn't mean to leave for good. I got a room at the motel in town, plan on staying for a while."

"Oh. Okay." Dez rose from the bench, stepping in front of Sasha. "You think I'm stupid. The second I turn my back, you're gonna grab Tyler and run."

Sasha didn't think Dez was stupid, until now. That ridiculous idea never crossed her mind. What the fuck would she do with a kid, alone?

"I would never take Tyler from his family."

"What, you're not his family?"

"I'm a stranger to him. A face from a picture. He probably wouldn't dig me very much if he got to know me."

Dez snickered, but he didn't crack a smile. His face stayed blank, cold, hurt. "Why'd you leave? What did I do?"

Sasha wanted to hold Dez, attempt to soothe his broken soul, but fear of rejection held her hands to her sides. "Nothing. You don't understand. I woke up and my mom was dead, found out I had become a science project to grow a baby. I freaked. It wasn't real."

"The only thing that wasn't real was your love for me. The only person you ever loved died, and you rolled."

Dez walked away, and Sasha fought to keep from chasing him. To make a scene would only freak out the kid. It'd be the worst move to plea her case of I'm-not-a-fuck-up.

In a slump, Sasha walked off the porch.

"You just taking off?" Vinny barked from the clubhouse steps, and Sasha groaned. It took all she

40

had not to scream at the sky.

"I'm not leaving town. I'm staying—"

"I don't give a fuck where you're staying," Vinny said, his face twisted in anger. "Don't you think you should say goodbye to Tyler. You know, in case he never sees you again."

Sasha expected this type of treatment, even from Vinny, but Jesus Christ it hurt more than she could ever imagine.

"Look, Vinny. I—"

"If I would've known seeing my face would make you bolt, I wouldn't have wasted four years at your bedside."

"Well, maybe you should've lied to me. Told me everything was fine, then eased me into this future of horrors," Sasha yelled, before she could stop her jaw from flapping.

"I can't believe you're gonna stand here and blame me. You think I haven't beaten myself up over that while I was driving all over the country looking for you."

"Vinny, I'm…" Sasha grabbed Vinny's hand, and he yanked his arm back.

"Don't fucking touch me, and don't you dare apologize. It won't mean shit."

Sasha glanced around at the people pretending not to gawk as Vinny stomped away. Thankfully, Tyler was nowhere in sight, but Dez had caught the full show from the doorway. For the first time since setting foot on this cursed land, she saw a smile on his lips. Even though Dez was mocking her, his grin was a view she'd drive to the ends of the Earth to glimpse.

Dez stepped back, melding into the crowd, and Tyler pushed his way onto the porch. The kid's little face scrunched as he looked around, his tiny fingers balling the ends of his shirt. He was looking for her. She'd strolled into this kid's perfectly fine life, threatening to devastate it if she left.

"Hey, little dude!" Sasha yelled out, almost by instinct.

Tyler jumped off the porch steps, stumbling over his own feet as he ran across the lot. "Are you going back to the hospital now?"

"Nah," Sasha said, waving her arm. "I'm all done with the hospital. I got a place in town, so I can be close to you."

"Why don't you just stay here?"

"Maybe, one day. I…gotta take care of some stuff first."

"Yeah." Tyler smiled a tiny little Dez smirk. "I got stuff going on too. You should come over tomorrow. We can play with my Hot Wheels."

"Okay!"

Tyler wrapped his arms around Sasha's waist, and she melted.

"Love ya, Mommy."

Sasha stood there, mesmerized by the little kid's enormous embrace. Even after Tyler ran back into the clubhouse, she remained frozen in place. Only once the shakes left her body, and the tears decided to stay put, did she walk to her truck.

Chapter Five

Sasha sat on the edge of a stiff mattress in a skeevy motel room, breaking out roaches on a wobbly nightstand. It had been a good, long while since she'd had to do this. Not even ten miles from the biggest drug traffickers in the Midwest and here she was, with no weed.

After rolling the remnants of once glorious joints into a passable bone, she sparked it up and settled back. Just as a mellow buzz filled her head, a knock shook the door.

Sasha hopped off the bed, dropping the joint on the nightstand. Shag carpet tickled her toes as she hurried across the room. She hoped it was Vinny, prayed it wasn't Otis, would totally take Kev's company right now.

The face she saw when opening the door forced her legs back. "Dez?"

Dez didn't say a word, didn't have to. His eyes said it all. A world of hurt had come to pay a visit.

"What's up?" Sasha muttered, scanning the floor for her gun.

Sasha flinched as Dez reached out, her eyes snapping closed. Whatever he had in store for her, a beating, a blade to the throat…fuck it, she deserved it.

Fingertips ran along her cheek, sliding into her hair, and she opened her eyes. Hate still burned inside Dez's gaze. Its fire snuffed out any trace of affection, but Sasha wasn't afraid. She should be. A smart person would flee from that glare. Then again, nobody had ever accused her of being smart.

Dez gripped onto the back of Sasha's neck, pulled her close, and she crumbled inside his tight clutch. Their lips connected, syncing together like they'd never missed a beat. Dez's strong arms holding her tight, his solid chest gliding along her own, hadn't felt this safe before. Their bodies had never fit so perfectly all those years ago.

Dez's leather jacket hit the floor, its clink sending chills up Sasha's spine. Dez kicked the door shut without breaking her kiss or missing a swirl with his tongue. Her hands left the ripples of his chest only long enough to tear off her own shirt. She wanted to feel his skin on hers, needed to.

Somewhere between sinking her teeth into Dez's neck and running her nails down his back, she lost her pants. Not a problem, since his were gone too. He guided her to the mattress, his weight covering her in a blanket of tingles. Before he could even creep inside her, a flood of heat shuddered her body and forced the deepest moan from her lungs. Damn, only he could make her cum with a look and a touch. It only got better when he slid inside her. His lips floated along her skin as his teeth grazed her nipple. He gripped onto her hips with his strong hand. This moment, when her will fell under Dez's control, was all that she'd missed and everything she loathed. To think she couldn't be complete without him, a man, warped her mind.

Dez flipped Sasha over, on her hands and knees. The way he pulled her hair, rammed into her, he probably thought this was a punishment, but goddamn did she like it. Her mouth locked tight, sealing in moans. Best to let him believe he was punishing her good and proper. Then maybe he'd love her again, the way he used to.

"Oh fuck, Sasha."

Hearing her name roll from his lips in a soft quaver broke her moans loose and crippled her ability to keep rhythm with his thrusts. She cried out, her elbows sinking into the mattress. Shivers nearly took her all the way down but Dez held tight, drawing her to his chest.

His rough hands ran over every inch of her body, trailing sparks. He drove into her, letting out a long groan, and she grinned at the feel of his legs quaking. This would be the part where he showered her with kisses, whispered into the back of her neck, except that shit didn't happen. Dez climbed off the bed, pulling on his pants.

"What's this?" He grabbed his shirt from the floor, looking at the scatter of burnt paper that littered the nightstand. "You're smoking roaches?"

His little half-snicker/half-snort was too cute, so Sasha didn't hurl sass.

"I burned through my bag on the ride here."

Dez dressed like the room was on fire. Fuck, it

could've been. The way her flesh vibrated, she wouldn't feel a thing nor give a shit.

The click of Dez's jacket lured Sasha's stare. He dropped a baggie of green buds on the nightstand and walked to the door.

"What's that, my payment?" It was meant to be a joke, but something told Sasha she hit the nail on the head.

A smirk lit Dez's eyes as he glanced back. He shrugged, stepped into the night, and slammed the door closed behind him.

"Whatever." Sasha sat up, breaking out a joint. The joke was on Dez. That was the best sex she'd had since waking from a coma, and she got a bonus bag of weed.

Dez's coldness left a sting, and a hollow vibe circled the room, but Sasha chose to ignore those things. Her focus lingered on the way Dez's fingers trembled against her back, how he'd held her body so tight. They were signs. Maybe, somewhere amongst shattered heart pieces, Dez still craved her as much as she craved him.

A few more days, that's all Sasha could take of this martyr bullshit. If tunes didn't start changing by then, she'd break the fucking record.

***

Vinny

Vinny hopped off his bed when a knock shook his door. It had to be Sasha. No one else would be rude enough to fuck with him after the day he'd had.

A lump rose in Vinny's throat, higher the closer he got to the door. He hated the shit out of Sasha right now, but he couldn't wait to see her face. His hands were actually shaking. Vinny took a deep breath, clicked on the internal switch for coolness, and opened the door.

Crystal waved from the landing, her smile like a blade piercing Vinny's chest. He'd slam the door shut, close off her needy leer, but she'd probably set up camp out there.

"I think we need to have a talk," he said, blocking the doorway.

"I see. Sasha's back, so now I'm out."

"You were never in."

"We've been together for six months!"

Vinny almost busted out laughing. If Crystal thought degrading sexual acts were a relationship, the bitch had to be straight-up delusional. He had to keep shit on the real, or he'd never shake the woman.

"No, honey. I've been trying to dodge you for six months while you begged me to fuck you."

Her jaw dropped, a tiny gasp squeaking out. And then came the waterworks. It seemed like the best time to slam the door in her face, so he did.

Vinny shook his head as he trudged back to his bed. He should feel like shit, but he was so relieved he didn't. Fuck Crystal. Fuck all them bitches. He'd never trust a woman again. Every piece of tits and a smile that wormed into his life left it in tatters. His own mother walked out on him without a glance back. He wasn't good enough. Ellen, the mother he thought would never betray him, only kept him around as a pawn. Ellen's betrayal was a lack of strength and smarts on his part. But Sasha? That dirty bitch was the devil in disguise. He gave Sasha his soul, and she split without giving it back. It was empty. His chest, that section of his brain reserved for compassion. Empty.

Vinny leaned against the pillows, looking around the room. A week ago, this place was a shrine to Sasha. Her shit had been scattered on every surface. The makeup she left on the dresser, the clothes strewn in every corner were things that once kept him going. By now that shit should be ash, at the bottom of the bonfire that raged outside the clubhouse. Sasha wouldn't care. If she had wanted any of that crap, if she had wanted him, she would've come back seventeen months ago.

An entire joint, half a bottle of whiskey, complete darkness, nothing would stop Sasha from grating his mind. Her wicked grin clung to his eyelids. That sweet voice haunted him, her moans, giggles, even her asshole jabs. They'd all be his right now, to savor, relish, fall into, if only he were enough for her.

Heat rolled beneath Vinny's skin, and he sat up in bed. Any second now, a flood of tears would burst free. He couldn't do it. He couldn't spend another night crying over something he'd never had, something that almost was.

A roar burst from his mouth, and he hurled the bottle in his hand across the room. Glass shattered. The jingle of fragmented pieces raining to the floor cut through the darkness around him, slicing the edge off his wild thoughts. The whiskey would stain the floor. It already left one hell of a stench, but braking that bottle stopped his tears, so fuck it.

Before a load of self-pity could crash back down, Vinny dropped his head to the pillows. He closed his eyes without bothering to undress. If he didn't beat the demons, catch sleep before his twisty thoughts returned, he'd never get any rest.

***

Dez

Dez sat in his truck, staring at the big house. What little shit he had was sitting in that grand Victorian. His son called the place home, but it didn't give off that home vibe to him. Not that he would know. The inside of a jail cell was the closest he came to home, before holding Tyler. He could be in the middle of a fire-laced cyclone, and as long as his boy was in his arms he'd be happy. Up until an hour ago, he thought he'd already gotten the best part of Sasha. He'd forgotten. The softness of her skin, that glimmer in her eyes were memories he had to let go. He should've known they'd come back with a vengeance, seeking to fuck up the life he'd been forced into.

A tap rattled the window and Dez flinched, groaning at the sight of Otis's smile. He opened the door, climbing from his truck. "Is Ty good?"

"Yeah. Put him down about twenty minutes ago."

Otis's voice held an icy tone, frostier than his

narrowed eyes. Dez slammed his door shut and crossed his arms, preparing for a lecture. "What?"

"I didn't say anything."

Dez leaned against his truck, straining to shake the guilty vibe. "You want me to give Sasha the cold shoulder."

"Didn't say that."

The words came out casual, but the hard stare lingered.

"She was young," Dez said, not exactly sure why he was defending Sasha. "A lot of shit got dumped on her all at once."

"That's your dick talking."

"Fuck you." Dez walked toward the house, thought of a great comeback, and then doubled back. "You wanted to forgive her the second you saw her, and you know it."

"She'll hurt us again."

"Probably," Dez yelled, his arms out at his sides, "but at least we'll be ready this time." Otis seemed more terrified than consoled by the notion, and saying it out loud shook Dez to the core. He might not make it, when Sasha ran off on him again. None of them would. "Come on, I got a bottle of the good stuff I've been saving for a rainy day."

"Crystal's in there," Otis said, following Dez onto the porch. "She's bawling her eyes out, talking about quitting."

"Fuck! She's one of our top earners."

"Why do you think I listened to her shit for the last fifteen minutes?"

"What does she want?" Dez headed for the door, running through the nice guy routine a few times in his head.

"You," Otis said with a snicker.

Dez walked inside, following light sobs to the parlor. His girls were lucky. Tyler honed his patience skills on a daily basis, making it possible for him to deal with their shit and not dish out slaps.

"What's wrong, babe?" Dez sat on the couch, and Crystal dove into his arms.

"Vinny was way harsh."

Dez rolled his eyes, catching Otis's smirk from across the room. "He didn't put his hands on you, did he?"

"No! That's like, the problem," Crystal said, as though Dez were thick-headed. "I think maybe I should get away for a while, decompress."

"Is that smart?" Dez asked, scooting closer to Crystal. "You're hot right now. I've been getting a lot of calls about you, from important people."

"Really?" Crocodile tears were replaced by a flirty gaze as Crystal ran her hands under Dez's shirt. "You'll take care of me, won't you?"

Dez glared at Otis, silently begging for a reprieve, but got a goddamn shrug.

"Absolutely," Dez said, gripping onto Crystal's wrists and prying her hands off his body, "but I'm your boss."

Crystal jumped up off the couch, her pout warping into a scowl. "Guess I'm not that hot."

Otis lifted his arms as Crystal stormed by, offering to take care of her.

"Ew." Crystal raised her hands, keeping them high in the air until her long legs stomped from view.

"See!" Otis pointed with his cigarette-filled fingers. "Told you Sasha would hurt us."

Chapter Six

Sasha

Sasha pushed her old pickup's engine, ignoring the clunks it emitted as it struggled up the mountainous road. Sunlight glinted off the compound's dented gate and Sasha squirmed, setting off a concert of squeaks from the truck's worn bench seat. In the light of the day, one glimpse of the compound's gravely slope should trigger a scorching wave of sadness, except it didn't. She drove up the steep hill and actually felt giddy. It was a first. Relief, dread, terror, those were the emotions she'd always experienced when driving onto this property, never any variation of excitement.

The motor chugged, cutting itself off as Sasha parked in front of the clubhouse. Before she could climb from the rusted cab, Vinny was on the clubhouse porch. He sneered, and she smiled. That seemed to royally piss him off, since he charged down the steps.

"What the fuck do you want?" Vinny yelled. All venom, every sharp syllable. The dude was taking grudge to a whole new level.

Sasha opened her door a crack, and Vinny didn't budge so she squeezed out of the truck.

"Tyler invited me over, to play Hot Wheels."

Vinny stepped back, snickering. "Good luck getting past Dez."

Sasha followed Vinny's pointed finger farther up the hill. There were those good ole feelings. Dread for sure, terror so strong it left a sour taste, and enough fear to ward off a six-foot biker. The big house. Its shadow fell over Sasha as she walked up the hill, cooling the area by ten degrees. The sudden chill weakened her legs, but the need to talk to that kid, hang with him, run her fingers through his thick hair drove her onward. When she got to the porch, her body froze. It didn't seem right to just walk in, but she'd never knocked on this door before.

She lifted her arm then ran her fingers through her hair. "Smooth," she muttered beneath her breath, "play it off. 'Cause nobody will notice this retarded shit."

Sasha stared at the door, willing it to open, and it flew open. A flinch took her back a step. She peered up into Dez's cruel glare and willed the door to shut. It didn't work this time.

"Hey," Sasha said, her smile fading as Dez's glare deepened. "I was, umm…hoping I could hang with Tyler for a bit."

"He's napping. Come back in an hour."

He shut the door in her face, pulling a gasp from her lungs. Dez must have thought he was big shit,

54

playing king in her castle, using that kid as a pawn. The similarities to her dear-departed mother locked her fingers into loaded fists. If it was games that dumb bastard wanted, she was down. Dez would be sorry, though. She was schooled by the master.

Sasha turned from the front door and there was Vinny, arms crossed, standing in the middle of the lot. From this distance, she couldn't see his smirk but goddamn she could feel it. That bastard totally set her up for this. That was fine too. Now, he'd have to deal with her ass for the next hour.

It was not easy, but Sasha forced her body loose and slapped on a smile. After all these years, Vinny had to know. This meant war. Sasha walked down the hill, mirroring Vinny's defensive stance. Phase one: kill him with kindness and let his own conscience do the work.

"The kid's crashed out," Sasha said, letting out a sad little sigh. "I'm just gonna chill here 'til he wakes up, if that's cool?" Two tiny eye bats and a gaze drop shattered Vinny's tough guy act. It was too easy to play him and a bit too fun.

"Yeah," Vinny said with a shrug. "I mean, whatever."

Sasha looked at Vinny, catching the tail end of his frown. It wasn't fun anymore. To top the whole shit sundae off, watching his pain through blonde-streaked hair really gave off an Ellen vibe.

"Vinny, I—"

"Just stay the fuck out of my way."

Sasha leaned back but couldn't escape the sting of his words. Vinny headed for the clubhouse. She almost wormed away into her truck, but decided *fuck that* and then hurried after him.

"Hey!" Sasha yelled, and Vinny spun to face her. As he leered at her, her brain turned to word soup. All those comebacks, harsh demands, fell victim to his hard glare.

"You have to forgive me." It was simple, whiny, but everything she needed to convey.

"The fuck I do," Vinny said, his face a ripe mixture of sorrow and spite.

There had to be a rebuttal, yet Sasha came up blank. Vinny turned his back, walking up the clubhouse steps, and she wandered toward the back lot. A row of gleaming stacks sent a surge of warmth through her veins. Just a few minutes behind the wheel of a big rig with a joint in her mouth, and she'd be set to perma-chill. It didn't even have to be moving. She could pretend.

Her feet went into double-time, and Vinny grabbed her arm.

"Where the fuck are you going?"

"I just wanna chill inside a rig." Sasha yanked herself free, glaring. "Mean fucker."

"You can't," Vinny said, rocking in place. "They're busy."

Sasha looked at the line of semis, each wide windshield covered in a thick layer of dust. "They're just sitting there, rotting away." She took a step, and Vinny ran in front of her.

"I'm not playing," Vinny damn near growled, his face backing up his words.

Now Sasha was way too curious to let this go. "Please tell me the product isn't loaded in those trucks, on the property."

"We don't run drugs anymore. Nobody would deal with us without you."

"Oh." She hadn't considered that. No Ellen, no Sasha, no Ashby in a stone's throw. "I didn't realize. Sorry." Vinny still blocked her path, his face a bundle of nerves. "So whatcha got going on in those trucks?"

Sasha bobbed, Vinny weaved, and she bumped him aside, hurrying to the trailer.

"Don't," he yelled softly, seizing her by the wrist. "You'll fuck up the scene."

"Scene?"

Vinny's grip tightened as he pulled Sasha from the blue truck, toward the green one. He opened the trailer's back door, and her eyes grew wide. It looked like a dungeon. Fake stones in the corners, a rack with leather straps in the center, tables of whips and dildos.

"What is this?" Sasha asked with a chuckle. She climbed into the trailer, scooting between two cameras on stands.

"One of our sets." Vinny's eyes stayed low as he climbed onto the bumper. "We've been shooting pornos."

"Shut up!" The smile came too fast for Sasha to stop. "Are you in them?"

"No," Vinny snorted, creeping past cardboard cutouts of rock walls. "I'm the director."

His face lit up when he said that, so fucking cute. Sasha grabbed onto the leather straps hanging against the rack. "I'll be in one. Turn on that camera, director-man."

"Stop fucking around." Vinny almost toppled a

57

camera to get out of the trailer.

No-fun Vinny sucked. Sasha missed awesome Vinny and refused to let her weaknesses steal his light from the world.

"Wait!" Sasha jumped out of the trailer, rushing after Vinny. She reached for his arm, clipping the edge of leather. "Vinny."

Vinny stopped short, turning on his heels, and Sasha skid on gravel to keep from crashing into his chest. Damn, she could've just crashed into his chest. Their eyes connected and he shrank back, losing his hard edge for just a second. Then it all rained back down. His hurt, anger, even hints of love clouded his stare. He probably would've stormed off if a pack of black sedans followed by a line of police cars didn't tear ass up the hill and surround them.

"Oh shit," Sasha muttered as the click of guns loading echoed over shouting voices. She turned toward Vinny and someone gripped her neck, slamming her face onto the hood of a car.

"Sasha Ashby," her legs were kicked apart, arms yanked behind her back, "you're under arrest for the murder of Federal Agent Rebecca Prescott."

Handcuffs dug into Sasha's wrists, nicking bone, and she jerked her arms only to have the metal rings clicked tighter.

"Stop!" Dez yelled, pushing rifles from his chest and barging into the crowd of pigs. "I have all the permits—"

"We don't give a shit about your Podunk business, Mr. Archer," some fat, bald jizz-rag of a man practically spat in Dez's face. "Fan out," the man said to his group of commando wannabe men who jumped like cowboys to trample the property.

"If you're not here about my business, then what are you searching for on my property?" Dez asked.

"What?" the man pinning Sasha to the hood of a hot car asked.

"Can I see your warrant? Please," Dez said as calmly as one could through clenched teeth.

The clutch on Sasha's neck tightened, and she was pulled from the car's scorching metal. Through a crowd of SWAT, feds, and state police, she found Dez, but he didn't look up from the papers in his hand.

"This says you have the right to search the property for Sasha Ashby," Dez said, thrusting the papers at the pig's chest. "You found her. Now leave."

A car door opened, and the asshole fed gripping onto Sasha twisted her arm. The burn forced a cry from her chest. She lunged into the douchebag, cracking the back of her head against his nose. Now he cried out. She couldn't help but giggle until a solid punch replaced her grin with split lips. Blood pooled in her mouth, like gas fueling a flame. Sasha stood up straight, spitting a wad of blood in a fed-pig's face.

Knuckles pounded her body from all sides, and she charged forward. Her shoulder connected to a chest, and she drove it into the side of a car.

"Sasha, stop!" Vinny shouted and Sasha froze. A knee crashed against her stomach, dropping her to the ground. Sharp rocks scraped her face as boots punted her sides. Each hit stole the air, robbing her

59

cries.

"I think our girl's had enough," the fed with the busted nose said, peeling Sasha from the gravel. She searched the sea of faces for Vinny, Dez, but only glimpsed cruel grins as she was tossed into the back of a car.

***

Sasha sat handcuffed to a metal table, staring at the wide mirror on the wall. She wasn't looking at her split lip. That rainbow of a bruise on her cheek was pretty, but didn't hold her gaze. She was looking beyond the glass. She couldn't see the group of men gawking at her, but she could damn near smell their frenzy.

The door squealed open, and the pigman whose nose Sasha had cracked walked into the small white room and sat across from her. A young, black woman brought up the rear, shutting the three of them inside.

"Don't I get a phone call?" Sasha asked. The feds glared with their hard stares, their cocky smirks flinging her way. "A lawyer? Cigarette?"

A file slid across the table. Sasha tried not to look, strained to keep her head high, but the gleam of blonde hair snagged her attention. She stared at a picture of a woman she never expected to see again. Misty, the girl who never was.

Sasha veered her gaze to the man sitting across from her. Other than the lovely purple mark she'd left on the bridge of the man's nose, his face was as empty as the wall behind him.

"Where is she?" the man growled.

"Who is she?" Sasha asked, sliding the file away with one finger.

"We know you picked her up at a rest stop outside the city, on your last run."

"Last run." Sasha leaned back, snorting. "You must have me mixed up with someone else, Pigman. I've been out of commission for a while."

"Before the coma, five years ago."

Sasha let out a huff, shaking her head. "That was a long time ago. A lot of shit's happened since then."

"Are you saying you don't remember what happened before your accident?" the woman fed asked from the corner.

"Oh no. I remember just fine," Sasha said. Her cuffs scraped the solid bar welded to the table as she glanced at the woman behind her. "I remember picking up a girl who sort of looked like the woman in your file, but more…what's the word, rough. Ratty clothes, dirty hair, not fancy like this bitch." She gestured to the file but didn't look, couldn't risk breaking her poker face.

"Then what happened?" the woman asked, lighting a cigarette and handing it to Sasha.

Sasha sure did love the good cop routine. She needed a few puffs of a smoke, because goddamn she was fucked.

"This girl, the one I picked up," she said, nice and slow. She wanted to drag it out, so she could get a few more drags on her cigarette. "The chick kept trying to get me to do drugs. I don't fuck with that shit, so I dropped her at a rest stop."

"Bullshit!" The man crashed his fist on the table, the bang circling the small room.

"I swear to fucking God."

Good cop plucked the cigarette from Sasha's bloody lips, crushing it under the tip of her boot. That was quick. Must be time for another beating.

"Let's go," the lady fed grumbled. She unlatched the handcuffs from Sasha's wrist, but the sting left by the jagged metal remained. The man who fancied himself Howdy Doody pulled Sasha from the chair, and the bitch fed slapped the cuffs back on.

"I think a night on the top level would do you some good," the man sneered, slamming Sasha against the wall beside a closed steel door.

***

Dez

Dez stood in the doorway of the parlor, watching Tyler bash toy trucks together. The kid was playing it cool, only looking out the window every other minute. Poor little guy was waiting for Sasha. The endless wait was a pain Dez had become numb to, one he'd hoped to protect his son from.

Otis slammed the phone to its receiver, and Dez turned toward the kitchen. It was hard to gauge Otis's expression. The man grew stiff, turned pale, when Dez had asked him to call New York and it hadn't worn off yet.

"So?" Dez asked.

Otis lit a cigarette and leaned against the counter.

A slight tremble ran through his fingers as he lifted the butt to his lips. It scared the shit out of Dez. He'd never seen Otis so rattled, so full of hurt. The plague of Sasha held no bounds. There really was no end to the misery she spread, and no stopping the compulsion Dez felt to help her at anybody's cost.

"Tony said he'll send a lawyer on the first flight out," Otis said, staring at his smoke lingering on the ceiling. "To tell Sasha to hold tight and stay quiet, if we can get to her."

"She's gotta be at county lockup by now." Dez took a step back, peeking into the parlor. Tyler had abandoned his trucks to stare out the front window, his little hands leaving marks on the glass.

"I'll go first thing, try and see her." Dez looked at Otis, struck by the levels of fear in the man's eyes. "I'm sorry. I know how hard it must've been to make that call."

"No, you really don't."

Otis bumped Dez's shoulder on his way out the kitchen. He listened to the sound of Otis's boots stomp through the house, ending with the slam of the front door.

"Fuck." Dez slumped against the wall, fishing a pack of smokes from his pocket. Otis was right. He had no idea what that call meant to the man. All he knew was Otis and the Lazzaris were connected, somehow. He should've asked his friend to make that call, instead of demanding it. But Sasha had crept under his skin, setting off a tidal wave of destruction once again.

"Where's Uncle Otis going?" Tyler asked.

Dez looked down into eyes he'd kill for, into the

stare that drove his irrational decisions. "To work."

"No. He got in his truck and left."

"Oh." Dez crushed out his cigarette, straining to keep the sadness from showing in his stare. "He probably just went to the store for something."

"Is Mommy coming back soon?"

Tears welled inside Dez's eyes. He couldn't break, not in front of his boy. "Yes. She has to take care of some important shit before she can come live with us."

"Awesome!" Tyler ran into the living room, returning to the window. "Uncle Vinny's here!"

"Great," Dez said, his sarcasm coming off as a weak version of enthusiasm. He strolled to the fridge, grabbing two beers.

"Where'd Otis go?" Vinny barked, storming into the kitchen.

Dez held out a beer and got a sneer before the bottle was snatched from his grasp.

"I asked him to call New York, make the Lazzaris help Sasha."

"I...can't believe you did that."

There was that look again, shock. Only this time, it colored his brother's face in shades of white.

"Fuck, man!" Dez popped the cap off his beer, leaning against the counter. "Nobody tells me shit. I didn't know it was some kinda big thing." He killed half his beer, waiting until Vinny's stiff body thawed. "How is Otis connected to them, the Lazzaris?"

"There used to be three Lazzari brothers. The oldest one, Stefano, ran it all until he turned up dead. The other brothers split up the turf, but nobody knows what happened to Stefano's son, Othello. Some people say he was killed. Others say he went underground."

"Otis?"

Vinny shrugged, downing his beer. Dez would follow suit, but he'd become too nauseous for drinking. He'd just made the long lost heir to the mafia throne ask for a favor from the people who killed his father.

"You'll throw us all away for her," Vinny said, almost to himself, "won't you?"

"Hungry," Tyler yelled from the living room over the TV's blare.

"Not him." Dez patted Vinny on the arm, heading to the fridge. "Or you."

Chapter Seven

Sasha

Sasha couldn't stop her hands from twitching. Today had been a fucking picnic. She'd been stripped, probed, blasted with a hose of burning chemicals, and left handcuffed to a wall for hours, all without a single puff on a joint. Now some inbred fuck in a prison guard uniform was marching her down a platform. Steel grate rattled under her feet, showing hints of the floors below. One of the many hands reaching through the bars on her right snagged her arm and she pulled back, only to be shoved from behind.

"We put the worst of you sick fucks on the top level," the guard behind Sasha said, practically shouting over the jumble of catcalls. "Murderers, child rapists, baby killers...the feds wanted something special for you, and I got just the thing."

They stopped in front of a cell and a large, bulky woman rolled off the bottom cot. A buzzer sounded, making every one of Sasha's muscles flinch. The bars slid open, and she was pushed into a chest twice as wide as her entire body, looking up at a woman double in size.

"Here's a special treat for ya, Martha. No holds barred." The cell slammed shut, and the guard laughed as he strolled away.

"Nice." The woman cracked her knuckles, which seemed bigger than the normal man-sized knuckles that usually pounded Sasha's face.

"Hey, Martha. I—"

"You're in my cell now. That means you're my bitch."

"Oh," Sasha said, taking a deep breath. This was gonna be painful, for the ugly cunt in front of her. She scanned the tiny space, searching for anything sharp enough she could stab Martha with, something heavy enough to swing.

"You're gonna give me a piece of your sweet ass, or I'm gonna take it."

Sasha took a step back, curling her fists. "You ain't taking shit from me, you oversized nasty bitch."

Giant knuckles barreled Sasha's way and she ducked, hurling her fist into a solid stomach. The bitch didn't move except her head, which cocked to one side. Sasha scurried back, her head clunking against bars. A churning firestorm whirled inside her chest, sucking the air from her lungs.

The huge woman closed in and Sasha swung, but it did nothing to stop fingers from clamping onto her neck. Martha gripped so hard her nails broke into Sasha's skin. Sasha kicked, landing a few good hits before a fist rocked her gut.

Martha slammed Sasha against the bars, cracking the side of her face. The world flashed to black, and blood filled Sasha's throat. She gasped for breath while thrown facedown onto the bottom cot.

A crushing weight pressed down atop Sasha, pushing her face into the thin mattress. Heavy breaths flowed over the back of her neck, choking her in their stink. She jerked her hips, tossed elbows as Martha's hands slid under her shirt.

"How about now, sweet ass?" Martha hissed.

Sasha was flipped to her back, a thick arm dropping across her throat. Tears blurred her eyes, the strangling grip blocking out the flow of air. Her pants were bunched down at her ankles, and fingers rammed inside her.

"Am I taking something from you now, bitch?"

The arm on Sasha's throat pressed harder, the other hand pounding faster. The burn, the rip of her skin, was nothing compared to the agony of her soul. A red haze crept over the world. She'd claw at the arm crushing the life from her neck, but she wanted to die. She prayed for death. The last thing she had left was being torn from her body, and she couldn't stop it. No more pride, no more worth. She was an empty shell, hollowed out by the ugliness of humanity.

A numb prickle swept over Sasha. Darkness crept up to claim her senses, and she dove into it.

***

"Get up!"

Sasha groaned. Hints of light trickled in and she

tried to pry her eyelids open, but the throb in her head kept them sealed shut. A palm slapped her cheek. The throb jacked up to a thud, and her eyes snapped open.

A guard smiled down at Sasha. His crooked teeth gleamed in the harsh light, begging to be knocked out. He lifted his arm, dropping bright orange clothes on Sasha's chest. "Get dressed. You have a visitor."

Sasha sat up, looking down at a hospital gown. Rows of cots filled with battered bodies lined the wall, leading to a big infirmary sign.

"The feds?" Sasha asked, pushing her shaky body to its feet. A million red-hot pinpricks erupted between her legs, and she choked down a scream.

"Your husband."

"Husband?" Sasha muttered. She turned her back to the guard, since he wasn't going to look away. Sunlight beamed through the window, glinting off the bars.

"It's morning?" she said, mostly to herself. Beyond the thick iron bars, she glimpsed her reflection in the cloudy glass. A kaleidoscope of colors painted one side of her face, scrapes and bruises littering the other.

Sasha squirmed out of her gown, every move spreading liquid fire. Streaks of blood crusted along her inner thighs, staining her skin. She looked for something to wash them off with, maybe bleach, but found nothing. The guard behind her snickered, and she hurried to dress. She should be enraged, but all she felt was fear. Terror that the man behind her would start in on her next, shame that she probably wouldn't be able to stop him. Before the coma, when she was strong, she could fight off an entire bar of bikers. But now, with only half her muscles and no brass to cover her fist, she really was just a little girl.

Her eyes stayed low as she turned back toward the guard. If something horrible was headed her way, she didn't want to see it.

"You got lucky," the guard said, pushing her toward the door. "I was just about to dump you back in Martha's cell, but rules say your husband has the right to a visit."

A cringe ran through Sasha's body at the thought of landing back in a cell with that bulldyke of a woman. Whoever this man pretending to be her husband was, she owed him big time.

***

Dez

Dez took deep breaths, but his foot wouldn't stop tapping the floor. He swore he'd never get this close to a jail cell again, but fucking Sasha. There weren't even bars on the windows in the family visiting area yet the walls were spinning, closing in on him. He should bolt, send Vinny inside this hellhole. If only. His dumb ass couldn't go anywhere, not without seeing Sasha and making sure she was all right.

A buzz rang out, flaring his nerves. He hated that fucking sound. The solid steel door at the end of the room opened, and Sasha limped through it. Dez shot to his feet, gawking as she hobbled over. Them motherfucking feds must have worked her over all night. When she sat down and a cry escaped her lips, he knew this wasn't the feds' doing. It was worse, so much worse.

Sasha's eyes stuck to the floor, a messy tangle of blonde streaked hair failing to hide her trembling lips. Dez grabbed her hand, and she flinched.

"Are you okay?"

"No touching," a guard yelled from across the room.

Sasha pulled her hand back, glancing at Dez for a second. "Husband?"

"It's a long story. Otis called New York. A lawyer should be here soon, hopefully work some mobster magic."

"Really!" Sasha said, her voice cracking.

It took every bit of willpower for Dez to keep his ass in his chair, to keep from wrapping his arms around Sasha's quaking shoulders.

"Listen," he leaned on the table, bobbing to catch her gaze, "the next time that bitch gets on top of you, go along with it. When her guard's down, bash her head against the top bunk and knee the bitch in her snatch. The top cover of the toilet makes for a great weapon. It comes right off and its heavy as shit."

A hint of a smile lifted Sasha's swollen cheeks. "I love you." She latched onto Dez's hand, pulling it to her chest. "I wish I never left you. I'm so sorry."

"That's just prison sadness talkin'." Dez caressed the back of her hand with his thumb, sliding his fingers between hers. "You'll be singing a different tune once you get out."

Sasha shook her head, and a guard seized her by the arm. Dez almost jumped up and decked the fucker, but the guy yanked Sasha away too fast.

"Come on," the guard said, pulling Sasha toward the door. "The feds wanna see ya."

"I meant it, Dez," she said before a metal door slammed shut, stealing her away.

The low buzzers, the clink of metal, sent Dez's head into a whirl. He had to get out, drive his fist through someone's face, hug his fucking kid. The image of Tyler's smile cleared a thick cloud of rage from his mind. Dez climbed his sorry ass out of the hard metal seat, hurrying from the room.

***

Vinny

Vinny sat up straight, rocking the pickup when Dez walked from the county jail. He had a few seconds to clear the worry from his face and go back to pretending not to care about Sasha before Dez reached the truck.

Dez climbed into the driver's seat, slammed the door shut, and started pounding the shit out of his steering wheel.

"Dude!" Vinny shouted. He reached out, then his brain clicked on. No way was he touching that man's bulging arm, especially when it was in full-on rage mode.

In a rush, Dez turned to face Vinny. Instinct forced Vinny's body to recoil, even though he was so ready to throw down. Then Dez collapsed against Vinny's chest, sobbing. Vinny's spine locked stiff. He didn't know what the fuck to do. Dez had never cried before, ever, let alone seek out an embrace for comfort.

"What the fuck happened in there?" Vinny asked, patting Dez on the back.

A sharp ache sliced into Vinny's chest, cutting deeper as tears soaked through his shirt. He wrapped his arms around Dez. Instant comfort stemmed from the embrace, sending waves of security that shocked Vinny's core. He didn't expect this. He had never touched Dez without fury motivating the action. If he had known hugging his brother would feel so good, it probably wouldn't have changed shit, but he would've done it more.

"Whatever it is, Dez, I'm here."

Dez pulled away from Vinny, wiping his eyes. "That didn't happen." Dez hurled a sharp glare, starting the truck.

***

Sasha

Sasha yelped as the guard pushed her into a hard metal chair. Her glare veered to the man, who looked so proud in his stupid uniform. One day, she'd slice the smile from his nasty face.

"Looks like someone had fun last night," the same fat fed from the night before said with a wink.

"Or someone had fun with you," his lady fed sidekick added.

Sasha glared at the two fuckers responsible for her torment. Just two more people for her shit list.

"I never caught your names," she said, staring across the table.

"You ready to talk?" The man leaned back, crossing his arms atop his big belly.

So much fat, Sasha would have to cut through so much fat to nick an organ.

"We can get you transferred to a private cell," the woman said, sliding back into her good cop role.

These pigs had nothing on her, and even if they did she'd never talk. Just to spite them, just to keep them guessing forever, she'd never talk.

The door opened and a fancy suit walked in, setting Sasha's heart to flutter. She knew a city lawyer when she saw one, cleaned plenty of messes for them.

"What's going on here?"

Both feds stood, puffing out their chests. "Who the fuck are you?" the man asked.

"Lucio Spengotti. Ms. Lazzari's attorney."

That took fed man back to his seat and made the bitch fed squirm.

"What's the charges, Agent Daniels?" Spengotti asked, eyeing the bruises that colored Sasha's body. "Can I see her rap sheet? I'm having a hard time tracking it down."

"There aren't any charges yet," the fed uttered into his lap. "She's being detained for questioning."

Spengotti dropped his briefcase onto the table, propping his hands on his hips. "Then why is she in county lockup?"

"The holding cells at the station were full." The

bitch fed was a pro at the hard stare. It must be a requirement for a woman in their clique, especially a black one.

"I was just at the station. There's only one person in the drunk tank." Spengotti had better dagger eyes than the feds. It warmed Sasha's heart. He turned to her, running his finger along her cheek. "Did they do this to you?"

Sasha shook her head. While the rips and scars were indirectly the fed bastards doing, lawyers liked proof, and she had none.

Spengotti glanced at his watch then back at the feds. "Your twenty-four hours are up. I want my client released, immediately."

The feds got up, muttered slurs about Italians, and then headed for the door.

"I'll be waiting at outtake," Spengotti said. "If she's not there in thirty minutes, I'm calling the attorney general."

Once the feds left the room, Spengotti sat on the table in front of Sasha. "Your uncle sends his love."

"Thank you, Mr. Spengotti—"

"Lucio."

"Mr. Lucio. You saved my fucking ass." That could be said on two counts, literally and figuratively.

"It's not over yet. What do they have on you?"

"Nothing, 'cause I didn't do shit," Sasha said, which was mostly true.

"That's a good answer."

The door squealed open, and two guards walked in. Sasha grabbed onto Lucio's hand. She didn't want to leave this room, go where he couldn't see all the horrible things that could happen to a woman in thirty minutes. A wide arm wrapped around Sasha's throat, and both the guards practically dragged her from the room.

"It's all right," Lucio said, stepping back. "I'll be waiting for you."

Sasha took one last look at her savior, an angel sent straight from Heaven, before the guards yanked her down the hall.

Chapter Eight

Dez

Dez parked in front of the big house but didn't kill the engine or look up from his lap. He was too embarrassed. Some man he was, weeping like a bitch in his little brother's arms. Vinny better not talk about this, ever, to anyone.

"Can you watch Ty for a bit? Kev and the twins together only equal half an adult."

Vinny chuckled, a sound Dez hadn't heard in a while. It was nice, brought a bit of warmth into his chest to chase away the coldness that lingered.

"Yeah," Vinny said, reaching for his door. "Where you going?"

"To find Otis, apologize."

The passenger door opened but Vinny didn't get out and Dez wasn't about to glance over.

"I'm sorry," Vinny said in a low tone. "What I said last month about me and Sasha being together behind your back all those years ago...it wasn't true. You shouldn't believe it."

"It was true." That was where Dez intended this topic to end. His now white knuckles should tip Vinny off loud and clear.

Without another word, Vinny climbed from the truck. As soon as the door shut, Dez took off. It wasn't the bullshit Vinny couldn't stop talking about that he sped away from. He already knew Sasha and Vinny were fucking back then, a lot, which implied other things. However, beating Vinny's ass last month over the matter had purged his hatred for their indiscretions.

Dez turned onto the road. His tires skipped on sand-covered pavement as he raced up the mountain. There was something much heavier he sought to escape from than Vinny's bullshit truths. Ever since Sasha was torn from his grasp at the jailhouse, he hadn't been able to get the visuals of her being raped from his head. The truck's engine screamed. Not even the rough bounce of the cab as he cut onto a dirt trail could shake the thoughts loose.

The top of a camper peeked over the trail, and Dez slowed his truck. He parked beside a concrete slab which used to hold the warehouse of Ashby Trucking and shut the motor.

"How'd you find me?" Otis asked the moment Dez stepped out of his truck.

"If I were a lonely old dude who lost everything in one day, I'd set up camp in the ashes of my happiest place too."

"Oh yeah," Otis said, dropping into a lawn chair outside his camper. "Then how come you haven't set up shop in Sasha's bedroom?"

"Asshole," Dez muttered, standing in front of Otis.

"What'd you want?"

"Come back," Dez said, before his mind had a chance to think up a non-whiny way to beg.

Otis climbed to his feet, grabbing onto Dez's shoulder. "What happened?"

"Nothing." Dez shrugged away from Otis's grip. "I just...need you home, man."

"Bullshit." Otis folded the thin plastic lawn chair, tossing it inside his camper. "I know that look. Something happened."

Dez almost broke. How free his mind could be if he let the ugliness out of it, but Sasha's secrets weren't his to share.

"Tyler keeps asking about you," Dez said in a somewhat convincing tone. "I had to shut down production today. Kev's been running the sets, and the clips I'm getting are shit."

"Right." Otis shut the door of his camper, fastening its padlock. "Let's go and pretend like you're not a lonely old man trying to get back the shit he lost."

A rumble filled the air as Otis started his truck. Dez strolled toward his own pickup, holding in the witty comebacks his mind was brewing up. He just wanted his family home, under one roof, which wasn't too much to ask for. So he kept his lips zipped, sunk behind his steering wheel, and followed Otis down the rocky trail.

***

Vinny

Vinny kissed Tyler on the head and scooted off the couch. He could only take about five minutes of that *Fraggle Rock* shit before flashbacks of bad acid trips streamed through his mind. Right now, a doobie and a beer was required.

He slipped into the kitchen, pulling a joint from his cigarette pack. A flame and a puff later, he could breathe. Smoke wafted around his face as he opened the fridge, finding an empty twelve-pack. He snickered, which cleared the smoke from his eyes for a brief second. With a soft sigh, he sat at the table. Just like with every bone Vinny had blown for the last five years, he wished Sasha were there to share it.

"Mommy's here!" Tyler yelled from the living room.

"Not yet, buddy. Maybe soon."

"No," Tyler said, long and loud. "She just got out of a fancy car."

The joint slipped from Vinny's hand, landing on the floor as he rushed from the kitchen. When he hit the foyer, the front door creaked open. Vinny stopped short, and Sasha peeked inside. That one glimpse rekindled his anger and soothed his soul at the same time. He would tell Sasha to fuck off, relieve the anguish of having to choose whether to love or hate her, but his weak heart jumped into his stupid throat.

"Can I come in?" Sasha asked, stepping inside without waiting for an answer.

The scatter of bruises that decorated Sasha's face

stole Vinny's words. Her swollen, cracked lips didn't hinder her smile, though. In fact, the black eye and puffy red marks were exactly how her face looked in his memory.

"Yeah—"

Tyler pushed Vinny aside, running toward Sasha.

"You came!" Tyler said, wrapping his arms around Sasha's waist.

Sasha cried out when Tyler squeezed. Tyler jumped, startled, sparking Vinny to rush forward.

"What happened to you?" Tyler asked, keeping a light hold on Sasha's arm.

"Umm…" Sasha took Tyler by the hand, limping into the living room. "Mommy fell down some stairs."

"You fall a lot."

Tyler hopped onto the couch, and Vinny leaned against the doorway. When he saw how Sasha winced as she sat, flinching with every movement, he knew exactly why Dez was fuming.

"Yeah." Sasha snickered. "I'll have to be more careful. Holding you makes me feel so much better, though."

Vinny watched Sasha pull Tyler close, resting her head atop his. God how he wanted to forgive her. It'd be wrong to do it now, just because she'd been…assaulted in jail. Only Sasha could fuck up a person's fortitude to hold a grudge. It hadn't even been a week.

"You wanna watch *Fraggley Rock*?" Tyler asked, clicking the buttons on the remote.

"What is it?" Sasha stared at the TV, narrowing her eyes. "I don't know, dude. This shit's kinda freaky."

Tyler giggled, clicking more buttons.

"What I really want is some ice cream," Sasha said, nudging Tyler. "What kind you got?"

"We don't have any ice cream."

"What?"

"Daddy doesn't like sweets."

"Say what!" Sasha steered her gaze to Vinny. "My mom always kept the ice chest loaded with treats."

"Dez don't like sweets."

Sasha snorted, rolling her eyes.

"We could go to the diner," Tyler said, hopping to his feet. "They have good ice cream."

Vinny walked into the middle of the room, waving his arms. "Nah—"

"Yeah!" Sasha climbed off the couch, groaning. "I can take you to the diner."

Tyler ran into the hall, tore back through the room, then headed for the stairs. "I gotta find my shoes."

Sasha chuckled, and Vinny charged forward.

"What the fuck are you doing?" He'd shove her, if she didn't look so beat-up already.

"What? I can't take my kid out for ice cream?"

"No," Vinny said in a hushed shout. "Not without Dez."

"Where is he?"

Vinny shrugged, gesturing to the window. "Out looking for Otis."

"That could take all night. What's the fucking problem?"

Vinny didn't want to say it, but fuck, Sasha

wasn't leaving him much of a choice. "What if...What if you take off, with him?"

"Oh my God. What kind of monster do you think I am?"

"I don't...I can't..." There weren't words to describe the type of monster Vinny thought Sasha was. Soulless, cruel, selfish wasn't strong enough to describe the woman who ripped out hearts for sport.

"I had a really fucked up night, Vinny. Can I just have one awesome thing? Shit, man, I'm looking at a life sentence."

This wasn't right; Vinny shouldn't have to make a decision like this. Tyler hopped down the steps, jumped over the railing, and pulled Sasha toward the door.

"C'mon, Mommy. I'm ready."

Sasha's pleading eyes clung to Vinny's face as her feet shuffled backward. A look he knew well radiated from her gaze. It was the one that told him she'd always have his back, but he didn't know. He couldn't trust her, but he couldn't stop her without hurting Tyler.

"To the diner, and right back," Vinny said, surprised at how firm his voice came out.

Sasha grinned, hobbling out the door, and Vinny rushed after them.

"Seatbelts," he yelled from the porch. She waved him off, and his stomach churned. He paced, lit a cigarette, then tossed it to the ground. A truck roared to life, its rumble competing with his heart's beat.

Vinny ran down the porch steps, stopping at the edge of the hill. "Fuck." Sasha's headlights flooded the lot, pulling him down the rocky slope. He should stop her. "Fuck!" Dez was going to kill him, peel his skin off in thin strips. An engine revved, growing fainter as it echoed down the mountain. It was too late. He just let that happen, let Sasha drive off with Tyler. Jesus Christ he was done, and she'd be done too if she fucked Vinny over.

***

Sasha

The feds had done a fine job of ransacking the truck. Tyler didn't seem to mind a few more rips in the already torn bench seat, and Sasha didn't give a shit about this old pickup. It was the precious cargo inside that mattered.

She peeked over, catching a goofy smile. Her foot eased off the gas pedal, the truck practically crawling to the stop sign at the end of the steep road. Man, this little dude made for one heavy load.

"It's right," Tyler said, his squeaky voice locking her boot even tighter to the brake pedal.

"I know, silly. I'm just...nervous. I never had a kid in my cab before." She turned right, heading toward town.

"It's cool. I've been in lots of trucks."

It was cool. Tyler's attitude, rolling tongue, his cute gestures with his little arms. He was like a tiny awesome person.

"Uncle Vinny let me drive his truck once. But don't tell Dad." Tyler turned toward Sasha, pointing his little finger. "He'll freak."

"Okay." Sasha couldn't help but laugh. The kid was just like her, which could be a bad thing.

A screech of tires lured her stare. She looked out her window, right at the grill of a dump truck. Her hand flew to Tyler. She had just enough time to curl her fingers into Tyler's shirt before a crash flung her to the side. Glass shattered, pelting her cheek as it flew across the cab.

The dump truck slammed into the driver's door of Sasha's truck, flipping it onto its roof. Metal screeched against pavement, sparks showering her skin as the truck grinded to a stop.

While hanging upside down, Sasha leaned across the cab. Blood dripped from her fingers, slapping the mangled roof below as she reached for Tyler. The steering wheel turned under her legs, and she fell to her side. Shards of glass burrowed into her elbows, slicing as she scooted toward the tiny, dangling lifeless arms. Warm drops rained down, splashing Sasha's cheek. She looked up, and a rush of panic forced a cry from her lungs. Tyler hung upside down, suspended by his seatbelt, blood pouring from his still face.

"No!" Sasha reached up, fumbling for the buckle. "Baby, please." The latch unclipped, and Tyler dropped into her arms. A groan trickled from his bloody lips and she grinned, hugging him tight. His pain-filled moan scraped her heart, but it was the most beautiful sound she'd ever heard. It meant he was alive, her baby was alive.

Sasha ripped off her flannel, holding it against a long gash on Tyler's forehead.

"You hit it too hard," a man's voice echoed

85

above the clink of falling glass. Sasha's entire body froze except for her right hand, which latched onto the butt of her holstered gun.

"The boss wanted her alive."

City folk. She could pick out that shrill tone in a crowded bar. Not New Yorkers, but definitely easterners. It didn't matter. Sasha pulled the gun to her chest, sliding away from Tyler. In a minute, they'd be bullet-riddled easterners.

The safety clicked off, and Sasha flinched. The soon-to-be dead men must not have heard it since wing-tipped shoes kept strolling her way. She took aim, glancing at Tyler. His little chest rose and fell, faster than it should. It sparked her own breaths into overdrive. She forced her stare back to the caved-in windshield, looking into a man's shocked eyes. She squeezed the trigger three times before her brain overrode her body's fear.

Above the buzz left by gunfire, Sasha heard the click of bullets loading into chambers. She laid down in front of Tyler, trying to follow the shuffle of feet. Not her son. This world could rape her, strip her down to ugly bits, but it couldn't take her son.

A wail of sirens bounced off the hills, and Sasha's body nearly crumbled. Never had she been so happy to hear the police headed in her direction. The tap of shoes faded, and her arm dropped. She waited until the sound of a dump truck's diesel motor drifted away and the sirens grew closer to toss the gun and grab Tyler. A gray haze rolled in to fog her vision, but she beat it back. She had to stay awake, hold this shirt to Tyler's head, be strong for her boy.

Lights flashed, tinting the crushed cab in blue and red. Voices shouted, telling her she'd be okay, yet her arms grew weaker. In a rush of hands and faces, Tyler was ripped from her clutch. Sasha rolled onto her back, landing in a bed of glass. Darkness crept up, dragging her from the whirl of lights and shouts of men.

***

Dez

Dez drove up the compound, slamming on the brakes when Vinny ran down the clubhouse steps. Without waiting for Otis to park, Dez shut his engine and climbed from the truck.

"I'm sorry, Dez," Vinny said, his brow scrunched.

Those three little words ignited a blaze of panic. Dez pushed past Vinny, looking inside the clubhouse. "Where's Tyler?"

Vinny shook his head, staggering away, and Dez reached for Vinny's throat. Otis held Dez back. Then Kev joined in, since Dez wasn't going to stop until his hand squeezed answers from Vinny's throat.

"Sasha took him," Vinny yelled, and Dez fell limp. "To the diner, for ice cream."

"You stupid fuck!" Rage swelled, and Dez broke free from the hands holding him down. Everyone jumped back, inching away. He'd bust Vinny's face right now, if he had time. "How long ago?"

Vinny flinched, continuing his slow backward

flee. "Forty-five minutes."

"Fuck!" Dez yelled, heading for his truck. "She could be two states over by now."

"She'll be back," Vinny said, in more of a question than a declaration.

Dez cocked his fist, lunging for Vinny. Then remembered, no time. "Fucking retard." Later, he'd kill his brother later.

The phone rang inside the clubhouse, and Kev ran to get it. Dez peeked through the window, catching an open-mouthed gawk. His chest clenched, tighter than his jaw as Kev dashed back onto the porch.

"Tyler's in the hospital," Kev yelled in a near hysterical pitch, his eyes wide with fright.

Dez's knees almost gave out. He couldn't breathe. What the fuck was wrong with the air? How could it abandon him when he needed it most? Otis nudged Dez's arm. It kicked his legs in gear, but did nothing to resolve the no oxygen problem.

"Come on," Otis said, guiding Dez to the passenger side of his own pickup. "I'll drive you."

Chapter Nine

Sasha

Clouds of smoke wafted in gentle swirls, circling Sasha. Through thick puffs of gray, she glimpsed the clubhouse walls. People stood all around her, frozen solid mid-party. Their cups were raised, halted from reaching their lips. Arms were in the air, stuck mid-sway as their owners hit pause on a dance. Nothing moved, except for a flash of red behind the haze.

Sasha only glimpsed a half-second of a maybe memory, but she felt the electric buzz vibrate her bones.

"Candy!"

Green eyes broke through the clouds, curvy hips swinging as Candy sashayed through the crowd of statue people crammed into the hazy clubhouse. Soft skin brushed Sasha's fingertips when she grabbed Candy, bringing warm tingles. It was real. Her lips pressed against the sweetest mouth she ever tasted, and a scent she never thought would flow again filled her lungs.

"I love you," Sasha said. She had to say it, just in case Candy didn't know, since she didn't have the balls to say it before.

"Don't forget your skin," Candy's silky voice whispered, echoing around the smoke-filled room.

"What?" Sasha asked. She reached for Candy, grasping only cold air. A steady beep blasted her ears, flashing the world in blurs of color. Sasha searched the whirlwind for Candy, seeking out any hints of red.

Fingers pried Sasha's eyes open, and light flooded in to slap her brain. She swung her arms, whacking a solid body.

"Calm down, Ms. Ashby," a woman said gently. "You're all right, at the hospital."

Sasha sat up, straining to see beyond the fuzz clouding her eyes. No Candy. No clubhouse filled with frozen people. Just a hospital room, also known as a waiting area of Hell.

"Tyler!" Sasha yelled to the woman beside her, who quaked in her crisp nurse's outfit. "My son."

"Your son is in critical condition, but—"

Sasha ripped the IV from her arm, pulling wires off her chest.

"Oh dear," the nurse said, backing toward the door.

"Where's my clothes?" Sasha shouted, stopping the nurse in the doorway.

"Closet."

"Don't go anywhere." Sasha leapt from the bed. Pain hit in waves, clawing every inch of her body, and she dropped to one knee.

"Please," the nurse cried out, only stepping one foot from the doorway. "You've sustained massive injuries."

"They're old." The mirror on the closet door showed fresh bruises on her side, matching the new scrapes on her arm and face. "Mostly."

"If you're in a bad relationship, we can help," the nurse said.

That brought a snicker. Her bad relationship was with the feds and apparently the mob. Sasha fastened her belt, crying out from the spikes of pain that accompanied her wiggle into a blood-soaked tank top.

"I got these in jail, by a giant dyke bitch who raped me. Aren't ya glad you're nosey?" Sasha walked past the woman's gawk into the too bright hallway. "Now, where's my kid?"

In a jumble of gasps and oh-mys, the nurse took off down the hall. Sasha followed, faster than her achy body would allow. Fuck the pain. Fuck people's mushy feelings. She couldn't give two fucks until she saw her boy, held him tight.

When she walked into a dimly lit room and actually saw Tyler, she almost ran the other way. Now, she didn't want to see. It twisted her stomach to glimpse her boy's beautiful face covered by a hard plastic mask. Her knees quaked at the sight of wires and tubes running into his pale bare chest. The group of doctors who hovered over Tyler's still body were doing fuck-all to wake the kid besides smoke cigarettes, and she could do that.

"The mother's awake, Dr. Woodrow," the nurse said, keeping her distance from Sasha.

An older man stepped away from Tyler's bedside, taking Sasha by the hand.

"Sasha. I was your doctor during your coma."

The doctor stared at Sasha, like he wanted a thank you for doing absolutely nothing while she was trapped in a sea of black.

"What's wrong with him?" Sasha asked, pointing at Tyler. "Why isn't he awake?"

"Your son lost a lot of blood. When patients are so young, we like to transfuse with the parent's blood."

"Here, take mine." Sasha held out her arm. They could have all her blood, if it brought Tyler's smile back.

"We would have, but you're B positive. Tyler is A positive. We've contacted his father. He should be here any moment."

"Then will he wake up?" Sasha glanced at the tiny body on the bed, only for a second. Gore had never turned her gut before, but this was different. She couldn't stomach the sight of Tyler's little body covered in scratches and welts.

"I'm going to do everything I can to help your boy," the doctor said, patting Sasha on the arm.

Dez pushed his way into the room, dropping to his knees beside the bed. He took Tyler's limp hand, casting a glare over his shoulder. "Dammit, Sasha. What did you do?"

"He needs your blood," Sasha said, still stuck in the middle of the room.

"Do you know your blood type, Mr. Archer?" The doctor asked, and Dez jumped to his feet.

"B positive."

The room took a quick spin. Sasha stumbled, bumping into the nightstand. "Oh no. I…"

"I'm sorry," the doctor said softly, "but we need the real father."

"What?" Dez growled. He looked at Sasha, but she couldn't speak. How could she, with the hurt slathered on his face? Without a word, Dez stomped to the doorway, grabbed Vinny by the collar, and dragged him across the room. He shoved Vinny into Sasha's chest and walked out the door.

"Is this the father?" the doctor asked.

"What?" Vinny damn near shouted.

"Do you know your blood type, son?"

Vinny looked between Sasha and the doctor before a meek, "A positive," streamed from his mouth.

"He's Tyler's biological father," Sasha said, pointing but not looking at Vinny. "But Desmond Archer is Tyler's legal father."

"I understand," the doctor said, ushering Vinny to the door. "I need you to come with me Mr.…"

"Archer," Vinny muttered.

The doctor stopped short, glancing back at Sasha.

She shrugged. What the fuck could she say, besides yeah, I'm a brother-lovin' whore. They left the room, but the nurses at Tyler's bedside hurled snotty leers.

Sasha staggered into the hall, following a slew of "Fucks!" and "Sasha's" to the waiting room. Her eyes connected with Otis as she stepped in the doorway. He tried to ward her away with his stare, but she walked inside anyway. When Dez saw

Sasha, he latched onto her neck and squeezed.

"Why'd you come back, ruin my life?" Dez shouted, snuffing out the flow of air.

The need to fight never came to Sasha. Her arms hit her sides, all her muscles giving in. Dez was going to kill her. Thank God someone was finally going to kill her, end the misery she spread onto the beautiful people of this world.

It took Otis, Kev, and a security guard to pry Dez's fingers from Sasha's neck. She dropped to her knees, hacking as cool oxygen rushed in to scrape her sore throat. Dez stormed off and she reached out, only grasping the edge of his pants. Kev took her hand, and she yanked it away. Nobody else should touch her. She'd infect them with her plague of tragedy.

Shame was a strong motivator, granting Sasha just enough energy to climb off the floor. She limped toward the door, keeping her eyes low.

"Where you going?" Otis asked.

Funny, how they all wanted to know where she was going. Probably had bets on when she'd split.

"To find out who tried to kill my son, so I can strangle them with their own entrails."

"She didn't mean that literally," Kev said to the security guard as Sasha slipped from the waiting room.

***

Dez

Dez paced in front of his truck, sucking down a

joint. The cherry singed his fingertips, and he chucked it to the ground. He'd been burned enough, wasn't taking that shit from his own joint. He would blow town, leave the fucking state, but he couldn't abandon Tyler. Just 'cause some doctor spouted out the same shit his brother dropped on him last month doesn't make it true. Why did it have to be true?

A roar streamed from his lips as his fists slammed against the hood of his truck, denting metal. He turned and Vinny jumped back, holding his hands up.

"Please don't murder me," Vinny said.

"Are you happy now? You were right."

"No, I wasn't."

Dez curled his fingers into fists. It was the only way to keep from grabbing his little brother's neck and choking the life from it. "You said Tyler wasn't even mine, that you had Sasha first and would have her last."

"I was an asshole." Vinny rushed forward, knowing full-well he was entering the strike zone. "Stupid blood letters don't mean shit, not to Tyler. Not to me. You're his dad. You can't leave him. He'll grow up alone, like I did."

Dez slumped against his bumper. Tyler was his everything, *his* son. He changed a million diaper, held the boy all night when he was sick, kissed scrapes and made them better. That made Tyler *his* son.

"They're taking him into surgery," Vinny said, slowly placing his hand on Dez's arm. "To remove his spleen. If you hurry, you can see him before he goes."

"Sasha?"

Vinny pointed across the parking lot, to Otis chasing Sasha down the sidewalk.

"Let her go," Dez said, heading back toward the hospital. "She's the goddamn grim reaper of agony."

***

Sasha

Sasha walked down the road, away from Otis and his stompy feet. She stopped at a payphone, dumped in a hand full of change, and dialed, waiting for a voice she knew she could trust.

"Fat Tonys," Enzo said through the receiver, only he sounded different, shaky.

"179, e, n, Boston," Sasha said, then hung up. She patted herself down, finding no gun, no smokes, even her zippo was gone. A lit cigarette drifted in front of her eyes, and she snatched it.

"Thanks." Sasha glanced at the man beside her, seeing the Otis she remembered, not the new one that despised her.

"I talked to the paramedic. He's a friend." Otis took Sasha's hand, dropping spent shells in her palm. "He said someone hit you with a dump truck, flipped your pickup. You fought them off while trying to stop Tyler's bleeding."

"I didn't know someone was after me, I swear. I would've never come here. I wouldn't have—"

Otis wrapped his arms around Sasha, triggering an onslaught of tears. She hurried to clutch onto him, just in case whatever drug he was on wore off and he went back to hating her.

"What was the call you made?"

Sasha drew back, taking a long drag of her cigarette. "Code. I gotta wait a few minutes for the capo to drive across town, then I'll call the payphone on—"

A smirk lifted Otis's lips, choking up Sasha's words. It felt like ages since she'd seen the man's smile. "What?"

Otis shook his head, leaning against the building. It didn't look like he wanted to spill, and she was in no position to push him, not anymore.

"You got any quarters?" Sasha dumped the rest of her change into the phone along with most of Otis's quarters. When the ring was replaced by her name, spoken in Enzo's sharp tones, a sigh flew from her chest.

"I was hit," she said, sharper than intended. "With an actual dump truck, by made men."

"Shit, Sasha. I would've called, warned you, but we were hit too. AJ and his crew are gone, along with a bunch of other men."

"AJ's dead?" A stab tore into Sasha's chest. She didn't even like the guy, but he was family, and not just legit family but high up on the mafia chain.

"Who did this?" she asked with somewhat of a sneer.

"The Mancini family."

"Mancini?" Sasha said. "Why does that sound so familiar?"

Otis let out a huff, tossing his cigarette to the street.

"They're your family," Enzo said, sending his bitter edge through the receiver. "Your mother's people."

Her mother had people? What a scary thought, more Ellen's running around out there.

After a short pause, Enzo said, "Tony needs you back here. Now," in an even shorter tone.

"I didn't know my mother had people, Enzo. You gotta believe me."

"No, Sasha. It's not like that. We need you to track down these bastards. They're your people."

They were *not* her people. Her people sat in a building a block away, loathing her very existence.

"My kid's in critical condition. They literally hit us with a dump truck."

The line stayed silent. Apparently the boss's son getting murdered trumped everyone else's tragedies.

"I'll be there as soon as I can," Sasha said with a huff. "Forty-eight hours, tops."

"Be safe."

"You too." Sasha hung up the phone and grabbed the back of Otis's jacket before he could sneak off.

"What do you know about the Mancinis?" Sasha asked.

Otis shook free from Sasha's grip, continuing to walk away. "They're dangerous."

Sasha ran in front of Otis, which wasn't an easy feat with her achy everything. "I'm serious. I plan on gutting every last one of those fuckers. I need to know about 'em."

The way Otis rocked in place, his eyes wavering, Sasha could tell he was about to clam up.

"They almost killed Tyler today," Sasha said, watching the fire return to Otis's glare. "What if they get it right next time?"

That was all Sasha had to say to sway Otis. It was apparent when the joint came out of his front pocket.

Otis pulled Sasha into an alley beside the hospital and sparked the bone. "Ellen's mom ran a money laundering operation out of North Jersey. She started getting into some heavy shit, blackmailing, kidnapping, jury tampering. When they forced your mother to bomb a black church full of children, she ran off. That's when I met her."

The topic of family had always enraged Sasha's mother, and now she understood why. The Mancinis sounded like demons, which would explain how so much evil was able to creep into Sasha's soul. With Ellen gone, there was nobody left who held the amount of depravity necessary to match such a wicked force, except for her. "Where do I find them?"

"All I know is your mom grew up on a farm."

"A fucking farm in Jersey." Sasha snatched the joint from Otis, taking a big hit. "There's as many of them as there is shit in this alley," she said through a stream of smoke.

"Your mama had a lot of brothers. Everyone knows the name. They should be easy to find." Otis stole the joint back, wagging his finger. "Don't you try and do this alone."

An entire pack of blood-thirsty Italians, probably holding pitchforks and torches, were waiting for Sasha to lead a good ole fashion lynching. "I won't be alone."

"I don't mean your mobster friends," Otis said, the bridge of his nose crinkling in disgust. "You need people you can trust."

Sasha snickered. That was a good one. "All the people I trust don't trust me anymore."

"That's the problem with burning bridges. You can't get across them again." Otis handed Sasha the joint, walking away. "You better run across the bridge you just set ablaze under Dez's feet before you lose him forever."

Solid advice, which Sasha was totally going to take after a few more hits on this joint.

Chapter Ten

Sasha didn't make it into the hospital. Everyone was out front, standing in a cloud of cigarette smoke. It was weird to see from the outside. She was used to watching assholes race by from within that cloud. It felt like shit to be the asshole on the other side of it. They all stopped whispering and looked at her when she pierced their imaginary bubble. Each of their stares could be labeled: furious, torn, leery, hopeful, and confusion. They reminded Sasha of the seven dwarfs, except there were only six of them and they were more like six-foot tall raging truckers than dwarfs.

"How's Tyler?" Sasha asked, once her mouth decided to cooperate with her brain.

"He's in surgery," Vinny said. "We won't know anything for a few hours."

They all stared, waiting for Sasha to leave, so she backed away. Against her body's wishes, she walked through the sliding glass doors and into the stench of disinfectant. It was a smell she'd hoped to never experience again. Her nightmares came with that reek. It'd cling to her hair for three showers but for Tyler, she'd soak in it.

A hand gripped onto Sasha's arm, and she swung her fist. Dez caught her knuckles midair, the slap echoing down the hall.

"Fuck! I'm sorry," she muttered, pulling back.

Dez lunged forward, and Sasha flinched. He didn't strangle her this time. This time, Dez held her softly. He caressed her battered body instead of trying to quash the life from it. If he picked her up and carried her to her old room, to her old bed, it'd be a dream come true.

Reality flooded in the moment Dez pulled away, letting all the pain of her throbbing muscles and agony of her vile mind return.

"Thanks," Dez slid his arm around Sasha's waist, gentle, tender, "for protecting our son."

Sasha fell against Dez, feeding off his energy as they walked to the waiting room.

***

Dez

Dez drummed his fingers against his leg. The whole setup of a hospital was bullshit. It was almost 1990 for Christ's sake yet he was expected to sit in a room, jumping at every white coat that walked by. They should have monitors in here. He should be allowed to see what was happening to his kid every second he was away from his kid's side. The world was headed into a downward spiral, and it all started with the barbaric system they were running 'round here.

"What time is it?" Dez asked, shifting in his stiff chair.

"Five minutes later than the last time you asked," Vinny said, tossing a magazine on the table.

"It's been three hours!" Dez slammed his fist against the armrest, and Sasha jolted up in her chair. Now, on top of being on edge, he felt like a total ass. He'd been trying to keep quiet so she could sleep but fuck, it'd been three hours.

"What happened?" Sasha asked, sitting up.

"Dez was announcing the time," Kev said from the corner. "Again."

Sasha rubbed her eyes, looking at the clock. "Fuck! It's been three hours."

A tiny groan seeped from her lips as she turned, staring into the hall. Dez grinned. Finally, someone was getting it.

"You need anything, Sasha?" Kev asked, pulling Sasha's gaze back to the tiny depressing room.

"Stop kissing her ass," Otis grumbled.

Kev dropped into a chair, crossing his arms. "Can you not see how fucked up her face is?"

"Thanks," Sasha groaned. "You look like a pile of fucking sunshine."

"That's not what I meant. Just, never mind. Fuck it."

"You're my wife." Dez covered his mouth. He wasn't trying to lay that down, but the sparkle in Sasha's eyes forced it out of him.

Sasha sat up straight, a half-smile lifting her swollen cheeks. "What's that now?"

"We were gonna lose the holler," Dez said,

staring into Sasha's eyes even though everyone else looked away. "Ellen was gone, you were in a coma, and Dante was trying to put the property in probate." Sasha cringed at the word Dante, which made Dez want to beat the man's face in even more than before. "I bribed a priest to sign a marriage certificate, and Vinny fucked the county clerk so she'd backlog it a week before your…accident."

Vinny squirmed in his seat, elbowing Dez.

"It was my idea," Otis said, the only person in the room who seemed to be enjoying himself.

Sasha lowered her head into her hands, and Dez leaned forward in his chair. She was grinning. It was hidden behind her hair, but he could see it.

"We were married before Tyler was born?" Sasha asked, staring into Dez's eyes. "On paper?"

"Yeah." He wished Sasha was sitting next to him, so he could hold her hand, feel her skin radiate warmth against his own. "We can…undo the whole thing, now that you're awake."

"We did consummate it," Sasha said softly, a smile spreading across her split lips. "In my motel room."

Dez didn't think *that* gleam would ever shine in her eyes again, didn't expect lust to burn. Not after what happened to her, but the lust was there, and it was for him. He'd walk across the room, curl into the chair next to her, but the doctor was headed their way.

Before a white coat could brush the doorway, Dez was on his feet. The doctor stepped into the waiting room, holding a blank stare. Dez couldn't tell if it was time to celebrate or wreck shit.

"Tyler pulled through like a champ," the doctor said, flashing a grin at the hoot that streamed from Kev's mouth. "Barring any unforeseen circumstances, I think he'll be just fine. He's awake now, asking for his daddy."

Although Dez wanted to run down the hall calling out Tyler's name, his legs were locked tight. Tyler had to be asking for him. His boy couldn't possibly know the truth. Dez glanced at Vinny, and a spike jammed into his heart. Tyler had to be too young to understand, he just had to be.

"Go, man," Vinny said, pushing Dez toward the door.

Sasha wormed away, and Dez grabbed her hand. "Come on, stupid," he said through a grin. Her fingers slid between his as they followed the doctor into the hallway.

***

Sasha

Sasha circled the bed, scanning Tyler over. He looked so weak, fragile. She cataloged every scratch, didn't miss a single mark on his tiny body. The fuckers who did this to him would get it all back, and then some.

"You weren't careful, Mommy," Tyler muttered. His sleepy eyes scolded her, forcing a laugh from Sasha's chest.

"I'm so sorry, little dude." She leaned over the bed's rail, kissing the only spot on Tyler's forehead without a bruise.

Dez lowered the bedrail, kneeling at Tyler's side. "How do you feel?"

"My tummy hurts."

The sad little declaration struck Sasha like a fist. She staggered back, fighting the urge to flee. Other than giving the kid a shot of whiskey, she had no idea how to comfort his pain. She'd run and get a doctor or nurse but a fuckload of them already littered the room, watching Tyler whimper just like her useless ass.

"It's okay, buddy." Dez kissed the top of Tyler's head, wrapping his strong arms around the boy. Tyler scooted as close as he could get to Dez, latching on. Sasha knew exactly what her son was after. She'd felt Dez's soft lips kiss her cheek and melt the pain away. The man emitted safety in a way she was never capable. Of course the kid went straight for it.

It only took one big hug and a few minutes of a story about a sleeping princess for snores to replace Tyler's groans.

"He's been sedated," a nurse said, adjusting Tyler's IV. "He'll be out cold for at least four hours." The nurse stopped fiddling with a machine to shoot Sasha a sideways glare. "You might want to clean up, get a change of clothes."

Sasha looked down at her shirt and pants, cringing. What wasn't torn was stained in deep red. It didn't seem appropriate to fuss over her outfit at a time like this. The bloody tatters actually fit with her mood quite well, but she didn't want to scare the kid. At least, not any more than she already had.

"I'm gonna run to the motel, get washed up."

106

Sasha patted Tyler's hand, backing toward the door. She would've kissed Dez, but the way he'd embraced that little boy created an impenetrable field of safety around the two of them, and she couldn't risk breaking it.

"I *will* be back," Sasha said from the doorway.

For the first time since entering the room, Dez looked away from Tyler. "We'll see."

"We will," Sasha said, walking out the door. Vinny rushed down the hall the instant he saw her, followed by Otis and Kev.

"Well?" Vinny asked, practically shouting.

They crowded Sasha, crowded the entire hallway without giving a fuck.

"He fell asleep, drugs and shit, but he looks all right." Sasha gestured to a group of nurses who were gathered around a large desk, whispering and gawking. "I think I'm freaking 'em out."

"You got, like, a gallon of dried blood in your hair," Vinny said, tugging the end of a near dreadlocked strand.

"And streaks all down your neck," Kev added, not that Sasha needed his two cents.

"Listen," she glanced around, making sure no Italians lurked in the halls, "I'm going to my motel room to clean up. If I'm not back in forty minutes, something bad happened to me." She had to make sure they knew that, since her track record stated otherwise. Before she got to the front door, Vinny ran beside her.

"I'll take you home," he said, following Sasha out the wide sliding glass door. "You can shower there."

Home with Vinny sounded amazing. She had to jump on this offer, before it got rescinded. "Thanks."

Vinny handed Sasha a lit cigarette once their feet hit the sidewalk. For just a second, while breathing in pine-scented air, staring up at stars she could actually see, she felt like herself. She could be that girl again. Her son deserved a vicious, killing-machine of a mother. She'd had one, and it did wonders for her personality.

"We saw your truck on the way over here," Vinny said as they walked across the parking lot.

"Oh yeah. Did you see my weed, because that was in there?"

"No," Vinny said through a chuckle. "I got a joint in my ashtray."

That bit of info helped Sasha move her achy legs faster.

"When I saw your truck all smashed up, on its roof, I thought I lost you forever. I thought I lost both of you."

It was the moment she'd been waiting for, his forgiveness. It should've brought relief, not self-loathing. She hadn't earned shit, just capitalized on the chaos that followed her.

"They'll need to hit me with something bigger than a dump truck." Sasha reached for the passenger door and Vinny brushed past her, opening it.

"Don't do that," Sasha yelled, slapping his hand away.

"What?"

Sasha climbed into the truck. Razor-tipped prickles spread between her legs as she slid onto the seat, but she stifled her groans. "I'm good, don't need a butler." She slammed the door shut, leaning against the open window. "You've seen me fucked up worse than this."

"No, I haven't."

Vinny hurried around the front of the truck, dropping behind the steering wheel, and Sasha grabbed a joint from the ashtray.

"Are we gonna talk about the blood type thing?" Vinny asked, although it didn't sound like a question. It sounded like he wanted some kind of omission, perhaps an apology, except he'd find neither in the cab of this truck.

"No." Sasha snatched the zippo from Vinny's hand, avoiding his glare. "Dez is Tyler's father. That's what we decided, in the woods that day." Vinny had his chance, they both did, and blew it. How different everything would be if only they'd told the truth. She wouldn't have fell in the cellar, her mother would be alive, and the kid in there would cling to her, not Dez. None of that mattered. It was a life that didn't belong to her, in a world that never existed. A wise person once told her not to dwell on what-ifs and should-haves. She had to live in the now, and all the slaughter to come in the future.

Chapter Eleven

Just like old times, Sasha hobbled up the stairs beside the garage. Wooden boards creaked as she stepped onto the landing. The squawk of old wood, also known as the sound of home, sent flutters of warmth that melted the icy shell that had become her self. Her excitement grinded to a halt when the door squeaked open. Bare dresser tops gleamed in the overhead light, just as shiny as the freshly swept floor. Wait, a floor?

"Where's my shit!" Sasha said, barging into the room.

"I burned it."

Vinny said it so casually, as if it weren't a lifetime's worth of memories. "Dude!" she yelled, gawking at the hollow, near-empty room.

Vinny tossed his keys on the nightstand, sliding out of his jacket. "You pissed me off."

It was a pretty valid reason, one Sasha couldn't rebut. "Did it make you feel better?"

"Yeah," Vinny said, without thinking twice.

"Then I guess it was worth it." Sasha shrugged.

The fire gods could have her shit as long as Vinny found a fraction of solace.

"I saved some stuff." Vinny opened the closet, pulling out a cardboard box.

Sasha knelt down as he unfolded the top. The first flap peeled back, revealing a hint of flames. With the shedding of the second flap, a bright emblem of a semi truck's grill filled her view. Vinny didn't get to open the rest of the box. Sasha sprang forward, grabbed onto her father's old jacket, and pulled it to her chest. Smooth leather tickled her fingertips, its soft crinkle sending shivers. It smelled the same, felt fucking great as she hugged it tight.

"I couldn't burn that."

The box was a treasure trove of awesome. Clothes Sasha really missed, bottles of perfume she'd never use again, and little wooden boxes filled with value-less yet priceless keepsakes.

"This is, like, everything," Sasha said, her smile growing wider the deeper she dug through her crap. "What'd you burn?"

Vinny dropped to his ass, leaning against the wall. "Some bloody clothes, a mountain of empty cigarette packs."

Sasha's chuckle couldn't be stopped, and it carried away at least ten pounds of stress as it escaped.

"I need a shower." She wobbled to her feet. An attempt to lift her tank top sparked a blaze in her shoulder, ripping a cry from her chest.

"Let me," Vinny said, jumping up off the floor.

"Seriously?"

"I won't look." Vinny walked behind Sasha. His hands fell to her waist, and she flinched. His grip remained light, gentle, yet she couldn't make her stiff body relax.

"Besides," he said, leaning closer. "I already have every curve memorized."

Warm breath flowed over Sasha's neck, igniting a tingle that hurt her most tender of places more than it excited. Vinny lifted the end of her shirt, peeling the blood-crusted fabric from her skin. A hand glided down her back, so soft. She forgot hands could touch in such a loving way. When his fingers hit the snap of her pants, he froze.

"Can I?" Vinny asked in a whisper.

Lips landed on Sasha's shoulder, and a tear skated down her cheek. She almost said no, almost pushed him away. But the image he still held of her, an undefeatable force to be reckoned with, was something she didn't want to lose. Plus, the notion of bending down to remove her pants seemed like torture.

"Yeah," Sasha said, twice since the first attempt only erupted as a stutter.

Vinny dropped to his knees, taking Sasha's jeans with him. She ignored his gasp, stepped out of the clingy denim, and walked into the bathroom.

"You can burn those too," she said, turning on the hot water.

***

No matter how shitty the water pressure, there was nothing better than a shower in your own home.

112

The harsh man-stink shampoo dampened the experience, but not enough for Sasha to give a shit. It was weird to smell Vinny on every inch of her body, and strangely comforting.

The clothes he'd left on the sink fit like a glove. Her old baggy cargo pants were pure bliss to slide into. Vinny even hung one of her ratty bandanas on the doorknob, cleaned and pressed.

Sasha grabbed the bandana, its soft fabric wrinkling in her grasp. For a good, long minute, she stared at herself in the mirror. She wasn't the girl who could pull off that black and red bandana, or carry the weight of that skin lying on the bed. The scatter of bruises on her face seemed right, and a cold leer filled her eyes, but her head wasn't right. She wasn't ready to be that girl, not yet.

Carefully, she hung the bandana back on the doorknob and walked from the bathroom.

"You look much better," Vinny said, sitting up on the bed.

"I feel almost much better."

Vinny lifted a joint and flashed a smile.

"Now I'm much better." Sasha eased onto the bed, dropping to her back. "Weed me." A deep chuckle pulled her glare. "What?"

"It's just...fuck!" Vinny rolled onto his side, staring at Sasha beyond the smoke that wafted from the joint in his grasp. "This. You."

"Don't get dorky on me now." Sasha snatched the doobie, taking a long hit.

"Sasha. I was trying to tell you something, before the coma, but you kept cutting me off."

Sasha hit the joint a few more times, since Vinny

was too busy blabbering to smoke.

"I love you."

Vinny said the words so firmly, so genuinely, it sucked the pot smoke right out of Sasha's lungs in the form of a cough. She handed him back the joint. It looked like he needed it more than she did, unless she also had that yellowish tinge to her skin.

"I love you too," Sasha said, failing to hold back her smile. "More than a friend, and not like a brother. But…"

"Dez." Vinny snickered, his head shaking.

"I can't hurt him again."

"You got no problem hurting me."

"You're special." Sasha thought it was funny, but Vinny didn't laugh. A bit of an asshole vibe snuck in and she shrugged it off, sitting up to face him. "I didn't come back here to make trouble, fuck up everyone's shit."

"Really?" Vinny snorted, crushing out the tiny stub of a joint in an ashtray.

"Really. I wanna do right by Tyler, give him a mom and a dad."

"That's…" Vinny hopped off the bed, grabbing his jacket. "Your line of thinking is straight-up retarded."

Sasha rolled off the mattress, climbing to her feet. Flashbacks of her mother's viper tongue started to crowd the room, scorch the air, so she made her way to the door.

"Want your jacket?" Vinny asked.

"No." Sasha didn't look back, didn't want to see her old skin calling out to its owner. As she stepped onto the landing, a cool breeze ran over her bare shoulders, cutting through her tank top.

"It's chilly," Vinny said, lifting the faded leather coat.

No shit it was chilly, but Sasha couldn't put that jacket on. Everything it symbolized was the opposite of who she had become.

"You got a flannel?" she asked, crossing her arms to combat the mountain's icy winds.

***

Sasha walked across the parking lot, peeking inside the hospital's wide glass door. Dez paced in the hallway then thrusted his pointed finger at a doctor's chest as Kev wedged himself between them.

"This can't be good," Vinny said, rushing inside.

As Sasha tossed her cigarette to the ground, a hand gripped onto the back of her neck. Her fist cocked back, and the barrel of a gun jammed into her side.

"Come with me now, and I won't have your boy clipped," a man whispered into Sasha's ear.

That slimy sharp accent, spewing out threats to her child, boiled Sasha's blood. She nodded. The asshole behind her probably thought she'd agreed with his demand, but she was giving her fist the go-ahead to fly. She shifted her weight, ready to swing, and the gun pulled away from her back, clanking against the sidewalk. Garbled words filled her ears, and the fingers clutching onto her neck fell limp.

Sasha turned and Otis winked, squeezing a greasy-looking wiseguy tighter in a chokehold.

"Shh," Otis said, the muscles in his arm flexing. "Go to sleep."

The man's arms flopped, his legs buckling, and Otis dragged him into an alley. Sasha scooped the fallen glock off the sidewalk, glancing around the empty parking lot as she followed.

"Friend of yours?" Otis asked, dropping the guy in a pile of trash.

Sasha stared at the man's face in the dim light. Something about his high cheekbones, pointed chin, looked familiar, but she couldn't place it.

"Don't know him, but those shoes." Sasha couldn't miss those dark-tipped loafers, especially not with the spot of blood on them, her son's blood. "I need to talk to this guy, someplace quiet."

"Wait here," Otis said, taking off across the parking lot.

With the gun high and aimed at the man's head, Sasha crept toward the end of the alleyway and peeked down the sidewalk.

"Sasha!"

Vinny's panicked call pushed Sasha's finger against the trigger. Thankfully, she didn't shoot. To kill this man here would be too easy, for him.

"What the fuck are you—" Vinny stopped just outside the alley, staring down at the pair of legs in the glow of streetlights. "What the fuck's going on?"

"What's going on in there?" Sasha tried to glimpse through the wide sliding door of the hospital, but a glare blocked her view. "Tyler?"

"No. Shift change. The new doc was trying to toss Dez out. Some bullshit about parents only."

"Awesome," Sasha groaned, as if Dez needed any more reasons to despise her.

"Don't worry. I set the doc straight."

"I bet you did, with a please and a smile."

Vinny frowned, kicking a can into the alley. "It's how you deal with propers."

In a screech of tires, Otis pulled his pickup to the curb.

"Help me with this guy." Sasha tucked the gun into her waistband, grabbing the man's limp hands along with bits of slimy papers.

"Dez is asking about you," Vinny said, lifting the guy's legs.

"Fuck, dude! It's not like I'm out here having a smoke break," Sasha grumbled, struggling to haul the body through a cramped, trash-strewn alleyway.

Otis opened the back door of his truck, and Sasha shoved the asshole who'd ruined her plans inside. Instead of jumping in the passenger seat, her legs scurried backward. She really wanted to torture this guy, but she *really* wanted to check on Tyler.

"I'm taking him to the old saw mill, outside town," Otis said, slamming the back door shut. "Meet us there, and don't be lollygagging." He tapped Vinny on the chest before rounding the truck. "You're with me."

"I gotta get involved?" Vinny asked, his tone of voice bordering on whiny.

Sasha pushed Vinny toward the passenger door of Otis's truck, holding out her hand. "Gimme your keys."

Vinny stood firm, a sour look scrunching his face, and Sasha dug through his jacket pockets. She pulled a keyring from his inside pocket, smiling at his frown.

"Thanks!" she said, jingling the keys as she walked backward toward the hospital. "See you in a few."

Her smile faded when she stepped under harsh fluorescent lights and choked on the stink of hospital. She strolled past the nurse's station, killing the perky chatter. The women's nervous eyes gawked, and Sasha flashed her now clean clothes on her way into Tyler's room.

Dez jumped up from a chair when Sasha walked in. His grin lit a spark in his beat eyes, and she hurried toward the shimmer.

"You came back," Dez said, only moving one foot away from Tyler's bed.

Fear had never hindered Sasha's steps until now. She was terrified to get any closer to either of them, afraid her unending cyclone of destruction would rip them to shreds. But the second her gaze landed on Tyler and the way his little nose twitched during sleep, her selfish desire to hold the child close overrode her logical decision to leave his life and never return.

"Vinny told me about the asshole doctor," Sasha said, glancing at Dez. "I'm..." Sorry didn't seem like the right thing to say. I'm a great big pathetic slut fit much better.

"Where is Vinny, Otis?"

"Yeah." Sasha squirmed away and Dez grabbed onto her waist, brushing the gun.

"What's going on?" Dez asked, with more annoyance than concern in his voice.

He looked so tired, so completely fed up with her shit. This bullshit with the mob might tip him over the edge, end her chance at redemption, but she couldn't rebuild their relationship on a foundation of lies.

"Somebody tried to nab me on the way in here, the same fucker who hit us with the dump truck." Sasha looked at her poor little dude, lost under wires and tubes. The scratches on his beautiful face warped her guilt to fury.

"What do they want?" Dez asked, stepping closer to Tyler's bedside.

"To die."

Dez smirked, which incited a giddy type of hum in Sasha's chest. It ran beneath her skin, growing to a warm tingle as it invaded every inch of her body. She reached for Dez, realized how desperate she looked, then jerked her arm back. Dez didn't let her get very far. His hands glided up her sides, along her neck, to her cheeks, and she didn't fight him. The fingers running into her hair gave off too much strength to part with, and the silky lips nearing her own were far too inviting to turn away.

"Is this okay?" Dez asked, pulling Sasha so close she could almost feel the tremble of his lips.

"Always." She kissed him hard, grinding into him even though it hurt like hell. Anything could happen between now and the next time Dez touched her body. She might not even make it across the parking lot. This moment had to count. The hands gripping her tight, that tongue skating along the roof of her mouth, those goddamn abs that had more ripples than the Hudson after a storm, had to be utilized. Dez gave her the tools to set the world aflame in this kiss.

A light sway set Sasha's feet to wobble as Dez pulled back. "Thanks," she said.

"Huh?"

Sasha pulled the gun from her waistband, holding it out. "People might be coming here, to hurt Tyler."

"Keep it." Dez lifted his shirt, showing the butt of a revolver tucked into a holster. "What crew are we wiping out?"

"Mobsters," Sasha said, also managing to convey a sorry with that one word.

"Like in the movies?"

Sasha shrugged, dropping a soft kiss on Tyler's forehead before backing toward the door. "I don't know. I've been kinda out of the loop for the last five years. Love ya." She stopped in the doorway, her mouth caught open. She didn't mean to say that last part out loud, but it was out there, in the air, causing a crinkle in Dez's brow.

"I love you too, you crazy bitch," he said, flashing a smile.

Although it actually hurt to do, Sasha walked away from the dimly lit room that housed everything she'd die for. The nurses stopped to gawk, again, as she strolled by. This time, Sasha blew them a kiss before strutting down the hall. That should keep them busybodies gabbing for at least an hour.

Kev walked from the waiting room as Sasha headed for the front door.

"What's up?" he asked, blocking her swift exit to

much needed revenge.

Sasha leaned close to Kev, eyeing the near empty hallway beside them. "You packing?"

"Hell yeah."

"Keep your eye on Tyler's room and your finger on the trigger."

"What am I aiming at?" Kev asked, his hand resting on the butt of his holstered gun.

"Any Italian mobster-looking motherfuckers." Sasha patted Kev on the arm, then strolled out the sliding glass door.

Chapter Twelve

Sasha walked through a kicked-in metal door of a long forgotten brick building. The thump of her boots echoed around the wide-open space as she crept deeper into the sawmill. It was perfect. Cobwebs hung from old steel machines, a man was tied to a logging table that had a giant saw protruding from it right above his head. There was even a flickering light that swung to cast shadows over Otis and Vinny, all perfect. Sasha grinned at Otis, and he nodded. She'd have to thank him later. This setup was like Christmas and her birthday all rolled into one.

She circled the table, glaring down at the man tied to it. The guy didn't cry out, beg to be freed; he just stared at her with a sneer on his now busted lips.

"Did he have ID on him?"

"No," Vinny said, holding out an envelope. "Just this."

Her name gleamed on the paper, in script she'd never seen before. Sasha grabbed the envelope, whacking it on the guy's face. "What's this?"

"Open it and find out."

"Damn. You got a nasty fucking attitude." Sasha pulled the gun from her waistband, pressing its barrel against the man's temple. He didn't squirm or break his hard stare, so she clicked the hammer back. "Aren't you even gonna try to grovel for your life?"

"There's no point."

"You're right." Sasha shoved the letter and gun into Vinny's hands, then pulled a knife from Otis's belt. "You see that there." She pointed the tip of the long, serrated blade at the man's shoe, tapping the little red spot. "That's my kid's blood. You made my kid bleed."

Sasha's hands trembled. She couldn't get the image of Tyler hanging upside down from her head. His little hands, dangling from a limp body, were seared into her eyes, and she couldn't shake it. She could still feel the drops of blood that rained from the child's cuts, even though she'd scrubbed them away. The only way to make it stop was to slice.

For every mark that blemished her son's smooth skin, Sasha left a gash ten times deeper. Skin ripped as she dragged the knife along the man's cheek, chin, the corner of his eye. Hints of tendons tore beneath her blade and peeked out from tatters of flesh before disappearing under pools of blood. Messy, things were getting messy and loud. The man's screams not only bounced off the wall but sprayed blood. Sasha's freshly cleaned clothes were now speckled in red and the man's face was a disaster, but she couldn't miss that one spot on his forehead.

"There we go," she said, stepping back to stare at her masterpiece. It was hard to tell if she got the placements of the cuts right. With all that blood and puffy skin, the guy's face just looked like chopped meat. She lifted the knife, pointing it at the man, and a stream of blood flew from its tip. "They had to take out my son's spleen."

Thick drops of blood dripped from the knife's teeth as Sasha cut the guy's shirt open. She had no idea where the spleen was. This guy's flabby stomach could be hiding three spleens. She'd just have to cut extra deep and take out everything.

Sasha drove the blade into the man's flesh. His howl shuddered her grip on the handle. All those layers of fat put up quite a struggle, which is why she put her foot on the table for leverage and pushed harder. A twist of her wrist sent a spurt of blood into the air, its splat lost under garbled cries.

"Sasha!" Vinny yelled, halting her tear of skin.

She veered her glare to Vinny, her hand still tugging at whatever bone the tip of her blade was stuck on.

"Aren't you supposed to be getting information?" Vinny asked, looking away from the blood-soaked table.

"Right," Sasha said through a chuckle. Since the knife wouldn't budge, she left it planted in the man's stomach. "I actually forgot." She wiped her hands on the guy's slacks, cringing at the puffy shards of flesh meant to be the guy's face. "Hey, asshole. What's your name?"

"F-Fuck, you," he managed to choke out

between groans.

"I don't think he's talking." Sasha glanced around the dusty floor, grinning at the sight of a sledgehammer. Another lovely gift this perfect place had to offer. It was heavier than she expected and felt better than she thought it would in her hand.

"Hold up," Otis said, lifting his hand to stop Sasha as she dragged a sledgehammer toward the logging table. He lit a cigarette, strolling next to the man who sniveled and gagged on his own blood. "Guess we better get Ellen in here," he said, nodding to Vinny.

"I knew it," the man stuttered, squirming against the ropes around him. "My sister can't die. She's like a cockroach."

"He's a Mancini," Otis said, dropping his cigarette in a puddle of blood. "Your uncle."

Sasha barely heard anything after get Ellen in here. How could she hear, with that pound in her temples? "Is she really dead?" Sasha clutched onto Otis, his jacket crinkling in her grasp. "Did you see my mother's body?"

"Yeah, I…" Otis laid his hand atop Sasha's balled fist, holding tight. "I did. She was really fucking dead. I'm sorry, Sasha. I didn't mean to…"

Otis was a liar to the core, but no one could fake the amount of sadness trapped in Otis's gaze. The second of hope twisted Sasha's mind. She couldn't take the aimlessness that came with not being told what to do. It could have ended, if her mother really was alive. Since only chaos remained, she figured, fuck it. Why not dive in headfirst?

The sledgehammer scraped the concrete floor as

Sasha walked across the room. She slammed its solid head onto the thick steel table, drawing a yelp from the man's split lips.

"Slide me that stool," Sasha said, glancing at Vinny. When the legs of a stool didn't grind against the floor, she looked over and into a leery glare. "Do you need to wait outside?"

Vinny kicked the stool, sending it in a skid to Sasha's feet. She climbed up the wobbly legs, standing tall atop the seat. "Hold me steady." The stool stopped teetering once Otis clutched her hips. She lifted the sledgehammer, glaring down at the bloody mess of a man wriggling on the table. "Why did you come after me?"

Sasha gave the guy all of two seconds to answer before letting the mallet's weight drop. The head slammed against the man's arm, cracking it sideways. His scream swallowed up the snap of his bone and grated Sasha's ears. She'd had enough. Answers didn't mean shit to her at this point, only silencing the man's agonizing shrieks.

"You should've changed your shoes, Uncle Asshole." Sasha swung the sledgehammer, bringing it down on the man's face. The massive splatter of pink and scarlet clumps jolted her body back. It was like a watermelon hit with a twelve gauge, surprising. A clump of skull-laced brain dripped from the mallet's head as she dropped the sledgehammer on the man's twitching body, easing off the stool.

"We're gonna need some gas," Sasha said, looking between Otis and Vinny's stunned faces.

***

Vinny

"That was…scary." Vinny strummed his fingers on the steering wheel of his pickup, speeding away from the sawmill. He didn't even want to look at Sasha. It wasn't the bloodbath painting her skin that bothered him. It was the bloodlust in her eyes.

"Yeah. So was seeing Tyler all busted up, unconscious, hanging from the seatbelt I'm glad you told me to put on him."

It was a good point. If Vinny were in her position…hell, he would've done worse. "Now what?"

"Turn into the motel. I wanna get my shit."

Vinny busted a left, driving along a row of doors. Only one was kicked open, spilling light onto the sidewalk. It had to be Sasha's room.

"Motherfucker!" Sasha jumped from the cab before Vinny could shift into neutral.

"Wait." Vinny grabbed his gun, hurrying after her. Mobsters didn't materialize from the woodwork with Tommy guns, which was always a plus, but Sasha was fuming. Her shit was strewn on every surface. Ripped flannels scattered the stripped bed, pieces of denim covered the orange carpet in blue, and a little card with the Federal Bureau of Investigation's seal rested on the nightstand.

"That's real fucking mature," Sasha grumbled, climbing atop a long dresser.

"What are you doing?"

"I stashed something up here." On the tips of her

toes, she reached up and pushed aside a square of tile. "Hopefully—Yes!"

A black briefcase slid from the ceiling, and Sasha jumped to the floor. Headlights flooded the room, a rumble silencing the cricket's chirp. Vinny glanced out the open door as Otis pulled behind his still running truck.

"We should get back to the hospital," Sasha yelled from the bathroom, over the stream of running water. "What time is it?"

Otis leaned against the doorway, lighting a cigarette. "They're gonna send more, smarter people."

"Let 'em." Sasha strolled from the bathroom, tossing a blood-stained towel to the floor. "I'll pick 'em off one by one."

"Aren't they your family?" Vinny asked, snatching the cigarette from Otis's hand before it could reach the man's lips.

"No. Tyler's my family, and you guys."

Otis grabbed his cigarette back, glaring at Sasha. "The Mancinis are gonna come here, come for Tyler as retribution."

"No, they won't." Sasha snatched the cigarette from Otis's lips, taking a long drag. "I'm gonna find them first."

Vinny had no intention of letting Sasha run off on her own. By the looks on Otis's face, that guy wasn't down for murdering Ellen's kinfolk. Vinny didn't care. Ellen never gave a fuck about hurting his people and she knew them, supposedly loved them.

"I have this." Vinny pulled the letter from his

pocket, waving it in Sasha's face. "I bet it's important."

Sasha reached out and Vinny lifted the letter high, far from her grasp.

"Give it."

"Not until you—"

The tip of Sasha's boot slammed into Vinny's shin. Sharp prickles took him to a bend, and she plucked the letter from his grasp.

"Damn." Vinny rubbed his leg as Sasha ripped open the envelope. When snickers didn't fill his ears, he looked up and into wide eyes. "What does it say?"

It looked like she wanted to talk, the way her mouth inched open, but nothing came out. Otis took the paper from Sasha's tight grip, stepping into the light.

"Hey, little girl," Otis read out loud, "been waiting a long time for you to wake up. We need to talk. Call me, when you're done with your temper tantrum and ready to have a civilized conversation. No games, little girl. I'll know." Otis folded the paper and Sasha snatched it from his hand.

"You gonna call the number?" Otis asked.

"No. I'm gonna have the Lazzaris use their connections to trace it. Then I'll pay Dante a visit, in person."

Otis grabbed Sasha's arm, stopping her mad dash from the room. "He's with the Mancinis."

"I'm going with you," Vinny said, trying his damnedest to keep from sounding like a whiny sidekick. Sasha grinned, and not the snarky yeah-right one. It was relief.

"I can't go back there." Otis released Sasha, backing out the door. "Sorry, Sasha." He got into his truck without another word and drove from the motel's parking lot.

"You ready?" Sasha asked, heading to Vinny's truck.

"What, we're leaving right now?" Vinny followed Sasha to his truck, standing outside the passenger door.

"No." Sasha slid onto the bench seat, fishing through the ashtray, probably in search of a joint, which she'd most likely find. "We have to face someone much worse than my psychotic father and long-lost mobster family. Dez."

***

Sasha

A ray of sunlight peeked over the hospital's west wing, beaming down to hit Sasha right in the eye. She'd been left shade-less, thanks to the douchy feds and their teenage girl hissy-fit.

It would've been ridiculous to think Otis had run here just to check on Tyler and not tattle on her planned rampage. Judging by the huddle going on in the corner when she walked into Tyler's room, tattling was exactly what Otis was doing.

"Mommy!" Tyler reached out, groaned, and then grabbed his stomach.

Sasha ran to the bed, beating Dez in a race to hold the child's quivering body. "Careful, little dude. You're on the mend," she said, keeping a light clutch on Tyler's arm.

Tyler nodded, leaning back against the pillow. "I wanna go home, watch my *Fraggly Rock* video."

Sasha laid her lips atop Tyler's head, hiding her frown in his messy hair. "Did they say when he could go home?" she asked, looking at Dez.

"Why? You won't be here," Dez sneered, and Tyler tensed up.

"You're leaving?" Tyler squawked.

"Yeah," Sasha said, and Tyler clung to her arm. "But only to go get my stuff, so I can move in with you."

That brought a smile to Tyler's swollen lips, and he settled back against the pillows. Sasha stood, pushing Dez into the farthest corner of the room. "What the fuck is wrong with you?"

"What the fuck is wrong with *you*?" Dez grabbed Sasha's hand, pulling it to his chest. "I just got you back."

"I have to go. It's the only way to protect Tyler."

Dez slid his arms around Sasha's waist, holding tight. "We can protect Tyler here, together."

The comfort that came with Dez's touch almost crumbled Sasha's will. She looked away from his soft gaze. The blaze that lit his eyes would scramble her brain and force her to stay, which would bring two mob families to her son's doorstep.

"No. I can't take that chance," Sasha said.

Hurt spanned Dez's face. Sasha braced for it, but his shove still knocked her back two steps.

"You just wanna run in and save the day for the Lazzari family."

"That's not what this is about. I don't give a fuck

about the Lazzaris or the Mancinis." Sasha wanted to throw her arms around Dez, hug him tight in case it was her last chance, but fear held her back. An attempt to embrace that man was like trying to pet a stray dog. Fucker could bite. "I want to build a life with you and Tyler, but my shit list is a mile long and it just keeps getting longer every day. I can cross almost everyone off in one trip, three days max."

Dez sneered, turning away. "Yeah, well, maybe I won't be waiting around for you this time."

This conversation was going fucking swell, and she didn't even drop the Vinny part yet. As if on cue, Vinny walked into the room holding her briefcase. He handed it to Sasha, shooing Otis away from Tyler to go in for a hug.

"What's that?" Dez asked, tapping the case.

"I brought this for Tyler," she said, holding out the briefcase. "You'll know what to do with it better than I will."

Dez hesitated, almost like she was handing him a bomb.

"It's forty-eight g's," Sasha said, and Dez snatched the handle.

"What the—"

"My earnings, for the last year. I thought the kid should get it."

For a second, it looked like Dez might give hating her a rest. Then she remembered, there actually was a bomb she had to drop.

"I'm taking Vinny with me."

"Right," Dez said, like he'd just figured out the secrets of the universe. "Of course you are."

Vinny, with his stupid knack for horrible timing, stepped beside Sasha and Dez's glare warped from fiery to inferno. "You're both assholes!"

"Dude," Vinny drawled, and Dez snorted.

"Just go," Dez said, waving them off. "Have fun."

Through sheer luck, Sasha was able to grab Dez's hand. More luck allowed her to pull him close. Either that, or he'd gotten weak in his old age.

"This is some kind of revenge, isn't it?" Dez dropped his stare, squeezing Sasha's hand. "For what I did, with…her."

"No!" Sasha could slug Dez for bringing that up. A coma, months playing hooky, all the beautiful women she'd fucked, and she still couldn't scrub away the vile thought of Dez's hands on her mother's body.

"We'll bring Cash," Vinny said in a rush. "He can be your spy."

If it wouldn't make her look guilty, Sasha would slap Vinny upside the head for cooking up such a stupid idea. She didn't even know which one of those twins was Cash.

"Just come back alive." Dez didn't look at either of them as he brushed by. He just passed the briefcase to Otis and squeezed on the bed beside Tyler.

Sasha stared at her son who was cuddling under Dez's arm, his deep brown eyes fixed on her. The announcement of her departure was supposed to be the hard part. Boy had she been foolish. It was the actual leaving them, here in this hospital room, that turned out to be damn-near impossible. Her knees quaked, threatening to give out. She could do this, she could walk over there and kiss her son goodbye, for what might be the last time and not weep like a baby.

Chapter Thirteen

Both of those Neanderthal looking twins dashed from the clubhouse when Vinny's truck pulled into the lot. The sight of their dewy eyes laid a ten-pound load on Sasha, which was awesome 'cause the weight on her shoulders just wasn't heavy enough.

"Are we really taking one of them lunkheads along?"

Vinny shrugged, parking beside the garage. "Why not? It's always good to have backup."

The prospect's sloppy steps kicked up gravel as they hurried to Sasha's door. Those two didn't look like backup. The poor naive bastards were walking casualties, having had only broken soldiers to train them.

"We're gonna get Cash killed," Sasha muttered, opening her door.

Vinny hesitated, clinging to his open truck door. Sasha hoped he'd changed his mind, decided not to drag some wet-behind-the-ears farm boy into a big city wolf den, but he just said, "I gotta grab some

135

shit."

Sasha climbed from the pickup as Vinny headed for the stairs beside the garage. She turned from the thump of boot on what should be her steps, glaring at two jacked-up versions of Kev. "Which one of you is Cash?"

They both stood up straight, shooting a near identical dumbass stare at each other. The tall, wide one stepped forward and gulped. At least the guy had enough sense to be terrified.

"Sorry bro, you gotta come with us to New York. Go pack a bag, be sure to put some clothes in with the guns. Other guy," Sasha racked her memory for a name, coming up blank.

"Cory."

"Right." Sasha didn't have time to feel like an asshole, and the men in front of her didn't have time to be offended. "Cory. Go bring Tyler his freaky rock video and the VCR. Maybe the TV too. The ones they got there are shit."

They scurried toward the big house, and Sasha headed up to *Vinny's* room. The second she crossed the threshold, Vinny tossed a backpack at her chest.

"What's this?" Sasha asked, holding up the jean bag.

"I packed some stuff for you."

"Weed and weapons!"

"Clothes," Vinny said through a chuckle, handing Sasha a duffle bag. "This one's weed and weapons."

Sasha dropped the bags to the floor, making her way to the nightstand in search of a pre-rolled joint. "I don't know, man."

"About Cash?"

"Well yeah, but…"

"Dez," Vinny said, in almost a sneer.

Vinny's attempt at tough did little to mask the hurt in his voice. It seemed wrong for Sasha to talk to him about Dez, but he was the person she always turned to for this kind of shit…before. If the crease on his brow got any deeper, then she'd stop.

"Dez looked at us like he's been waiting for us to take off together," Sasha said, abandoning her search of the ashtray to comb through the scatter of cigarette packs. "He wasn't even surprised when he found out you were Tyler's—" She slapped her hand over her mouth. Some idiotic part of her brain actually believed if it weren't said aloud, it wouldn't be true.

"Yeah," Vinny said, low and drawn out. He walked toward Sasha, her every muscle growing stiff. His arm brushed her chest as he reached down, opening the top drawer of the nightstand. "I might've said a few things to Dez." He pulled out a joint, its white paper gleaming as he lit his zippo. "Things we said we wouldn't say, that day in the woods."

Vinny's words came out between puffs of smoke. The sweet aroma cloaked the stench of betrayal, so she didn't lay into him.

"You can bet Dez was surprised then." Vinny took another hit, passing the joint to Sasha. "So was my face, when it started getting pounded."

"Why'd you do it?"

"When I got those pictures, Dez freaked. Said we should all forget about you. That you forgot about us."

"What pictures?" Sasha asked.

Another trip into the nightstand's drawer and Vinny pulled out a manila envelope. He dumped the envelope, spilling large, glossy prints of her face onto the bed. Half the pictures had Rosalie's address in the background. The others, close-ups of her kissing Rosy, and Liz, and Michelle, were tasteless jabs. No street signs in those photos. Their sole purpose was to turn those who loved her against her. Only one kind of evil would deploy such a vicious tactic.

"Fucking feds," Sasha yelled, pushing the photos to the floor. "I was wondering why they didn't pick me up a year ago. They wanted me on the property so they could poke around."

"They weren't the only ones who wanted you on the property so they could poke around." Vinny jabbed his finger at Sasha's stomach and she swatted his hand away, biting back a smile. Hope brimmed in his eyes. He wanted so much from her, a kiss, her love, the recognition of fathering her child. All she had to give was the roach burning her fingertips and a pat on the arm.

Sasha walked to the door, grabbing the bags from the floor. Huffs and grumbles flowed behind her. It wasn't easy to ignore her best friend's pain, but she stepped into the sun's warmth without looking back.

***

Special Agent Philip Daniels

"Agent Daniels! We just got word on the bug. She's leaving town."

Daniels jumped up from his desk, pushing past the young agent and tearing ass down the hall. According to his watch, he still had two hours before he could legally pick the Ashby perp up for questioning again, but time zones confuse things.

The director looked up from a stack of papers on his desk, grumbling as Daniels burst into the makeshift office in this commandeered building. Must be the hideous view of a shitheel town that had his superior in a huff. He'd turn around, wait 'til the old crab downed a pint of scotch, but that hillbilly bitch wasn't getting off that easy.

"Sir, our girl's leaving the state. I'm gonna bring her in now. I'll take the slow route back, circle the town to stall for time."

"Agent!" the director hollered, stopping Daniels in the doorway. "I just got my ear chewed off for forty-five minutes by the attorney general. This Ashby case is closed."

"But sir—"

"No. It's over, Daniels. She's got friends in high places, and their feet stomp hard from up there."

"That bitch murdered Rebecca." Daniels tried to stop it, but his fist drove into the wall through the crumbling plaster and hit a beam.

"You've been working this case hard, Phil," the director said in a stern tone. "You're overdue for a vacation. Why don't you take a week off, get your head together?"

"I don't need a week off."

The director rose from his chair, his large hands clamping onto his thick leather belt. "Well, now I'm not asking. Go get yourself a bottle of Makers Mark and get past this."

"I can't do that." Daniels stormed down the hall, past his office and the agent still waiting in his doorway. He didn't give a fuck about grabbing his shit. All those years of compiling case files could've been spent watching his daughters grow. The countless hours of footwork should've been time he used to flirt with his wife. It would've meant something, if he had taken out the heart of organized crime. But because one skanky cunt fucked all the right people, everything he'd worked for was circling the proverbial drain. There was no way he could just let this case go.

***

Sasha

The clunk of a semi as it hit a pothole ripped Sasha from sleep, and the hum of tires brought a smile to her lips. She rolled onto her side in the sleeper cab, staring out the wide windshield of her father's old semi. A thin beam of the setting sun cut through bushy trees. The flashes of light, the whirl of green leaves whizzing by, let her forget. For just that minute, while tucked between backpacks and fleece blankets, life was normal. She was just a girl in a truck, with her best friend riding shotgun. She could hold onto that fantasy, but it would only be for herself. Everyone else would still see the empty shell of a woman she had become.

A jolt shook the cab, carrying Sasha's body up. "It's bumpy as a motherfucker without a trailer." She leaned against the passenger seat, and Vinny handed her a lit cigarette. It still didn't sit right with her. Not the cigarette, that hit her nicotine deprived spot just right. It was Dez. He should be sitting in that driver's seat, not some man she barely knew. They couldn't have gotten that far. She should make them turn around, swap out the dud for Dez.

"Where are we?" Sasha asked, coughing as cigarette smoke stung her parched throat.

"We just cut into Maryland," Vinny said through a yawn, stretching.

"What!"

Leather crinkled as Vinny turned in his seat, staring at Sasha with judgemental eyes. "You've been asleep for six hours."

"Shit." There goes her plan of kidnapping Dez. "I hope you got some sleep."

"He's been snoring this whole time," Cash said, pulling a joint from behind his ear.

Cash only took one quick puff then passed it directly to Sasha. The dude wasn't so bad. He just...wasn't the person she wanted in that seat at this moment.

"You want me to take over?" Sasha asked, almost nervous to wield a big rig after so long.

"Nah," Cash said. "I'll sleep when we get there, figure I'll be doing a lot of motel squatting."

Sasha passed the joint to Vinny, leaning back to take a good look at the man behind the wheel. A

Colt .45 tucked in a holster, outline of a snubnose through the jeans at the calf. Cash wasn't as dull as the sack of muscles he looked like. Maybe he would prove useful.

"It's not that I don't trust you," Sasha said, still staring at Cash. "It's just, your big ole backwoods ass would stick out like a sour thumb."

"What about him?" Cash pointed at Vinny, who paused mid-toke.

"Vinny's good with propers, always has some smart-ass shit to say, like them. Probably all them thick books he's always reading."

"I am pretty damn refined," Vinny said, tugging the ends of his coat, the joint flopping in his mouth.

"Oh yeah, just look at you, man." Sasha plucked the doobie from Vinny's lips, handing it to Cash.

"It's cool," Cash said after a quick hit. "I know why I'm here, but I ain't no snitch. You know what I mean?"

Sasha did, and it meant everybody knew about her and Vinny. How Dez could even look at her face without slugging it, she'd never know. The shame he must feel. Just the sound of her name must twist his stomach, the way her gut twisted in his absence. She should've stayed gone, but fucking Vinny. When she got back to Kentucky, if Dez was still there, she'd find a way to make it up to him, whether he liked it or not.

***

Dez

Dez pulled a picture from his pocket, gliding his thumb along its worn surface. This photo had gone everywhere with him for the last five years. He'd squandered hours staring at it. A long crease ran across its center, but that didn't matter. Sasha's face was etched into his brain. He thought this faded image of her scowl was the only thing that kept his heart beating. That was before he touched her, got dosed with her electric vibe.

"That was Sasha," Otis said, hanging up the phone.

It was news Dez already knew, he could tell at the first ring, but hearing her name set off a whirlwind of shivers.

"And?" Only one word, yet it still erupted from Dez's mouth in a pathetic quaver.

"They just got to Queens. I wrote all the motel's info down."

It sounded like Otis wanted to say more, but that was all Dez got. Not one hint that Sasha missed him, loved him, needed him. The TV cut off, replaced by a VCR's whirl. Tyler was rewinding that video, again, to watch it for the billionth mind-grating time.

Otis's hand landed on Dez's shoulder, and he almost swung. He wasn't even angry, yet the strongest heat prickled every stitch of his skin.

"Why don't you take a break?" Otis said, ripping the picture from Dez's grasp. "Have a cigarette."

Fresh air, and the ability to listen to his own thoughts instead of doped-up muppets, would be amazing. A soft mattress and a Sasha that hadn't been trampled under the world's heavy boot would be even better. In this life, he took whatever he could get.

"Thanks, man," Dez said, rising from his chair and snatching the picture back.

While kissing Tyler on the head, Dez got sucked into an ice cream run. Not a bad task. Any excuse to keep busy seemed all right in his book.

Dez only got two steps away from the hospital's front door. The aim was to sneak into that alley and spark a bone, but damn it was far from Tyler. He had the rest of his life to smoke joints, but the hospital cafeteria would be closing soon and he had ice cream to fetch.

After one last drag, Dez flicked his cigarette to the ground. He turned toward the hospital's door, catching a glint of metal in the glass. A crack rung in his ears. Pain didn't even become a factor until his knees hit the ground. That's when the thump in his head pulsed so hard it blurred his vision.

The curve of a baseball bat raced into view then…black.

Chapter Fourteen

Vinny

Vinny thought he'd get at least twenty minutes to stretch, shower, roll a few joints. These were important things, necessary things, that Sasha was grossly neglecting. He got two phone calls worth of weed into his system, which equaled to half-a-joint, and she was standing in the motel's doorway tapping her foot.

"Just hang out with Cash then," Sasha said, walking out the room. "I'll be back."

"No!" Vinny practically shoved the joint in Cash's hand, running out the door after Sasha. "Damn girl, trying to ditch me already?" He'd be pissed, except the buzz of the city around him sent him into a trance. Eight o'clock at night and people still hustled along the sidewalks. So many buildings, packed in rows and twinkling as they rose to the dark sky. Some dude in a suit, holding a clunky device to his ear, plowed into him then had the nerve to yell, "Fuck you!" It was awesome.

"Hey! Fuck you, buddy," Sasha shouted, turning to flip the guy off.

"This place is cool," Vinny muttered, gawking at the line of taxis they strolled past, all filled with more people.

"No, it's not. It fucking sucks here."

"C'mon." Vinny nudged Sasha with his elbow, and she grumbled. "You think every place fucking sucks." More grumbles, laced in crystal-clear obscenities. Just like old times. It should've brought tingles, but all Vinny felt was a slice to the heart.

"We're here." Sasha stopped beside a long red carpet, leading to two large men blocking a glass door. "Just be cool, which means quiet, and do everything I say. These guys have a bunch of weird rules."

"I feel like we should've prepped for this more," Vinny whispered, smoothing back his hair.

"Nah, it's good. You're cool. Come on."

Vinny was cool, all right. In fact, his spine was frozen stiff. Unless he wanted to stand on the sidewalk all night, gawking at city folk, he needed to plant his hip at Sasha's side.

The men nodded at Sasha, opening the doors, and Vinny forced his legs to hurry after her. He stepped through the double-doors, and his jaw dropped. By the looks of the old stone building, he was expecting a wide-open room with a single table. Maybe even a boxing gym. Yet he stood in the lobby of a classy restaurant. It was like walking onto a fifties movie set, fully equipped with the big-titty tiny-dress hostess who flounced toward them.

"Sasha!"

A rush of perfume struck Vinny first followed by the sight of a curvy woman groping Sasha. The woman dragged her red-tipped fingernails up Sasha's back, brushed her lips along Sasha's neck. Vinny adjusted his now tight pants, looking away to hide his grin.

"They got AJ," the woman said in her shrill eastern accent.

"I know." Sasha tried to pry the hands off her body, but the woman was going strong. "That's why I'm here. Tony's waiting for me, doll. I gotta run."

"Come see me later?"

Sasha walked away from the chick's whiny plea, and Vinny followed. Before he could get out one snarky comment, a waitress latched onto Sasha while balancing her tray of drinks.

"You're back!" the waitress said, kissing Sasha on the cheek. "Did you hear?"

"That's why I came," Sasha said, gliding her hand down the arch of the woman's back.

The waitress pulled Sasha to an empty spot at the bar. Vinny looked around, but not one head turned their way. The waitress didn't even glance at him as he walked next to Sasha. Everything about the place, its tables full of robot-like people, the dim lights and glimmers of jewels, left an eerie vibe.

"I've been so scared," the waitress whispered, setting down her tray to run her hands up Sasha's chest. "I thought they'd run in here and shoot up the place, but now you're back." A bare knee slid between Sasha's legs, the woman holding tight. This chick was laying it on thick, right in front of him, in the middle of this creepy restaurant where

147

people didn't notice shit.

"I got business to take care of, babe."

With that, the chick dismounted, grabbed her tray, and winked. "Call me later."

Vinny watched the woman's hips sway as she headed toward the scatter of tables. "You've been busy." He didn't tear his gaze from the eye candy around him. He already had Sasha's glare down pat.

"It's…not what it looks like."

"Uh-huh. Doll? Babe?"

Sasha leaned closer to Vinny, shielding her mouth. "So I don't mix up names."

"Uh-huh!"

Sasha's smile lit up the smoky room, blocking out everything else. It'd been ages since he'd seen that glow, a glow capable of blinding the average man not accustomed to such a shine.

"Just hang here." Sasha slapped the bar and like magic, a clean-cut, thin-mustached man appeared to wipe the pristine area in front of Vinny. "Get whatever you want. I'll be right back."

Vinny almost chased after Sasha, but the weird mobster rules she mentioned kept him rooted in place.

"What can I get ya, sir?"

"Sir," Vinny muttered. Jesus Christ. He would've run a comb through his hair if Sasha had bothered to tell him they'd be traveling back in time to hit the swankiest club in 1950.

"Whatever's on tap," Vinny said, watching Sasha cut across the room.

"We have seven drafts on tap and one specialty barrel."

Vinny's gaze remained glued to Sasha as she walked up three small steps to a private dining area. The men sitting around the long table up there were different than the other people in the restaurant. For starters, these guys were looking right at him.

"Budweiser," Vinny said, leaning against the bar to commence a proper stare down.

***

Otis

Otis peeked into the hallway, again. Dez should've been back by now. Hell, the man could've driven to Tennessee, got thirty ice cream cones, and still would've been back twenty minutes ago.

"Where'd Daddy go?" Tyler asked, snuggling into the pillow.

"He'll be right back, buddy," Otis said from the doorway.

"You already said that, twice. I'm tired. I need Daddy to tell me a story."

Tyler's lips started to pucker, his eyes squinting. The kid would start bawling any second, and Otis wasn't high enough to deal with that shit.

"Hold tight, little man. I'll go look for him." Otis hurried down the hall, poking his head into the waiting room.

Kev jumped up from a chair, away from his flock of porn stars who had come to check on Tyler an hour ago and never left.

"You seen Dez?" Otis asked, keeping his eye on

149

Tyler's door.

Kev shook his head, stepping into the hallway. "Not since before the girls showed up."

Barbed wires of panic spread out beneath Otis's skin. This wasn't right. Dez definitely wasn't the take-off type, not even when pushed out the door.

"Go sit with Tyler," Otis said, and Kev ran down the hall toward Tyler's room.

Otis walked out the sliding glass door, looking around. Dez's truck sat under a flickering streetlight, in the same spot as it had been when parked two days ago. This was bad. It wasn't his damaged mind overreacting. A wickedness clung to the air. Otis could almost smell its bitter residue. It was a foul mixture of burnt soul and Dakkar Noir.

"City folk," Otis muttered, dropping his gaze. A scatter of red on the curbside caught his eye. His stomach dropped. He didn't have to inspect the stains. It was Dez's blood.

A fiery scorch shot through Otis's chest, its raw ache strong enough to bring tears to his eyes. The man he had once despised and grown to love as a brother was gone, most likely dead. There wouldn't be a body to bury, no goodbyes. Dez was gone. When those scumbags finish off Sasha, Tyler will have nobody.

"Tyler!" Otis ran back into the hospital. Nurses jumped up at the squeak of his boots, and people backed against the walls as he sprinted by. He didn't give a fuck about making a scene. If anyone but Kev was in Tyler's room, the people in this hospital would get one hell of a scene. They'd get to watch him put a bullet in some asshole's head.

150

Otis burst through Tyler's door, pulling his gun, and Kev dove in front of Tyler.

"What?" Kev yelled, reaching for his holster.

"I want my daddy," Tyler cried out.

The kid's sad whimper echoed the same thought in Otis's head. He really fucking wanted Dez too. "I'm gonna take you to him, buddy. We're blowing this popsicle stand." Tyler giggled, which dulled the scorching blaze in Otis's chest to a searing flame. He shut the door and grabbed a bag. All the medical shit he could stuff in this sesame street backpack was coming with them.

"Dude!" Kev tried to block Otis from clearing out a cabinet, only to receive a hard shove. "Where's Dez?"

Otis froze, his eyes veering to Kev. The look on his face must've said it all because Kev staggered back.

"I gotta call Sasha," Kev said, reaching for the phone.

"No." Otis snatched the paper with the motel's phone number off the nightstand, tucking it into his pocket.

"They're not just gonna let us take the kid out of the hospital," Kev said, way louder than he should have. "We're not his parents."

Otis pulled Kev across the room, far from Tyler's earshot. "If we split Sasha's focus, she'll get killed. Her and Vinny."

"Is Dez—"

"I don't know." Otis didn't want to hear it, couldn't admit that Dez was dead. Not yet. "There's blood on the sidewalk outside. His truck's still in the parking lot."

"What if he just ran off with one of the girls? Maybe he's at the big house, crashed out."

"Call." Otis said, knowing it was a useless task. "Call everyone you know. I'm still packing all this shit up." He pushed Kev out of his way to see Tyler hobbling across the room. The kid's little gown flapped behind him, showing a complete blast of a full moon.

"What are you doing out of bed?" Otis asked, rushing to Tyler's side.

"I need my VCR," he groaned, tugging at the wires.

"I'll get you a new one, buddy." Otis reached for Tyler's arm only to get a tiny hand in his face.

"I'm not going anywhere without my *Fraggly Rock* video."

***

Dez

A steady hum filtered in, cutting through the haze that clogged Dez's mind. Cold metal vibrated beneath his cheek. That sound, the way his head floated on top of its skull-shattering throb, he could swear he was on an airplane.

His eyes only opened halfway, hindered by crusts of dried blood. Shoes. Fancy, glossy loafers filled his view, their polished soles tapping shiny metal.

"The ape is stirring."

A man's voice echoed in Dez's ears, one he

could barely register over the drone in the air. The voice was impossible to trace, so he followed the legs attached to those shoes. He never got a glimpse of the man he planned to kill. Curved walls stole his gaze. The riveted steel, that small round window...he really was on an airplane.

"Boss said this one's an animal."

They got that goddamn right. Fuckers were about to find out how much of an animal he could really be. A squeak rang out beneath Dez's fingertips as he dragged himself across the steel floor.

"I got something for him," a man said, his snide voice booming right above Dez's head.

Dez rolled over, grabbing onto a calf, and a sharp pinprick stung his neck. A chilled warmth rushed through him, gathering in his fingertips and toes. His clutch gave way without consent. Dez looked up as a needle drifted away from his neck. A whirl took his face back to the metal floor, and a haze of gray rushed in to veil the world in its fuzz.

Chapter Fifteen

Sasha

The table in front of Sasha used to fill her with a sense of belonging. Now it sent chills. It seemed longer, wider, with all those empty seats. The eyes staring at her had changed as well, but she couldn't place their new glares. Maybe that's how *friends* looked right before they killed you.

Sasha pulled out her chair slowly, giving Antonio enough time to tell her to fuck off. After all, her mother's people, whom she didn't even know, did just murder his only child. These guys were big on retribution, but wasn't everyone?

"No," Antonio said and Sasha froze. "Sit here."

Eyes lowered as Sasha moved toward the seat closest to Antonio. Enzo grumbled the moment her ass hit the solid wood, his arm sliding away. If only they'd slit her throat and get it over with. Except hands didn't move under the table to reach for knives, and eyes didn't grow harsh.

"Tony. I'm sor—"

Antonio grabbed Sasha's hand, and she flinched.

"Relax. You're safe now," Antonio said, squeezing Sasha's hand. The brief but tight grip emitted more love than her mother had ever spared. That feeling had tethered her to this place once. She couldn't let it creep up on her again.

"Jesus, Sasha." Enzo slammed his fist on the table, squirming in his chair. "I didn't know you were so...I should've came when you called. I'm so fucking pissed, I'll never forgive myself."

"Nah. I'm good." Sasha sat up straight, even though it spread fire between her legs.

"You look bad," Marco said, only flashing his gaze to her face for a fraction of a second. "Like you got hit by a dump truck."

"Yeah." Sasha forced a snicker. Though she hadn't dared to peek in a mirror, she could only imagine how colorful her face must be. "Wait 'til you hear about what I hit one of them motherfuckers with." The levity broke, and the air seemed to grow thick. Vengeance tends to do that. "I have some really bad news, Tony."

"That's funny," Antonio said, in a tone that hinted otherwise. "I have some really bad news for you too, Sasha. But please, you go first."

Sasha barely knew these people, and for no sane reason, she trusted them. She'd spill all her secrets onto this table. It'd make one hell of a mess, but the men here would help her clean it up.

"Dante's working with the Mancinis."

"Donatello? My brother?" Antonio's fist curled, and Sasha shrank down. At least she wasn't the only person at the table to do so. Every one of them

155

tough guys cowered in their chairs.

Sasha pulled the envelope from her flannel pocket, strategically placed so the top peeked out to prevent any shady reaching movements. "Dante's the one who sent the Mancinis after me." Her fingers shook as she slid the letter to Antonio. It wasn't fear that rocked her core. It was the idea of causing the man any more suffering than he'd already endured.

"It's his handwriting," Antonio said the moment he pulled the letter from its envelope.

"The men who came for me had this." That's when it hit Sasha, men. There was still another Mancini in her town. She had to warn Dez.

Sasha looked across the room, catching a glimpse of Vinny practically nose deep in a waitress's tits.

"Did you call this number?" Antonio asked, folding the letter and placing it on the table in front of him.

"No. I was hoping you could trace it so we could have a face to face with Dante."

"You brought backup?" Enzo asked, gesturing to Vinny acting like a straight-up redneck at the bar.

"Yeah. I got another, more brutish guy back at the motel."

"Smart," Enzo said, leaning back in his chair. "Have him lose the jacket."

Sasha sat tall in her chair, glaring at the side of Vinny's face. His gaze shot to her, as though he could hear her silent call. A light tug to her collar was all it took for Vinny to strip off his coat and drape it over a stool, emblem down.

"I would like to have a talk with my brother. This changes everything." Antonio looked at Enzo, who nodded.

Secrets didn't usually fester at this table, which must mean Sasha's bad news was next.

"Sasha." Antonio paused, staring off into the crowded restaurant below their platform. For the briefest of seconds, he looked so weak, so broken. Just another victim of this city, lost amongst smiling faces. Then, as though a switch flipped, the steel returned to Antonio's stare.

"Sasha. I had intended to declare you as my heir, since I no longer have any living children, and bring your father back into the fold. But if Dante has…done this thing, *his* seat as underboss passes to you. Since he won't be breathing any longer."

The part about Dante no longer breathing left a giddy warmth in Sasha's chest, but she wasn't taking up anybody's seat. Decision making was never her strong suit. She had always been more of the vicious bulldog type. "I don't want either position."

"That's too bad," Antonio said, the way one would scold a child. "It's the burden that comes with your blood."

Sasha would bitch, moan, storm out, but Antonio's glare kept her lips sealed shut and her ass glued to the seat. Apparently, this decision was final. Her, a boss in America's largest crime syndicate. Every day would be half-naked women and breaking bones, fucking paradise, except the current boss was about to put his son in the ground and kill another one of his brothers. That would not

157

be her life. A high seat at a table of death couldn't be the legacy she'd leave for Tyler.

Antonio leaned forward, his elbows crashing against the table. "I declare my nephew, Othello Lazzari, as my heir." A hint of a smile cracked his grief before he settled back into his seat. "In the case of my death, Othello will inherit everything, including my position in the family. It'll make things right again."

"I don't know, boss," Enzo said. "We don't know what Othello's been up to. He could be a cop."

Sasha snickered as visuals of Otis decked out in a policeman's get-up streamed through her mind.

"I know what he's been up to," Antonio said. "He's one of Sasha's men."

A screech of chairs chirped like a choir. Everyone had to be sure Sasha could see their shock beyond their unnecessary hand gestures. Italian men, they sure did have a flare for the dramatics.

"I was one of *his* men, actually, but Otis won't accept this title. He won't come back to the city, or this family."

"Like you, my dear, he won't have a choice," Antonio said. The way his eyes narrowed when he pushed those words through his clenched teeth turned Sasha's stomach. It was going to be a fun call home. Not only would she have to warn Dez about a stray Mancini in his town, but she'd have to tell Otis the life he knew was over.

Antonio grabbed the letter, scooting his chair away from the table. "It'll take me a few hours to get a lead on this number. Do you mind if I hold onto this?"

The man could hold onto that letter forever. Sasha wanted nothing that Dante touched. It was bad enough she had to live in this skin he helped spawn.

"Keep it," she said, looking away from the curvy script of her name on the envelope.

"Go get some rest. You had a long drive." Antonio rose, waving to a man in the lobby. "We'll call you when it's time to move out. Marco, do we have her information?"

"Yeah, boss. She's right down the road."

The lawyer who boosted Sasha from the clink, Spengotti, met Antonio at the bottom of the steps. Sasha watched Antonio shake the man's hand, ushering him toward the backroom. It was impressive. A glaze coated the man's stare, and a slight tremble disturbed his fingers, yet Antonio walked through the room without missing a single one of his powerful steps. If her son had been killed, there'd be no discussions, no plans to put in place. She would've went bat-shit crazy. The world would be burning as she ran through with a flamethrower. Just the thought sent the room into a whirl. She needed to talk to Tyler, to Dez, right now before an irrational frenzy took hold of her mind.

After a quick nod to the men around the table, Sasha was on her feet. Vinny separated himself from a waitress's wandering hands the second her boots thumped down the steps. He grabbed his jacket, slinking beside her. What a sight. She couldn't have choreographed it any better if she tried. Two backwoods truckers stomping across fancy carpet, holding hard glares and forcing those around them back with their invisible wave of badassery. They watched way too many fucking movies.

***

Otis

Otis carried Tyler across the hospital room. It was just like old times, the boy wrapped tight in a blanket, cradled in his arms. Except now, the kid weighed a goddamn ton.

Kev stuck his hands through the open window, and Otis passed Tyler off.

"This is fun," Tyler all but yelled as Kev maneuvered him through the window frame.

"Shh." Kev crouched low, hiding behind thick bushes. "We're being sneaky, little man."

After tossing the backpack at Kev's feet, Otis climbed onto the window sill and slipped outside. He'd stolen lots of shit in his long life, but never a kid. This kid was practically his, sort of club property, but it still felt skeevy to nab him.

"Act natural," Otis grumbled, since Kev had decided now was a good time to play ninja and duck behind every object.

"Right." Kev stood up straight, clutching Tyler tight as he walked beside Otis across the parking lot.

They made it into the pickup, and Otis peeled wheels. Scary, how easily a person could steal a child from a hospital. Even more scary was the thought of how easy it could've been for another person to steal his child from this particular hospital. Now they'd have to take Tyler from his cold, dead hands, which was fine with him. Otis glanced across the cab, catching the kid's smile in a flash of streetlights. What a smile, like Sasha's when she was that age. He'd die a million deaths to protect that grin, slaughter any person who tried to snuff it out.

"We can't take him to the holler," Kev said, still snuggling Tyler like a baby.

"I wish we could put him in an indestructible box, under the ground, in the middle of a mine field."

Kev tapped Otis's chest seven times, which was six too many.

"There's a fallout shelter on my uncle's farm. A small TV, bed, shelves of canned fruit…it's done up nice."

"Yeah?" Otis said, speeding away from the town's bright lights and into the darkness of the mountains. A secret fallout shelter that even he didn't know existed sounded pretty damn good right about now. It's not what Sasha would do, or Dez. They'd run into the fight headfirst and get everyone killed.

"I can get all my cousins to come over with sawed-offs," Kev said, unraveling the blanket so Tyler could move his arms. "Nobody'll get past us, if they can even find us."

An army of Kevs, brandishing sawed-offs. It could be enough brainpower to take out two, maybe three, men.

"It's good." Otis busted a right, heading for the freeway. "What do you say, buddy?" He glanced at Tyler, forcing a smile. "Want to check out uncle Kev's farm?"

"Is Daddy there?"

Otis squeezed the steering wheel so tight his fingers burned. "Not yet. He will be, though."

Kev shot Otis a hopeful glare, matching the one beaming from Tyler. The tattered pieces of Otis's heart shattered into dust. It couldn't be too late to save Dez. He had to find the man, bring him back to his kid.

"Sasha's gonna freak if she tries to call the room." The way Kev said it, you'd think he'd just figured that out.

"You'll call her, say Tyler got his room switched, give her your uncle's phone number."

"Me!" Kev cried out, leaning against his door. "No way, man. You should do it."

"I can't. After I make sure Tyler's all set-up, I'm jumping on a plane to New York."

***

Sasha

Sasha slammed the phone down. Twice she'd called Tyler's hospital room, and the fucker just rang. Granted, she did place the calls within a twenty second timespan, but still.

"Everything cool?" Vinny asked, poking his head inside her motel room.

"Nobody's answering at the hospital."

"Maybe they let Tyler go home," Vinny said, strolling inside.

Sasha grabbed the phone, dialing the big house, and Vinny sat beside her. Another ceaseless ring grated her ear. Same shit from the clubhouse's line, not that she expected any different at this point. She'd freak out, wreck the place, but Vinny had just sparked a joint and she didn't want to miss a puff of sticky buds.

A few deep hits and ideas started to pop into Sasha's head. "I could call the operator, have her connect me to the hospital's main line."

"Yeah," Vinny said through a stream of smoke. "Kev's probably still in the waiting room. He'd be the easiest to track down."

A ring filled the room, rattling the phone against the nightstand. It was a goddamn beautiful sound, but Sasha wasn't letting it flow a second time. She snatched the phone from the receiver and said, "Hello," before it reached her ear.

"Hey, Sasha. I'm glad I caught you," Kev said.

Even through hundreds of miles of telephone wire, Sasha could smell Kev's bullshit. It was uncanny. "I need to talk to Dez," she said, making a mental note to slap Kev the next time she saw him.

"Oh," Kev said, his squeaky tone vibrating the earpiece. "Well, Dez just crashed out."

"Otis then."

"Fuck. Otis just split to run home for a shower."

"How come nobody answered Tyler's line?" Sasha yelled into the phone. "What the fuck, dude?"

"They moved Tyler to a new room. You want the new number?"

163

"Yeah, asshole." Sasha scribbled down the number, which looked vaguely familiar. "Are you there now, with Dez and Tyler?"

"Uh…yeah," Kev said, in squeaky liar's tone. "They're both snoring. I can wake them up if you want."

Sasha did want that. But if they really were sleeping, and after the day they'd had, it'd be a dick move to wake them just so she could hear their voices. "No. But listen, there are still people in town looking to hurt me. Y'all need to be real careful. Don't let Tyler out of your sight. Tell Dez as soon as he wakes up."

"Don't worry. I got this."

Those five little words were enough to make Sasha want to hop a jet and fly home.

"Just tell Dez and Otis what I said and kiss Tyler for me." She hung up before Kev could utter some dumb shit to rile her last nerve.

"All good?" Vinny asked, relighting what was left of the joint.

Sasha flopped back on the mattress, staring up at the sparkly ceiling. "Kev's lying. I wish I could see through the phone, take a peek at what's really going on back there."

"That would be cool." Vinny dropped beside Sasha, propping on his elbow. "Like, we could do it with the TVs. They could be cameras and telephones too."

Sasha rolled onto her side, stealing the joint from Vinny's grasp. He'd obviously had too much. "That's just crazy. You're high."

"You're fucking high." Vinny reached for the

joint, and Sasha moved it farther away. "Give it, bogart."

"Nope. You're 86'd, man," she said through a snicker, falling onto her back to keep the joint from Vinny's reach. His arm glided along her chest, igniting sparks. He must've felt them too, because he stopped reaching for her hand and looked down at her face. A soft fire lit his eyes, jacking up the already too blue shade. It was like gazing into an ocean and staring at the morning sky all at once, magnificent, stunning, impossible to turn away from.

Vinny ran his rough fingertips along Sasha's cheek, gentle, slow. The tiny electric shocks of Vinny's touch cut her breaths short, fully disrupting her ability to form proper thoughts. A kiss. That should stop this assault of tingles and help her build an immunity to his entrancing stare.

All she had to do was lift her chin, and his lips floated in. Once again, she was wrong. Vinny's kiss didn't quell the tingles vibrating her skin. It turned them into a cyclone of warm prickles.

The mattress squeaked beneath them, and Sasha flinched. For a second, she was back in that jail cell, pinned under a bulldyke's grasp.

"Is this okay?" Vinny whispered between tender kisses.

Sasha's fists unclenched. She hadn't even realized how tight her fingers were balled until Vinny's breath rushed over her skin.

"Yeah," she mumbled. It had to be okay; she needed it to be. Vinny's hands had always soothed her soul. If she couldn't handle the most familiar touch in her life, she'd be damaged beyond repair.

Vinny's lips traveled down her neck, his hand sliding under her shirt. The weight atop Sasha no longer sent a blanket of comfort. It smothered. When his fingertips grazed her nipple, she jolted back.

"Stop," Sasha yelled, and Vinny's hands flew off her body.

"I'm sorry, I—"

"It's not your fault." Sasha jumped off the bed, pulling her flannel closed. She couldn't get covered up enough, hold herself tight enough. Vinny looked so let down. He probably wasn't used to the cold shoulder, not with those dimples. "I can get a girl over here in like five minutes."

Vinny sat up, scooting to the edge of the bed. "You think that'll help you?"

"For you, stupid," Sasha said with a chuckle.

"Shit. I can get my own girl here in five minutes, got lots of numbers at the bar."

"I bet you did." She grabbed her smokes from the nightstand, heading for the door.

"Wait!" Vinny hopped to his feet. "I can go slower, softer. I want to help you."

Although sweet, it was a completely ridiculous thing for Vinny to say. He could never understand. Her sense of worth had been stripped away, and that wasn't something a person could get back in one night.

"There is no helping me." Sasha stepped under the harsh glow of motel lights, shutting the door behind her.

Chapter Sixteen

Otis

Otis squirmed in the oversized leather seat within the tin can they called an airplane. It was nice of Sasha to spring for first class. She didn't know he'd taken cash from her briefcase of blood money to spring for this flight, but it was her fault he was on it so the deed seemed justified. He'd stalled in Kentucky as long as he could. A man only had to tell twenty rednecks it was cool to shoot any city folk they saw once. If he had hugged Tyler goodbye one more time, the kid would've gotten suspicious. There were no excuses left. He had to return to the city he'd wiped from his existence, or sit back like a bitch as his friends, his true family, got picked off one by one. He'd rather die than live life as a pussy, which was the reason his ass was planted on this airplane's cushy seat.

"Another drink, sir?" the stewardess asked, leaning against Otis's armrest.

He shouldn't. The tiny drained bottles were

starting to pile up, but it'd be rude to say no to a woman who'd spent so much time propping up her cleavage so high.

"Why not?" Otis said, admiring the tightly-fitted outfit the airline put their women in. "Do you know how much longer?"

She cleared away Otis's stockpile of empties, placing two fresh teases of a bottle on his tray. Her hand landed on his thigh, a coy smile lifting her tanned California-girl cheeks. Everything in this tin can was a fucking tease.

"About two hours, sir." The woman batted her eyes, then pushed her little cart down the aisle.

Otis cracked the lid on his tiny bottle of Jack Daniels, downing it in one gulp. Two hours, that should give him enough time to get his head on straight before Sasha chewed it off.

***

Sasha

A red-hot cherry sizzled Sasha's skin, and she dropped her cigarette. That was the second cigarette she let burn to the butt. At this rate, she'd never get the required amount of nicotine into her system.

Sasha slid down the brick wall of the motel until her ass hit concrete. One more try. If she couldn't get three puffs in before twisty thoughts dragged her into an abyss of self-pity, she'd fucking quit smoking.

She cringed, her shoulders slumping at the thought of quitting her favorite hobby of huffing toxins into her lungs. She thrust the cigarette butt to her lips, taking three quick puffs all at once. It was a bit extreme, but she wasn't getting fucked out of smoking.

"Hey." Cash sat on the sidewalk beside Sasha, handing her a big blue book. "I got something for ya."

"What is it?" Sasha opened the cover, smiling at Tyler's name spelled out in colorful block letters.

"Pictures. I took pictures of everything."

He sure fucking did. There were pages of photos. The pictures spanned from when Tyler was a tiny bundle of a baby in a dresser drawer on the pool table all the way to the little dude she knew in hiker boots and corduroys. Every holiday, every smile, even the bloody scrapes complemented with tears were here for her to see.

"I knew you'd be pissed when you woke up and all this shit happened. I tried to get it all. There was this diaper mishap I wanted to snap, but the stupid camera—"

Sasha threw her arms around Cash's neck, hugging tight. "Thank you. This is…" A lump lodged in her throat. It seemed to arrive at the same time as her tears, but she choked them both back. "…so awesome."

The look on Cash's face when she pulled back, like *he* was about to cry, pulled a chuckle from her mouth. If only she had a camera right now. That mug of his would be a perfect addition to the book.

A tap shook the window behind Sasha, and she turned to see Vinny waving the phone.

"Gear up, brother." She patted Cash's shoulder

on her climb off the sidewalk. "We got scores to settle."

***

Dez

Sounds jumbled, fading in and out. The one Dez heard loudest was a pound. It had to be his brain, since it was synced up with the throb in his temples. People hovered all around him. He couldn't see them, could barely hear them, but their thick presence clogged the air. It was the feel of danger. A man could sense something like that coming on, especially one who'd spent as much time in prison as he had.

Then he heard that word, the only one strong enough to replenish the energy in his muscles. Sasha. If these fuckers so much as tangled one lock of hair on Sasha's head, he'd feed them their own intestines. *Dead*. A man said dead and Sasha in one breath.

Rage warped to strength and set a course through Dez's veins. When it hit his toes, he jumped to his feet.

"Whoa!" a man yelled, stumbling back.

"Told you he was an animal," a deep voice rumbled from behind Dez. The boss!

Dez followed that deep tone to a dark smile. He'd never officially met Dante. It was no secret the guy called himself Sasha's father, but the resemblance was uncanny. It'd be impossible to deny Dante's claim, yet Dez refused to accept it.

Hands gripped onto Dez from all sides, forcing him back down onto a dusty concrete floor.

"You're gonna die screaming, motherfucker," Dez shouted, pushing against the men holding him down while glaring at Dante.

"Ha! *Mother* fucker," Dante said, chuckling. "That's a good one, coming from you."

Dez thrashed, getting one hand free. A solid hit to the nose on some insignificant douchebag was all he got in before knuckles and heels pounded him to the ground.

***

Sasha

Three black sedans crept along a dirt road. No lights, no brakes, just tires crunching gravel as they drifted to a stop. Sasha would jump from the back seat, sprint into the woods, and burst through the front door of a warehouse she couldn't even see. She would, if she wasn't sandwiched between Vinny and Cash.

"You ready for this, Sasha?" Marco asked from the driver's seat. He knew someone would kill her only living parent tonight. There was no other reason to come to an abandoned warehouse in the middle of the woods, in New Jersey, if not for serious-grade murder.

"That man is nothing to me. You should be more concerned with Tony's feelings." Sasha nudged Vinny's arm and he opened the door, sliding out.

Darkness hung thick under a moonless night.

Sasha couldn't see faces, only the silhouettes of the men gathered in front of the car. Antonio's was unmistakable and jarring to glimpse. He'd never been on a job before, at least not with her.

Sasha pulled Vinny and Cash back a few steps as they walked toward the crowd. "You see the guy in the center, the big one. Don't let anything happen to him or I'm fucked."

The click of bullets loading into chambers echoed over the rustle of leaves as Sasha joined the group of bloodthirsty mobsters.

"Sasha, you and your men take the front. Marco and Ricci take the rear. The rest of us will cover the sides."

Sasha nodded, and Antonio grabbed her arm before she could slink off.

"I will talk to my brother before he dies. Understand?"

"Well. There goes my plan of kicking down the door and unloading a clip into Dante's face."

Antonio narrowed his eyes, his stare as deep as a grave, which she'd be in if she crossed him.

"Yes, sir," Sasha said, shooing Vinny and Cash down the trail.

***

Otis

Twenty-five years hadn't been enough. Otis had to pry himself from a taxi and force his foot onto the dirty street. The first few steps weren't bad, then the stench hit him. That smell reminded him of death, misery, childhood. It fucking sucked.

His boots dragged, kicking up asphalt as he walked across a motel's parking lot. Sasha was going to burn this city down. She'd probably start with him for letting Dez get taken. He'd probably let her put him down, end this long road of shit called life. Dez was gone because his dumb ass had failed. Tyler was probably scared shitless, locked in a metal bunker, his little stomach ripped open, because he was weak. No more of that shit. Sasha was back now, which meant he had to man up to keep up with her set of balls.

Otis nodded to himself for encouragement. It didn't do a goddamn thing to boost his moral. Since standing outside Sasha's door all night like a pussy wasn't an option, he lifted his hand and knocked.

The door didn't fly open. Sasha's scowl wasn't piercing his eyes. Relief flowed in waves until he realized he'd have to track her down. No way was he stepping foot inside Fat Tonys.

"Fuck all that." Otis slid down Sasha's door. Red flakes of chipped paint rained to the sidewalk as he plopped down. Waiting would work for at least an hour, maybe two.

***

Special Agent Philip Daniels

The grease-ball sitting outside his perp's door might complicate matters. He could call it in, loitering of a suspicious character. Then the director would get wind of his location, send agents to shut him down. They were welcome to try. He was Special Agent Philip Daniels, decorated war hero, the top authority on street thugs like Sasha Ashby.

Not even an enigma like her could fool him. That monster was smart, disguising itself as a girl, but he caught every angle. Her coma was faked. He knew it. Why else would her top man go into that hospital room every day for hours? She was giving orders and laying low. A criminal mastermind. Those two undercover agents who went missing in Little Rock had to be her doing as well, instinct told him so. Sasha Ashby had her thumb on the pulse of all shady business across the map.

He shouldn't blame her. The Lazzaris and Mancinis had genetically engineered her to be soulless, trained her from birth to be a sociopath. Then again, they all had a sob story. Every piece of trash he swept off the streets cried about their shitty childhoods. *My daddy beat me. Mom turned tricks in the living room for drug money. I had no one.* She'd be no different when he dragged her ass to the pen.

The memory of slapping cuffs on her boney wrists, twisting her scrawny arms, stirred every part of him. He adjusted his belt, returning his gaze to the window. That scuzzy hillbilly was still camped outside her door. Maybe he'd get lucky. That guy could be there to kill the bitch. Then he could call it a day, go home, and crack open that bottle of scotch like the director had suggested.

Chapter Seventeen

Sasha

Sasha stood beside a dented metal door, battling to keep both her nerve and breaths steady. This place was the warehouse time forgot, grown over by the woods around them. It didn't look like a lair for a calculated family of mobsters unsuspectedly waiting to be massacred. It looked like a trap.

Vinny leaned against the doorway across from Sasha, and she attached to her gaze to him. She'd hoped to find some sort of signal that would assure her busting through this door was the right thing since Vinny considered himself the smart one, but she only got a shrug. A big fat nothing from the smart guy usually meant trouble, but fuck it. Sasha nodded at Cash, and he smashed his big boot against the flimsy door.

Metal hinges snapped, echoing through the darkness of the warehouse. As the door crashed to the ground, Sasha charged inside and the click of rifles cocking greeted her. A squeak erupted from beneath her boots as she stopped short, staring into shadows. Vinny collided with her back, and a bright light blinked on. The sudden glare of a floodlight stunned Sasha's eyes, her fuzzy gaze dropping to the cracked concrete floor.

"Took you long enough, little girl."

A white blur still clouded Sasha's sight, but the barrel of her gun veered straight to its target. Dante's grin filtered in, and her finger twitched against the trigger.

"Drop it!" a man yelled, his voice echoing around the wide-open room.

Sasha tore her glare from Dante. Men inched closer to her on all sides, each holding a cocked rifle and a hard stare. "Eight," she whispered to Vinny, and two guns clicked behind them.

"Ten," Vinny said, dropping his gun.

Cash's piece clanked to the ground next, but Sasha wouldn't drop her outstretched arm. She couldn't lower her gun from Dante's face.

"All right," Dante said, gesturing to Vinny. "Shoot the skinny one."

"No!" Sasha tossed her gun at Dante's feet, standing in front of Vinny.

"And the other piece," Dante said, pointing at Sasha's pants.

Sasha pulled a glock from her waistband and dropped it at her feet. Unfortunately, some asshole kicked it away.

"The pockets." Dante grinned, and Sasha rolled her eyes up to the cobweb lined rafters. No way in Hell was Dante getting the shit in her pockets. A smile spread across her lips and she shrugged, narrowing her eyes.

"Pat her down," Dante said, and two men gripped Sasha.

The men groped Sasha's waist and hips, and she hurled an elbow. "Back the fuck off." The man on her right clutched the back of her neck then slammed her face against a metal table while the other guy pinned her arms down.

"Fuckers!" Vinny yelled.

Sasha could hear Vinny and Cash struggle, which ended quickly with their groans. Beyond a growing pile of knifes removed from her every pocket, she glimpsed Dante stroll to the window.

"Hey, Tony," he yelled out the fractured glass. "You might as well come in through the front, cause the guys coming in the back are gonna get shot."

The grip holding Sasha down loosened and she pushed off the table, backing between Vinny and Cash. "You guys okay?"

"Yeah," Cash said, holding a puffy cut on his forehead.

Vinny rubbed his stomach, slightly hunched over. "Ask me in twenty."

"What is this, Donatello?" Antonio walked through the front door unarmed, unafraid, without a pause in his step, and every gun-toting man scurried back.

Dante closed his eyes, a long, slow breath sinking his chest. His glare flashed to Sasha, growing spiteful before he turned to face Antonio. "My exile is over, brother."

"Your exile is over when I say it is!" The rise in Antonio's voice shrunk Dante's shoulders. It was a beautiful sight, to see him cower.

"Your say isn't worth shit, thanks to my little girl."

Antonio looked at Sasha, hurt brimming in his eyes. Her jaw dropped. She didn't do shit, would slice Dante to shreds before help him. "I didn't..."

"Yes, you did," Dante said, hurling a sharp glare Sasha's way. "You marched them all to me, just like you did before." His eyes narrowed on Sasha, wavering. "I'm disappointed, little girl. Thought you were smart enough to learn from your mistakes."

Bursts of gunfire rang out through the broken windows, bright flashes bathing the trees outside in white.

"There goes your crew, Tony," Dante said, shaking his head.

The hard edge in Antonio's stare cracked. Sasha had never seen this side of the Don, the broken side. He looked so frail, so weak while trapped in the clutches of sadness. Sasha balled her hand into a fist, stepping away from Vinny and Cash. For killing her mother, and stealing what would've been the best years of her life, Dante would die. But for hurting the only man who'd spared the time to care about her, she'd be sure to make her so-called father's agony last for days.

"You actually think you can handle Lazzari business," Sasha sneered, creeping toward Dante. "You couldn't even run a two-bit biker gang."

"He has me now, darlin'."

A woman's smooth voice flowed through the musty air, sending razor-tipped prickles beneath

Sasha's skin. She turned toward the voice she'd never thought would tickle her ears again, and an old woman walked from the shadows. It could've been her mother, if her mother had lived to that age. The resemblance struck like a knee to the gut. She might not be able to kill this woman, who looked so much like the person she wanted more than anything in this world.

"And my boys," the woman said as the pack of lanky men moved in, creating a barrier of loaded rifles to follow her across the large room. "It seems my only daughter went ahead and got herself killed."

"By him," Sasha yelled, pointing at Dante.

"I know, sweetie. I already thanked him properly."

"Gross," Sasha muttered. Her entire family was fucking gross, on both sides. "I can see how you all think you're so clever, but not one of you found this." Sasha pulled a snub-nosed revolver from her bra, aiming it at Dante. There were only six shots in her chamber, but she just needed one. Antonio was going to be pissed. He'd have to scold her in Hell, because they weren't getting out of this one alive.

Dante snickered. He must have thought her hesitation was due to his smug face. Time to prove dear old dad wrong. A grin popped onto Sasha's lips as she squeezed the trigger. She aimed for Dante's heart, but the bastard moved. The bullet blew through his shoulder, lodging into the stone wall behind him. When the ring in her ears dulled, she caught the tail end of his cry. It was like music to her fuzzy ears.

The butt of a rifle struck her chest. Air turned to fire, singeing away oxygen, and Sasha dropped to her knees. A whirl took the room in circles, and a barrel pressed against her temple, but she wasn't letting go of her gun.

"Bring in the ape," Dante yelled, cradling his blood-soaked shoulder.

A door banged open, and a roar flowed into the room. Sasha knew that growl, but it couldn't be. He couldn't be here.

She looked up from the floor as two men struggled to drag Dez in front of Dante, a third man dropping blows every time Dez fought. Vinny shouted, boots shuffled over the slap of fists, then Vinny and Cash dropped to their knees on either side of Sasha. At least they tried to fight. She was stuck on the cold, cracked floor in a stupor. If Dez was here, where was Tyler?

The moment Dez saw Sasha staring up at him from the floor, his body locked stiff. "Sasha!"

Dante pointed his gun at Dez and pulled the trigger.

"No!" Vinny cried out. He thrashed under the grip upon him, providing just enough of a distraction for Sasha to jump up off the floor. She lifted her gun as Dez slumped over, dripping blood from his shoulder.

"An eye for an eye, little girl." Dante moved the barrel to Dez's forehead. "You want to keep going?"

Dez steered his gaze to Sasha, nodding. He wanted her to shoot Dante. The dumb asshole probably had some romantic scenario playing out in his mind where they'd all go down in a hailstorm of bullets, meeting in the center of the room to kiss one last time before they died hand in hand. That stupid shit wasn't happening. She, unlike the majority of people in this room, was a realist.

"Donatello, stop all this nonsense." Antonio's voice boomed throughout the building, shaking both her and Dante's gun hand. "Let us talk about this, like civilized human beings."

"Finish this already," the old woman barked, with Ellen's voice.

"Yeah." Dante moved his aim from Dez to Antonio, cocking back the hammer. "I'm sorry it had to come to this. Goodbye, Tony."

"Don't," Sasha yelled. The look in Dante's eyes rattled her knees. She'd seen that regretful stare before, the night her mother died. She couldn't do it. She couldn't watch another person she loved get gunned down by that man.

Her gun swung until finding the only thing that could affect every single person in the room, the floodlight. One shot and a thick veil of darkness covered them all.

A rifle poked Sasha in the back and she jumped aside, grabbing onto its barrel. The revolver slipped from her hand, its clank triggering a barrage of blasts. Each shot flooded a tiny space in white. In every corner of the room, bursts of gunfire lit a fraction of the scene. One flash showed Vinny, using her fallen revolver to blow the side of a man's head to red splatter. Another millisecond of light revealed Dez crawling toward a rifle. The glare from the gun now in her grasp displayed a lovely image, despite how annoying the loud blast was. It showed the man she stole it from gagging on a mouthful of blood, a result of the bullets she'd shot into his throat.

Sasha crouched down as the man fell to the floor. In every strobe of light, she took a shot at an unfamiliar face. Bullets whizzed by, searing streaks of fire along her arm and cheek as they grazed her skin. She took a step, tripping on a tangle of floppy arms. Her chin whacked concrete, and a buzz silenced the gunshots that rattled her head. She stayed down, rolling onto her side. It could've been two seconds, two hours for all she knew. The thunder of high-powered rifles didn't let up, and she never found the strength to push herself off the floor.

Fingers wrapped around Sasha's wrist, squeezing. She kicked, lifting the rifle, and Dez pushed the barrel aside. Time seemed to stop as his hand slid along her cheek. In the flashes of gunfire, they stared into each other's eyes. Her smile triggered his arms to circle her body. When lips brushed against her own, she giggled. Goddamn if she wasn't about to kiss him in the middle of this room, surrounded by gunfire. Dez always got his way.

Sasha locked onto Dez's lips, taking his back to the floor. A bullet struck the ground, kicking concrete onto her face, and she didn't even flinch. Her body was too busy crumbling to give a fuck. All that stupid shit going on outside Dez's grasp could wait, for just one more kiss.

Chapter Eighteen

The shooting must've stopped somewhere between that one last kiss and the five that followed, since Vinny started kicking Sasha's leg.

"Thanks," Vinny grumbled, glaring down at Sasha, "for starting a shitstorm and ducking out to fuck in the corner."

Sasha climbed to her feet, straightening her blood-splattered flannel. "I just saved our lives, asshole."

"Not all our lives," Vinny said, pointing across the room.

"Cash?" Sasha yelled, pushing Vinny aside. It was worse, much worse. Slumped against the threshold, Antonio sat in a pool of his own blood. A steady flow seeped between his fingers, rolling off his stomach to drench his lap.

"Oh fuck!" Sasha slipped on sticky puddles, hurrying to Antonio's side. "Tony! You can't die." Her hands covered his, and a warm flow gushed between her fingers.

"Don't worry, dear. I've already taken steps.

183

Othello's position is secured, right alongside your own."

"I know," Sasha said, unable to control the quaver in her voice. "That's why you can't die, you fat bastard."

Antonio chuckled. His hands flopped to the concrete, letting his guts spill into Sasha's palm.

"You'll make a great underboss."

"No!" Sasha yelled, looking over her shoulder. "Cash?"

"I'm here." Cash limped across the room, less with every step.

"You good?" Sasha asked Cash, removing one hand from Antonio's stomach to fish a set of keys from his pocket.

"Fuck yeah!"

"Go fetch Tony's car, and be careful. Those guys might be out there." Sasha took off her flannel, balling it over Antonio's wound.

"Where's Tyler?" Dez asked, kneeling beside Sasha. The way he clung to her arm when he asked, the tremble in his voice…she'd never heard that level of fright come from his mouth. It shook every one of her bones.

"He was supposed to be with you." It was close to an accusation, the way she flung it out there, but fuck. What kind of grown-ass man gets kidnapped? "When was the last time you saw him?"

"I don't know how long it's been. I was drugged. I think I was on a plane. He was in his hospital room the last time I saw him, safe with Otis."

"I couldn't get ahold of Otis earlier. Fucking Kev, I knew he was lying."

Vinny peeked his head outside, crouching low. "We might've killed them all. I didn't hear any cars pull away."

"Good," Sasha said. "Can you check around the side, see if any of Tony's men are alive?"

"Yeah."

Vinny ducked out the door and Dez reached for a rifle, groaning. "I should go with him," he said, teetering to his feet.

"Stop, dummy. You've been shot." She'd grab Dez's leg, but her hands were the only thing holding in Antonio's intestines.

"It went right through. I'm good."

"Then...stay here and protect me. I'm scared." Sasha tried to push out the statement with an edge of fear and failed miserably. The words together, they just came out all awkward.

"Yeah, okay," Dez snorted, walking toward the door.

"I'm totally unarmed here. Anything can happen to me," she muttered into her chest, feeling pretty stupid. "You just gonna leave your woman."

Dez stopped short, turning to face Sasha. "My wife."

"Wife?" Antonio said. "I missed the wedding?"

"Don't feel bad. I did too," Sasha said, masking her regret with a sad little smile.

"We can do it again." Dez knelt beside Sasha, leaning in to catch her gaze. "No coma, forged papers. If you want."

Sasha looked at Antonio, who grinned between winces. His sticky fingers clutched onto her own drenched hand, growing weaker with every shuddering breath. An untouchable was dying in her grasp. Anything was possible, and eventually everything faded away. Sasha had to take the things she wanted, before she became nothing but a memory.

"Fuck yeah! Let's do it." She'd kiss Dez, but headlights flooded the warehouse and she needed to get a glimpse of Dante's dead body. She scanned the still boots. There weren't many. It sure looked like they'd clipped more men when the bullets were flying.

"Four out of ten ain't bad," Dez said, moseying around to poke bodies with the barrel of a rifle.

No old woman, and no douchebag wearing way too tight tacky leather pants.

"Donatello?" Antonio sputtered.

"He lives." Her words came with a bitter edge, yet Antonio grinned.

Vinny called out to Cash, and Sasha leaned back, watching them load a body into the back seat. "Who is it?"

"I don't know their names," Vinny yelled, dragging another guy toward the car. "The tall one, and the guy who drove us here."

It had to be Enzo and Marco. That would perk Antonio up. "Enzo and Marco are alive," she said, looking down at Antonio. He stared up with blank eyes, beyond her face. Antonio's chest no longer rose and fell in quick fits. No more gasps trickled out.

"No!" Sasha grabbed onto Antonio's shirt, shaking. "Don't leave me alone with this shit, Tony." She dropped her head to his chest. Her warm tears sank into his shirt, his cold blood soaking through her tank top. "Please."

"Sasha." Dez pulled Sasha back. Antonio's limp hand slapped the ground, and she turned away. She didn't want Dez to see her cry. If he knew, really knew, how fragile she was, he'd leave too.

"Come on." Dez glided his thumb across Sasha's cheek, clearing away streaks of blood and tears. "We have to get your friends to the hospital."

Dez helped Sasha off the blood-soaked floor even though it must've scorched his shoulder.

"Not the hospital," she said, heading to the car. "We have a doctor. And a cleaner, to retrieve…the Don's body."

"We?" Dez snickered.

If only it were a joke. "Yeah. We. Me and Otis."

Dez stopped in front of the car, his wide frame blocking one of the headlights. "What?" That question came out in a sharp, short tone.

"I'll tell you about it on the way," Sasha said, dropping into the passenger seat.

***

Otis

After two hours of sitting on a sidewalk with no weed, Otis picked Sasha's lock. That girl thrived on pot, probably had at least three bags stashed around her room.

It only took opening one drawer to hit the jackpot. Sasha wouldn't mind if he helped himself to one, maybe two, joints.

Otis picked up the phone, dialing Kev as he rolled a bone. A squeal of brakes echoed through the open motel door, and he set the phone back on its receiver. Then came the click of a bullet loading into its chamber.

He reached for his side to find it bare, holsterless. Fucking airlines, dumping him, unarmed and with no weed, in a city that wanted him dead. Just the thought that he'd actually paid for that kind of treatment boiled his blood. Otis crept beside the door, waiting for some asshole to poke a barrel inside so he could grab it.

Sure enough, some asshole came through the door gun first, and Otis grabbed their hand. He recognized Sasha's wrist the instant he squeezed it, but his brain was too slow to stop his fingers from twisting. Sasha didn't drop the gun, not his girl. Her heel crashed down on the top of his foot, and he hopped back. The tip of her boot stopped inches from his balls, sending a rush of air through his jeans to raise all the little hairs on his skin.

"Otis!" Sasha staggered back, gawking.

This was the moment Otis had prepared for. He'd spent hours rehearsing a speech to let Sasha down gentle, tell her Dez was gone. What a waste of time, since his spineless ass refused to speak. His gaze fell to the ugly carpet, and that's where it stayed. Drugs, it had to be the lack of drugs. He'd never gone this long without a joint, had never been such a coward before.

"Where's Tyler?" Dez growled, pulling Otis's stare from the floor.

A smile spanned Otis's lips. Dez was alive.

Bloody, covered in cuts and bruises, about to rip his head off, but fucking alive. Otis didn't know what to do, wasn't used to happy. Before the strange feeling could crest, burst his skin, he rushed forward and wrapped his arms around Dez.

"Ah!" Dez cried out, flinching. "You're gonna rip my stitches."

Otis pulled back, caught Dez's harsh glare, and then went in for another hug.

"Jesus," Dez grumbled, pushing Otis away. "If it's gonna be like that, you should know I'm a power-top."

Sasha shielded her face, turning away. Bitch was probably snickering.

"Otis? What are you doing here?" Vinny squeezed his way into the room. He looked pretty beat-up, like he'd been fighting. Just like Dez.

Otis narrowed his glare on Dez, crossing his arms. "Please tell me you didn't run off to fight your brother for Sasha. I thought you were fucking dead. I got on a plane."

"I didn't run the fuck off." Dez poked Otis on the chest, forcing the man back a few steps. "Where's Tyler!"

"He's safe. In a fallout shelter on the Prichette farm."

"Are you kidding me!" Dez shouted, his curled fingers raising. Otis thought the dude would wring his neck, but Dez just stomped to the phone. "What's the number?"

"It's on the nightstand," Otis said in a rush. "The kid's good, I swear. All the women are doting on him, putting swamp mud on his wounds. Kev got like twenty of his cousins to show up with sawed-offs, ready for trouble."

"Swamp mud does work good," Sasha said, plucking the joint Otis just rolled off the bed and putting it in her mouth.

Otis followed Sasha to the doorway, snatching the joint and sparking it up. "What went down? You're covered in blood."

"I got some bad news for you, Otis."

The car doors of a black sedan opened and two men got out. Otis didn't know them, but he could recognize a wiseguy any day. Vinny stepped back, Sasha stared at Otis with regret, and Dez was busy yelling at Kev through the phone. These fuckers were going to let him get whacked. That's cool; he didn't need the clubmates he had thought were his ride-or-die family. The two assholes coming toward him were already limping. He'd finish them off in a heartbeat.

Otis curled his fingers into a fist and the tall guy bent over, kissing the skull ring on Otis' finger. Otis froze, staring at Sasha as the second guy did the same.

"What the fuck are they doing?"

"Pledging their loyalty," Sasha said, rubbing the back of her neck, "to the new Don of the Lazzari family."

An invisible fist swung in to strike Otis in the chest, robbing his lungs of oxygen. It must be a joke, mistake, a trick. It was a ploy, to get him to walk willingly into Fat Tonys.

"I-I. I don't—"

Sasha lifted her chin, her eyes narrowing. In this

moment, Otis could almost hear her thoughts. A warning. While in front of these men, he could only show strength.

"Tony died," Sasha's voice cracked, but her face stayed strong. "He had no sons, so he left everything to you, his brother's son." She stole the joint from his hand, taking a long hit. "Everything."

***

Special Agent Philip Daniels

Never in twenty-three years of law enforcement had Daniels witnessed something like this. If he wasn't watching it with his own eyes through binoculars, he'd never believe it. His perp was good. This little girl had accomplished what no others could, killed the boss of all organized crime and replaced him with her man. That must've been her plan all along. The fake coma, her conveniently timed trip back to Kentucky when Antonio's son got popped, she was running the long con.

Daniels shifted in his seat, tugging at his pants. That fucking slut. He hated how his body reacted to thoughts of slamming her against a wall. She made him get hard, evil bitch. The way she leaned back, moving her pawns around her chessboard. He couldn't wait to smash Sasha Ashby's face into a metal table and toss her ass in a cell, forever. He would get the girl no one else could get.

A throb spread out beneath his skin, cutting his breaths short. He had to stop this, had to concentrate. There was only one way. He loosened his belt, hiking down his pants. A gasp broke free as his hand glided up and down his shaft. He looked out the window, tightening his grip. Her wickedness wafted across the parking lot, seeped into his car, and infected him, making him do this vile thing.

Shivers ran through him but he kept his eyes on her and his hand in his lap, working it faster. He'd take her, break her, force a confession. And when she was alone in the dark, forgotten, he'd really take her. That smart ass would be his, to do with as he liked. Then, when she was too broken to fight, he'd leave her in a dark cell until the day she died.

Chapter Nineteen

Sasha

The moment Sasha stepped from the shower, Dez climbed inside. She wrapped herself in a towel as she walked from the bathroom. He'd waited on purpose. There was more than enough room in the shower for both of them, yet he stood in the bathroom and waited. His gaze didn't even flash to her naked body as she slinked by him.

Scratchy carpet tickled her toes as she walked across the room to her bag on the dresser. Most likely, Dez was trying to be respectful. His refusal to touch her, look anywhere below her face, was probably his idea of giving her space, his notion of comfort. It wasn't comforting. The only thing Dez accomplished by treating her like a wounded animal was making her feel like a wounded animal.

Sasha ripped off her towel and tossed it in a corner. Wet strands of hair slapped her arms as she pulled on her last clean tank top. She'd have to put her dirty pants back on, unless Vinny had a pair she could borrow. They'd be extra baggy, but that was better than bloody. Until she was forced to leave this room, a tank top and underwear would do.

The shower cut off and Sasha crept toward the cracked-open door, weaving to get a glimpse. Hints of inked flesh peeked through the slit, drawing her closer. The door flew open, she jumped back, and Dez smirked. It was the first hint of a real smile she'd seen from him in what felt like ages.

Her gaze dropped from the incredible sight of a Dez smile down to something even more magnificent, his bare chest. She wasn't able to get a good view the other day, when he was pounding her from behind, but goddamn. How could she have forgotten the cool shade of his tanned skin, the ripples that cut across his stomach?

"You trying to peep on me?" Dez grabbed onto the towel wrapped around his waist. "Wanna see?"

"Don't." Sasha shrank back, shocked by the levels of fear that ran through her body. Sharp arms of fire rose in her chest, her fingers trembling. She had to keep cool, play along. A half-smirk crossed her lips, but that was the most her punk ass could muster up.

"You're scared," Dez said softly. He turned his back, pulling on his jeans before losing the towel. It was classy, made Sasha want to rip his pants right back off. She would fall into his strong arms but that damn fear, which surged uninvited, rooted her legs in place.

"I understand, you know." Dez smoothed back his long, wet hair as he plopped on the bed. "It can be hard to get close to someone after something like that happens."

Dez stared at her, his eyes leering, wanting, the way they always had. That one look brought more confidence to her sorry self than all the stabbing, shooting, and sledgehammering she'd done so far.

The knots in her stomach unraveled, allowing her to walk across the room and sit on the far end of the bed. "Did anything like that ever—" She clamped her jaw shut. She really didn't want to know if Dez had ever been assaulted in that way. It could crumble the image she built of him in her head. Must be how he felt about her, now that she'd been ruined.

"Shit got close." Dez scooted over, just enough for his hand to brush up against hers. "Real close my first night in. My roommate was this huge woman-beating psycho. He said he'd choke me out and skull-fuck me if I didn't give him a blowjob and make it good."

"Fuck! What'd you do?"

"I bit dude's dick off."

Sasha turned to gawk at Dez. "No, you didn't."

"Well, it was just the tip."

"Oh my God!" A giggle took Sasha back, flat against the mattress. She rolled onto her side and Dez propped onto his elbow beside her, staring into her eyes.

"You want to burn one?" he asked without moving a muscle.

"Yeah." The bag of weed was on the nightstand, behind Sasha, but she didn't budge. The different shades of blue in Dez's eyes held her captive. Her body craved his soft kiss, his rough fingertips, his firm hold. Strength radiated around him, so strong it sent shivers beneath her flesh. If he touched her now, the shivers would grow to quakes and not even his strong arms could quell them. It made her want to both jump on his lap and crawl into a closet and hide at the same time.

"Thanks," Dez said, his breath running over Sasha's cheek. "For saving me from your insane father."

"Anytime."

Before she could smirk, his lips covered her mouth. The twisty thoughts in her brain fell silent. Heavy chains of fear shattered, leaving only Dez's hard body to glide, press, energize her soul. If only he'd reach around and grab her ass, she could be that woman again. The one people died for, killed for, feared.

Dez slid his hand down Sasha's side, and her throat sealed shut. His fingers traced her hip, skating down. Every light touch drove her lungs to pump, yet air refused to pass through her cinched airways. Then he clutched her ass. The imprisoned breath, which seared the walls of her chest, burst free as a laugh. Whatever magic Dez possessed, it somehow replenished the weakened muscles given to her upon waking from a coma. Just a little closer, and she could be her old self again.

Sasha pressed against Dez harder, gripping him tighter, and his shoulder flinched.

"Sorry," she said, gently pushing him back to the mattress. "I forgot, you've been injured." She climbed atop his lap. Her chest glided along his hard body as she leaned down to kiss the patch of fresh stitches on Dez's shoulder. "It must be throbbing."

Dez squirmed, grinding against Sasha. "You're about to find out."

A devious gleam ran through Dez's eyes, kick-starting a frenzy in Sasha's chest. Electric-laced tingles swelled, rolled, crawled beneath her skin. She thought the need to want another person this close was gone, yet the desire to feel Dez slip inside her surged so hard it left an ache. For returning her stolen mojo, Dez deserved a proper thank you.

With one finger, Sasha popped open the button on Dez's now super-tight jeans. She leaned down for a kiss when the motel's door flew open. Its knob slammed against the wall, almost at the same time as Sasha gripped onto the gun under her pillow.

"What the fuck is this?" a woman's grating, whiny, sharp voice rang out.

"Rosalie," Sasha grumbled, climbing off Dez. That bitch was like the clap. Sasha should grab the gun and use it on herself.

"You're in here fucking some guy!" Rosalie yelled, her bracelets clanking with every over-exaggerated hand gesture.

Dez jumped off the bed as Rosalie stomped toward it, but Sasha didn't move. She sat on the edge of the mattress, her gaze stuck to the floor. Once Rosalie's tanned leg, attached to a tapping red heel, broke her peripheral, she had no choice but to follow it up. Beyond the muscled thighs that peeked beneath a leather mini, past a tight waist strategically flaunted by a sheer top, she found a cute scowl.

"I thought you came back for me," Rosalie said, slapping on a thick pout.

"Jesus Christ," Dez all but growled, voicing Sasha's thoughts exactly.

Vinny and Otis ran into the room, guns drawn. They froze, bumping into each other when taking in the scene. It must've been a sight, Dez with no shirt and his jean button undone, Sasha on the bed in basically her underwear, and a saucy Italian woman dressed a bit like a hooker.

"What's all this now?" Otis snickered.

"Out," Sasha shouted. "Everyone, get the fuck out."

"No problem," Dez muttered, grabbing his shirt and pushing his way to the door.

"No, not you," Sasha said, reaching for Dez, but it was too late. He slipped out the door, walking into the night without a glance back.

"Fuck!" Sasha yelled, kicking the nightstand and sending the lamp crashing to the floor.

Vinny stood in the doorway, bobbing like a retarded duck, and Otis leaned against a dresser, making himself quite comfortable.

"Come home with me." Rosalie knelt down, maneuvering between Sasha's legs. "You're all beat up. Let me take care of you, baby."

Rosalie pawed Sasha, clutching onto her waist, draping her arms around Sasha's neck. Every time Sasha pulled away, the woman's hands came in stronger.

"We can take a bath," Rosalie whispered, licking Sasha's ear. "I'll make you some primavera."

The situation had grown far beyond the standard

limitations of annoying, and Otis snickering in the corner wasn't helping.

"Dammit, girl." Sasha took a firm hold on Rosalie's wrists. "How many times do I have to end it with you?" She jumped to her feet, yanking Rosalie up along with her. "You're making yourself look like a fool."

Amid an outburst of "No-baby!" and "Please!" Sasha dragged Rosalie to the door.

"Don't let me see you 'round here again." Sasha shoved the whiny bitch into Vinny's chest, pushing them both clear of the threshold, and slammed the door shut.

"That was harsh," Otis said between chuckles.

Sasha groaned, pointing to the door that rattled under a barrage of pounds behind her. "Bitch is crazy. The boys tried to warn me about her." She grabbed a pack of cigarettes from the nightstand, plopping onto the bed. "But goddamn, that woman could cook."

After a few seconds of listening to Rosalie yell her name while constantly pounding on the locked door, Sasha grabbed her gun.

"No," Otis said, plucking the glock from Sasha's hand.

"I'm just gonna scare her off." Sasha hopped off the bed, reaching for her gun as Otis lifted it higher.

"I'm the Don, and I say no."

"Fuck!" Sasha backed away, lit a cigarette, and slammed the lighter onto the dresser. Otis was un-fucking-believable. The dude hadn't even been officially titled yet and he was already playing the Don card.

"You know," Sasha said, dropping back against the headrest, "you're only half-Don. I hold fifty-percent of the interests in the Lazzari family."

"Okay." Otis popped out the clip, emptied the bullet from the chamber, then tossed the gun onto the bed beside Sasha. "Here's half your gun."

"Nice. Asshole." A long, loud huff slipped past Sasha's lips. She sat back, waiting for the psycho-bitch to clear her doorway. Otis smirked every time Rosalie shouted "I love you!" through the flimsy wood, which pushed Sasha's annoyance level up a notch.

"You better have a joint in your pocket," Sasha all but spat, narrowing her glare on Otis, "because this show ain't free."

***

Vinny

Vinny leaned against the wooden beam of the motel's porch. He couldn't help but stare and snicker. A scorned lover's spaz-attack was far more entertaining when he wasn't on the other end of it. He had to give it to Sasha, she had great taste. This woman had legs that lasted for days. And that rearview. Her hips swayed every time she banged on the door, jiggling that firm ass within the confines of its tight leather skirt.

The woman quit her screechy shouting and stopped pounding the door. She turned, yelping at the sight of Vinny. Guess the broad didn't figure on drawing an audience with her giant hissy fit.

"What the fuck are you staring at?" she barked.

She crossed her arms, which only propped her already overflowing cleavage farther out the top that barely held them in. Damn the woman was cute. Even with the flared nostrils and bonus crazy chick points, she was totally fuckable.

"I'm staring at a beautiful woman in need of a joint," Vinny said, flashing a smile as he pulled a doobie from his breast pocket.

The woman giggled. In the bat of a highly painted eye, her entire body shifted from attack to prowl mode.

"Are you in Sasha's crew?" she asked, slinking in front of Vinny.

The question came with a million bad intentions, mostly on her end. Thankfully, Vinny lived hundreds of miles away and really didn't give a fuck.

"Yep. Looks like you had a rough night." He brushed a stray hair behind the chick's ear, flashed a grin, and she nearly melted on the sidewalk. "Wanna burn one, talk about it."

"I love your accent," she said, running her hands up Vinny's chest.

"Damn," Vinny muttered, dropping his gaze. Experience taught him to stay away from women who dropped the L-word within the first five minutes of chatting, but he was headed for the hills come sunrise and wouldn't be returning to this hellhole. "Oh yeah." He reached for the woman's waist slowly, giving her plenty of time to slap his hand away. Since she didn't, he latched on and pulled her close. "What does my accent sound like?"

The broad draped her arms around Vinny's neck, rubbing against him. "Like a real man."

That was the cue. Vinny tightened his grip, backing the chick who didn't even bother to drop her name into his open motel door. Her lips locked onto his before one foot could brush shag carpet. Cash jumped up from the bed as they barged inside, wavering in the center of the room. Vinny tore himself from the tongue that had practically rammed itself down his throat and hurled Cash a leer. His buddy knew that stare and was out the door in seconds flat.

Now that they were alone, closed up in a tiny motel room, Vinny could peel that woman's tight top off except he didn't get a chance. She wiggled out of her shirt, then ripped his off in a heartbeat. Damn, these city women moved quick. Not to worry, he knew just how to slow her down.

Vinny clutched the woman's curvy hips, lifting her feet from the floor. She tightly wrapped her legs around his waist. He laid her down on the bed, keeping in sync with her rough kisses, but she wouldn't let go. Her thighs squeezed, back arching so she could press against him harder. He had to literally pry her off him, hold her down as he stood.

"Damn, girl. Simmer down. I wanna enjoy this."

She squirmed. Her eyes narrowed in the most playful, naughty way as her hand slid between her legs.

"Oh no," Vinny said, pushing her hand away. "I got this." He knelt down, yanking her to the edge of the bed. The gasp that followed sent a shiver up his spine. His jeans would've burst open, except that damn woman had unbuttoned them before they even got near the bed.

Her skirt slid up with ease, mostly because she tugged it out of Vinny's way. Her entire body shuddered with his slightest touch, and her fingers curled into his hair. A nibble to the inner thigh set off a series of loud moans. Fuck, this bitch was going to be a screamer.

Chapter Twenty

Sasha

Sasha took two hits before passing Otis the joint back. For the way he stood there, gawking like a perv as she lounged on the bed in her underwear, she deserved the extra hit.

"You gonna hide out in here all night?" Otis asked through a stream of smoke.

"Maybe."

"Do you know how many chicks Dez was with when you were gone?"

Sasha shrank back, despite the joint Otis waved in her face. This had been information she'd been dreading and dying to obtain, and now it dangled in front of her. Just like that roach in Otis's grip.

"Do I want to know?"

"None," Otis said, lifting the joint back up to his own lips.

A snort burst free, and Sasha snatched the joint. As if she'd believe that shit. "Yeah, okay."

"I'm serious."

"You guys were doing pornos."

"I know," Otis said.

"Them twats must've been all over Dez."

"They were, but he didn't touch a single one of them. And I'm not talking about this last year. He hasn't looked at another woman since the night we fished you out of the cellar."

Otis had always been a hard man to read. He seemed different now. His eyes didn't hold that cruel edge any longer; lies and schemes weren't circling behind his gaze. Still, she couldn't trust...anything.

"You don't know that. Dez could've fucked around when you went home."

"The big house is my home," Otis said in a sneer. "It has been for the last five, almost six years." He leaned over, taking the joint Sasha had completely forgotten to hit. "I tried to pull him out of the slump a few years back, but he said it wouldn't matter how many chicks he fucked. That it wouldn't do shit, cause none of them were you."

All the little hairs rose on Sasha's neck, her arms. Fuck. Her entire body had become a resting place for electric shocks. She shot to her feet, picking her blood-stained pants off the floor.

"Where you going?" Otis asked, stumbling away from the door to keep from being trampled by Sasha.

"To find Dez."

"What about that crazy bitch?"

For the last five minutes, Sasha had been subjected to the sound of Rosalie's sweet moans echoing through her motel wall. Once, for about a half of a second, she even heard Vinny grunt. The noises sparked so many uninvited feelings. Rage flared, jealousy burned, but the sensation that scorched the hottest really caught her off guard, lust. She shouldn't want to bust down Vinny's door and join him in that party, yet she did.

"Fuck that crazy bitch," Sasha said, shoving her feet into her boots. The fractions of warmth she could gain from the room next door paled in comparison to what Dez had to offer. His arms filled her body with such strength, recharged her broken will.

Sasha hurried out her motel's door without bothering to lace her boots.

"Wait!" Otis called out. He grabbed her gun from the bed, reloading the clip he swiped earlier. "Don't forget to use protection." He slapped the gun into Sasha's palm, winking.

***

Dez

Dez walked away from the motel, peering down the sidewalk beside a three-lane road. There were countless yellow cars, buildings that damn near glowed as they reached toward the sky, but no Cash. The dude must be in that room with Vinny and Sasha's sloppy seconds. This city seemed to bring out the nasty in everyone who set foot in it. He'd be damned if he let that shit creep up on him. He was getting the fuck out of this city before traces of its debauchery could seep beneath his skin.

Tiny chucks of pavement scattered as Dez stomped across the parking lot, toward the semi at the far end of the motel. He'd wait for five minutes. If nobody showed by then, he was splitting.

Dez climbed up the running board and opened the driver's door. As he dropped his ass into the cushiony seat, a sliver glint caught his eyes. The keys. His dumbass brother left the fucking keys in the ignition, in an unlocked truck, in the middle of New York City. Vinny was going to be one sorry motherfucker because this semi was getting boosted, by him.

The cool metal of the ignition brushed Dez's fingertips, the keys clinked, and the passenger door flew open. Dez jolted back, reaching for his gun. Just as his fingers wrapped around the butt of a revolver, Sasha poked her head into the cab.

"Hey," she said, crawling up onto the seat and shutting the door. "Going somewhere?"

"Home," Dez barked, making both of their bodies flinch with the sharpness of his tone. After a deep breath and a drag from the cigarette he'd snatched from Sasha's hand, he was ready to form somewhat non-spiteful words. "Since your fucked up family is done using me as bait, I'm getting gone. It looks like Vinny's pretty happy slopping up your leftovers so I guess you can keep him, but I'm taking Cash with me."

"Listen—"

"No!" Dez lifted his hand, blocking Sasha's pout from view. "Don't you goddamn talk to me. You're the fucking devil, Sasha. You'll spout out some lies about love, and I'll just hand over my heart. Even

207

though we both know the only thing you can feel is sorry for yourself."

Sasha jolted back, as though his words had formed into a hand and slapped her. A heavy silence clung to the cab, thicker than the stale cigarette smoke trapped within. Sasha's eyes glossed over, but only for a moment. Any second, she'd unload on him. Any second now.

Barbed slurs never erupted. Sasha remained still, quiet. Without her hurling back hate, his harsh words just sounded shitty.

"Tyler needs me." Dez reached for the ignition, and Sasha grabbed onto his arm.

"I need you!"

Her voice trembled, worse than the hand that clutched onto his wrist.

"Please," Sasha said in a near whisper, "don't leave me."

Dez jerked his arm back. That sounded real. He could almost hear the pain in her voice. "Jesus Christ," he sputtered. "You're serious, aren't you?"

Sasha looked up from her lap, and a tear rolled down her cheek. Dez flinched, holding back a gasp. All the screwed up shit he'd done to her yet she never shed a tear, until now. The pain behind her stare twisted his gut. Sasha had a million reasons to cry. He didn't want to be one of them.

Before his brain could get a say, he wrapped his arms around her. The instant Sasha's weight fell against his chest, a wave of heat rushed through him. Although he couldn't place the sensation, he cherished it. The ripples of warmth filled in all his cracks, somehow making him whole again. Then her lips pressed against his own. Fire drove her kiss, burning stronger than ever before and sweeping in to incinerate every thought in his mind. He squeezed tighter, clutched Sasha harder, yet he couldn't get as close to her as his heart desired.

"Stay," Sasha whispered between gentle kisses. "Stay with me, Dez."

Her soft plea sent chills. He'd stay with her forever, except there was someone even more fragile who needed him.

"Tyler," Dez said. He pulled away, and Sasha latched onto his shirt.

"He'll always be in danger," she said, her fingers shaking as she clung to his collar. "Unless you help me kill the fuckers who want to hurt him."

As much as Dez hated to admit it, Sasha's backward logic actually made sense. He'd be damned if his boy had to live with one eye over his shoulder. Dante had fucked with his kin for the last time, and whoever was stupid enough to follow the man deserved a bullet to the head.

"I'll sta—"

Sasha locked onto Dez's lips. The force of her body falling against his chest drove him back, between the seats and into the sleeper cabin. Her deep kiss robbed him of breath. He didn't need to breathe anyway. Her embrace carried the secrets to life. Only while lost in her grasp did every question clear. Without her touch, her lips, her hands running underneath his shirt, nothing made sense.

"We'll slaughter those bastards," Sasha whispered, unlatching Dez's belt. "Then we can go get Tyler, bring him here." Her breath flowed over his neck as her fingers slipped inside his boxers. "We can all be safe here." She gripped the one part of him that yearned for her the most, and he almost jumped out of his skin. How her clutch could be so hard yet soft, he'd never understand but forever appreciate. "We can be together."

Whatever the hell Sasha was saying, it all seemed just fine right about now.

"Yeah," Dez moaned. He just wanted to put that out there, let her know she was on the right path with the whole kicking off his jeans thing. That other shit could get sorted out later. First things first, her pants had to come off.

Dez held Sasha tight, rolling her back to the thin mattress. It wasn't easy to maneuver in this cramped sleeper cab, on a flimsy piece of foam meant to be a bed, but goddamn he made it look sexy.

"I love you," Sasha said, in more of a breath than a statement.

That stopped Dez's tug of Sasha's pants somewhere around the ankles. He looked up, into her smile. The blaze racing through his veins was just a flicker compared to the one that lit Sasha's stare. Her pants were in the way. They were always in the way. Dez ripped them off, easing between her legs. His heart jumped into his throat. He was about to have sex with his wife, for the first time since she found out they were married. She had to feel it, the electricity in the air. If not, he'd make her feel it.

Slowly, and with a slight amount of thrust, he slid inside her. "I love you too, baby."

*****

Cash

Cash walked across the motel's parking lot. As he neared his room, a loud moan streamed through the door. He staggered back. Vinny might have stumbled dick-first into a potentially deafening mistake. It sounded like a roomful of cats were fighting behind that door. The dude better be making good use of the box of condoms on the nightstand, because goddamn this place was filthy.

A cool breeze laced in the scent of week-old vomit ran over Cash as he turned toward Sasha's door. He stared at the faded number on her splintered door for what felt like five minutes. He lifted his arm only a tad then froze midair. No way was he knocking. Sasha scared the shit out of him. She'd probably unload a full clip before she asked who was there.

Cash took a step back, eyeing the semi across the parking lot. Nobody would toss him out of there. He could sit back, roll a bone, and actually smoke the fucker in peace.

The bag of weed was in hand before Cash climbed up the running board. He opened the passenger door, hopping inside. A quick glance into the back and his entire body froze. Except for his jaw, which dropped wide open. Somehow, he had climbed into a semi and stumbled into his wildest imagination. Sasha couldn't be naked in front of him, riding Dez in the sleeper cab. There was no way her tits looked that perfect in real life. It must be a dream. He would've noticed the curves of her hips, the ripples on her stomach before now if it were real.

"Fuck off," Sasha yelled, throwing a boot into the front.

The bag slipped from Cash's grasp as he nearly fell, backward, out of the truck. He reached for his buds when another boot sailed past his face.

"Oh fuck!" Cash slammed the door of the semi shut. His legs locked stiff, and his breath barely flowed. He stood in front of the semi's door, staring at his own shocked eyes in the shiny surface. The sweetest sounds flowed from within the slightly swaying cab. It was nothing like the screeches erupting from Vinny's room. The noises echoing from the semi were cries of passion, a wordless declaration of love.

Cash shoved his hands in his now empty pockets, turning away. Dez might be the luckiest bastard alive. Archer Brothers Productions was dominating the porn industry, the guy had the coolest kid ever, and then there was Sasha. The goddess of his fantasies had returned, shining far brighter than he remembered. Cash walked through the bits of paper blowing across the parking lot, back toward the line of motel doors. If ever he wanted to live in another's skin, it was now. He'd trade places with Dez in a heartbeat. To be the man enjoying the hot woman instead of chasing the hot woman's ghost all over the country was far better.

A throat cleared and Cash looked up, right into Otis's chest.

"Shit!" Cash stumbled back a few steps,

shrinking down at the hard glare beaming at him.

"Did you see where Sasha went?" Otis asked.

"I umm…I don't, umm…"

Otis pushed Cash aside, looking at the semi. "Was she in the truck?"

"I didn't see it," Cash mumbled.

"Was she fucking Dez in the truck?"

A snicker followed Otis's question, and a prickly heat crept up to sting Cash's cheeks.

Otis chuckled, backing toward Sasha's now open motel door. "Her mob buddies are on their way here. Go fetch her, let her know."

"I'm not going back over there. I'll get Vinny."

"You'll get them both," Otis said, his smile warping into a glower. He walked into Sasha's motel room, slamming the door shut behind him.

Cash peeked over his shoulder, cringing at the thought of opening that semi's door again. This time, Sasha would probably hurl a blade since she was out of boots. He'd get Vinny first. Hell, he might even get thanked. With that train whistle of a woman still piping, his buddy must be deaf by now.

Chapter Twenty-One

Sasha

Sasha leaned back, letting her weight fall against the firm chest behind her. Dez slid his arms around her waist as she twisted a joint from the bag thoughtfully left by a peeping prospect.

"I can't wait to bring Tyler here," she said, fishing a lighter from the pants beside her.

"What, like for a visit?"

"No. To live." Sasha got in two hits before Dez plucked the joint from her lips.

"My son ain't growing up in no city."

"We talked about this, like thirty minutes ago. You said yeah."

"I don't remember none of that shit," Dez said between puffs, reaching for his jeans.

This time, Sasha snatched the joint with no plans on giving it back. "Right before we had sex, I said we should bring Tyler here when shit cools down and you said yeah." She hurried to dress. Dez looked like he was about to bolt, then of course she'd have to give chase or he'd think she didn't care.

"Fuck, Sasha. I wasn't paying attention. Your hand was on my dick."

Knuckles banged on the passenger window, and Sasha almost grabbed her gun. "Dammit Cash—"

"It's Enzo."

Sasha froze, only her gaze moving to Dez. It was strange, the sense of wickedness that wormed its way into her gut. Enzo had dragged her from many beds over the last few months, but none had a man in them. For Enzo to see her tangled in the sleeper cab with Dez felt like a betrayal to herself. She couldn't accept the depravities of her own sexual appetites, which meant no one else would either. This could be the end of her very short reign, but she wouldn't live in lies again, so she yelled, "It's open."

The door squealed open, a shoe tapped against the running board, and Enzo poked his head inside.

"It figures," Enzo said, climbing into the passenger seat and shutting the door. "All these motel rooms, and you're holed up in the back of a semi."

Harsh leers of judgement didn't rear their ugly head, malice wasn't filling Enzo's eyes, only a slight hint of amusement. For the first time, Sasha was pretty damn happy to feel so stupid. The Lazzari family had always accepted her. To expect otherwise was asinine.

"Did you find Dante?" she asked.

Enzo dipped his head toward Dez, narrowing his gaze. "Is he one of your crew?"

Sasha glanced at Dez, catching a chill from his frosty glare. "Actually, this is my husband, Dez."

"Husband!" Enzo leaned back, staring Dez down even harder. "Since when?"

"Umm…" Sasha dropped her stare. That was a good question. She had no idea how long they'd been married. The date was supposed to mean something. Too bad nobody bothered to tell her what it was.

"Five years," Dez said, his sharp glare now fastened on Enzo.

"I see." Enzo tucked his blazer behind his holster, placing his hand on the butt of his gun. "You okay with that, boss?" He was speaking to Sasha, though his eyes never left Dez. "This man, forcing you into marriage while you were in a coma?"

Sasha shrank down. When put that way, it sounded pretty fucking harsh. "It's not like that. Dez is good people."

"Fuck this," Dez said. As if the cab were on fire, he jumped into the front and bolted out the driver's door.

The cab rocked when the door slammed shut, bursting the sanctity created by Dez's warmth.

"Sorry, boss."

"Stop calling me that!" Sasha leaned into the front, grabbing a pack of smokes. "So, Dante?"

"I got a lead, but that's not why I'm here. Word's out about Tony and Othello. A meeting's been called with all five families at Fat Tonys. Set for eight o'clock this morning. I wanted to give you some time to prep Othello."

"Who's gonna prep me?" Just the thought of sitting at the head of that long table brought on the urge to run screaming. All the weed in Cash's stolen bag wouldn't be enough to calm her nerves, and the dude had a lot.

"Please," Enzo said, opening his door. "You were born for this."

The cab swayed as the door slammed shut, leaving Sasha alone with the sad truth. She actually *was* born for this. Enzo hadn't meant to, but he'd just shone a glaring light over her entire life. She was a construct. Her mother had known this would happen, shaped her to fill the Lazzari seat. The moments of love, which carried her through a lifetime of cruelty, were never real. Her mother just used affection to keep her clinging so the training could continue. For some insane reason, it made Sasha proud to know she'd fulfilled her mother's expectations, which also made her want to retch.

Sasha jumped into the front seat, damn near bursting from the truck. Another second alone with her sorry self and she really might puke. Regret came quick when her feet hit pavement. Otis glared from the doorway of her motel room, Dez glowering from within. They were both waiting for her. That tiny sleeper, with its ability to conjure jagged memories, wasn't looking so bad after all.

"He came to call a meeting, didn't he?" Otis asked before Sasha could pick her boot off the dirty parking lot. "With all five families, right?"

"Yeah. To introduce you as Don and work up a strike plan on Dante and the Mancinis."

Otis crossed his arms, staring down at Sasha.

217

"And who'll be my backup?"

"What?"

"You're gonna put me in a room with people who swore to kill me if they ever saw me again. So I want to know, who's gonna have my back? Cause it ain't you."

The spite in Otis's tone drove through Sasha's chest like a knife. Then Dez strolled beside him, and she had two sets of harsh eyes to stare at.

"You know what..." Sasha strained, literally bit her tongue, but the pain of holding back was worse than her teeth digging into flesh. "Fuck you!" She would've unloaded on Otis and Dez, but those two little words seemed to do the trick. Otis staggered from her doorway and she pushed Dez aside, stormed into her room, and crashed the door closed behind her.

***

Vinny

Vinny pulled on his pants, stomping across his motel room. With all the shouts and banging outside his door, it was impossible to enjoy his post-sex high. Another one of the many reasons to hate a city that didn't sleep. He tore open his door, snickering. Of course everyone was crowded in front of the closed door beside his. It must be fuck-with-Sasha time. Why else would these assholes disturb his freaky stranger sexcapades?

"Thanks a lot, man," Dez said, glaring at Otis. "I was getting ready to lay into her."

"You'll have to wait your turn," Otis all but growled.

Now Vinny was pissed. These two jokers teaming up against Sasha sparked his instinct to defend her, but he hadn't officially forgiven her yet.

A groan rumbled past Vinny's throat. He ducked back into his room and grabbed a key from the dresser.

"Come back to bed, baby," the freaky chick whose name he didn't even want to know whined.

"Look." Vinny picked the woman's clothes off the floor, nightstand, and lamp, then dropped them on the bed. "It's been real, but you gotta split. And it's probably best if you don't come 'round anymore. Sasha wouldn't like it, and she is the Don now."

Finally, Vinny found something to shut that woman up. He turned from the mistake on the bed and pushed past Otis. In one swift move, he slid the key in the lock and slipped into Sasha's room. Dez tried to barge his way inside, but Vinny shoved the door shut and locked the deadbolt.

"What the fuck!" Sasha yelled, jumping up off the bed.

"I lifted the spare key from your crazy friend." Vinny walked from the pounds that shook the door, plopping on the bed. "All right."

Sasha stood, frozen, her stare bouncing between Vinny and the door that rattled against its seams. "All right what?"

"You've been punished enough."

Sasha's bright smile cast a veil of silence over the room. Dez's shouts didn't twist his stomach; the

219

bang of fists against wood stopped spiking his nerves. Only Sasha's raised cheeks and that sparkle in her eyes remained.

"Does that mean you're my friend again?" Sasha dropped onto the bed beside Vinny and Vinny clenched his hands. That sly grin, her electric vibe. It took all the will he had, which wasn't much, not to grab her up and hold her tight.

"I never stopped being your friend, but I am done being an asshole."

It looked like Sasha might hug him, until the door shattered open. Splintered wood slammed against the wall as Dez charged inside.

"You're just fucking everybody, huh?" Dez shouted.

Sasha flew off the bed. Her face scrunched as she pointed to Vinny.

"No. I already know you're fucking him," Dez sneered. "I'm talking about the greasy Italian."

"Enzo?" Sasha's laugh echoed over Dez's growl. Like a woman with a death wish, she walked right in front of Dez and stared into his eyes. "No, Dez. I don't fuck men."

"Unless their last name's Archer," Dez said, shoving Sasha away.

"Hey!" Vinny stomped forward. His hands grew a mind of their own, latching onto Dez's shirt and slamming him against the wall. "Don't touch her."

Dez lifted his chin, his big hands clenching. "You gonna stop me."

The blaze in Dez's eyes, which usually forced Vinny back, only sparked his rage. He'd had enough of his brother's shit. The dude wanted a fight, that's fine, but it wouldn't be with Sasha.

At the slightest hint of movement, Vinny drew back. He had to get the first hit, or he might not get any.

"Stop!" Sasha ran between them just as Dez swung. The edge of his fist clocked her chin, dropping her straight to her knees.

Both Vinny and Dez jumped back, releasing their clutch on each other to gawk at Sasha. She moved her hand from her mouth, and a thin stream of blood trickled from her lips. Vinny closed his eyes. The shock in Sasha's gaze, the bright red blood that stained her skin wouldn't fade from his mind. It only burned stronger, until his hands trembled.

Dez stared down at Sasha, his fists still balled at his sides. "I'm sorr—"

Vinny cracked his knuckles against Dez's cheek. The force of the hit took them both into a stagger and they fell against the dresser, sending the TV crashing to the floor.

A giant fist filled Vinny's sight. He shrank down, bracing for lights-out, when Otis yanked Dez away. A cool breeze, left by Dez's failed swing, didn't chill Vinny down. It boiled his blood. He dashed forward, drawing back before Dez could break from Otis's grasp, and Cash tackled him to the bed.

Vinny pushed, surprised when Cash's big ass actually flew off him. The cockiness of his newfound muscles quickly melted to fear once he realized Dez had thrown Cash aside and was coming in with a left hook. A gunshot filled the room, its blast bouncing off the walls.

Dez froze mid-swing, and Vinny jumped up. Chunks of ceiling rained down, bouncing off Sasha's arm as she lowered a gun.

"Stop," Sasha said through gritted teeth. "Please."

"Tell it to your baby daddy," Dez shouted, glaring at Vinny. "He came at me."

Vinny begged his mouth to keep closed but like the rest of his body, it had gone rogue. "That's 'cause you're fucking stupid. She didn't even like having sex with me. She just did it 'cause I wanted to. But she loves you, and you don't even care."

It looked like Dez might charge, again. Vinny was ready. Even though the steam had left his fists, he'd hurl them if he had to.

Dez pushed Otis from the kicked-in doorway, storming into the rays of morning light, and a crushing weight lifted from the entire room.

Sasha gestured to Cash and Vinny's stunned faces, pointed at Dez stomping past a row of motel doors. "These fools are your backup," she said to Otis before rushing after Dez.

Chapter Twenty-Two

Sasha

"Hey!" Sasha grabbed Dez by the arm. Although she wanted him to stop, she jumped back when he spun to face her. It was the rage trapped in his glare. She could still taste her own blood and didn't want another mouthful.

"I can't believe I hit you." Dez drew back, his white knuckles aimed at the brick wall.

"Don't!" Like the stupid idiot she was, her dumbass jumped right in front of his fist. This time, his arm locked up. As if the air had turned to glue, his hand slowed to a stop over her chest.

With Dez so close, and in the light of day, Sasha could see it wasn't rage clouding his eyes. Pain held his stare. The look had been easy to mistake, since she'd never witnessed such a deep twist of agony.

"I never wanted to hurt you like that again," Dez said, unable to lift his stare from the dirty pavement.

Sasha placed her hands on Dez's cheeks, almost feeling his entire body wilt beneath her fingertips.

"I know what you mean."

A light tremble invaded her body when Dez looked at her. Agony still lingered in his gaze, but a hint of shine broke through. This was her chance. She could sneak a kiss while his defenses were down before he could push her away.

"I'm out," Otis yelled, heading for the street. "I'm sick of you guys' soap opera bullshit. Nobody even cares I'm supposed to face the five families and walk straight to my death. So, fuck you all."

Sasha watched Otis stroll toward the busy sidewalk, looking back at Dez to find a scowl. "Fuck," she muttered. If Otis left, the families of the other boroughs would turn on her then each other. She'd never get revenge, never get her hands on Dante.

Dez took a step back, probably because her foot wouldn't stop tapping. A snort accompanied his head shake, and he waved toward Otis.

"I'm sorry." Sasha ran toward Otis, glancing back at Dez. "About everything."

Otis stomped down the sidewalk, waving for a cab, and Sasha slinked in front of him.

"You can't go," she said, reaching for Otis's arm.

"The fuck I can't." Otis turned to the side, keeping his hand high.

"Dude!" Sasha grabbed Otis by the jacket sleeve, pulling his arm down. "You can't just leave me."

"You left me!"

Sasha took a step back. The tremble of Otis's shout cracked her heart, but the wall of tears building in his eyes severed it in half. "Leaving was the biggest mistake of my life." She slid her hand into his and he didn't pull away, so she squeezed harder. "Don't go."

"If you make me do this, you're just a selfish bitch."

There was no legitimate argument Sasha could lay down. Even though she truly believed in Antonio's decisions, there was a small chance Otis would be walking into a trap. Antonio was gone. Dante had been legally stripped of his title, name, and possessions. Now that all the papers were signed, Otis was the last legitimate Lazzari. That made him the ultimate mark. He was right; she was selfish. She couldn't tell him to run for the hills of Kentucky, because her need to drive a blade into Dante's neck held her thoughts captive.

"If you go now, they will hunt you down. Put bullets in all of us, just to prove a point." Sasha pulled Otis closer, holding his hand to her chest. "We need to go in there strong, together. Slap our dicks on the table."

Otis snickered, his stare drifting down to Sasha's pants.

"Figuratively," she said through a grin. "Those other families work for us. They're in their seats, running the other boroughs, because we let them." She dropped Otis's hand to jab her finger at his chest. "Remember that."

A slice of cruelty cut through Otis's far-off stare. It was nice. A look Sasha hadn't seen from the man since her return.

"I guess it could be fun, to make *them* sweat," Otis said, nodding.

"That's what I'm talking about."

It only took a light tug, and Otis was on his way back toward the motel.

***

Vinny

After a shower and a shave, Vinny felt like a new man. A man who still regretted hitting his brother, but a squeaky clean one.

He latched his belt, walking from the bathroom. "You're up," he said to Cash, pushing dude's big ass off the bed.

"Why?" Cash groaned, walking into the bathroom. "I ain't been rolling around in a stranger's snatch."

If Vinny's mind wasn't a jumble of barbed thoughts, he might laugh at that. "We're representing Otis. You want us to look like a bunch of dirty hillbillies?"

"I don't think a shower's gonna change much," Cash said, closing himself inside the bathroom.

Vinny reached for his shirt, caught by his reflection in the mirror. He looked as good as any city folk. The shit-kicker boots, confederate flag belt buckle, and lightly faded bruises around his eye would fit in just fine.

A knock rang out and Vinny grabbed his shirt, opening the front door. Sasha stumbled back. Her eyes grew wide and stayed on his bare chest. That's right, girl, he had been working out.

"Where's Dez?" Vinny barked, instantly hating

himself for asking. He shouldn't give a fuck where that guy was, or if his brother was pissed or hurt.

"He's in my room, calling home to check on Tyler."

"I miss that kid." A churn started to whirl in Vinny's stomach after his first word. Then Sasha gave him *that* look. Fuck her, it wasn't inappropriate. He'd always loved Tyler, constantly thought about the boy. It shouldn't feel wrong now, now that he knew the truth, now that *the* kid was *his* kid.

Vinny pulled on his shirt, heading straight for his pack of smokes.

"You got any pants?" Sasha asked, creeping inside and shutting the door.

"What?"

"These were my last pair." She tugged at her cargo pants, but those dark bloodstains didn't need any help to be seen.

"Yeah." Vinny grabbed a duffle bag off the floor, digging through rumples of jean and black tees. "They're gonna be big."

"That's not true."

"How do you figure? You're all scrawny now."

"No." Sasha pushed the duffle bag aside, taking Vinny's hands. "What you said before. I enjoyed everything we ever did together, everything."

Vinny had to force a breath. Sasha was standing too close, holding his hand too tight. He could kiss her at any second, and it wouldn't be his fault.

The shower cut off with the squeak of a knob. Good thing. If he stared into Sasha's deep eyes any longer, he would've wrapped his arms around her.

227

Since Dez was within a five-mile radius, the guy would've sensed it. Then another door would get kicked in, and they'd have two wrecked motel rooms to pay for.

"Here." Vinny pulled a pair of cargo pants from his bag, practically throwing them in Sasha's face. To touch her right now was too risky.

"Thanks," she said softly, sadly. She opened the door, glancing back. There was something in her gaze. A look that told Vinny if he asked her to run away with him, she'd seriously consider it, except he didn't want that life anymore.

Vinny nodded and Sasha walked out the room, closing the door behind her.

***

Tyler

Tyler scooted to the edge of the bed. He wanted to run across the cold floor and peek up that ladder. If it wasn't for the mask, which was staring at him from the corner of this little steel room, he would've looked up that ladder by now. So far, the mask hadn't moved. It could be waiting for him. Maybe the squeaky bed beneath him was base. There were arms, legs, and a long rubber suit attached to that mask. That meant it could grab him up, if he left base.

"My daddy'll shoot you, mister. If you touch me," Tyler warned, but the mask didn't respond. Hopefully, the sucker got the message because he was getting off this bed.

Slowly, Tyler placed his foot on the frosty ground and…nothing. He must've scared that mask good and proper, since it didn't budge. That's what the mask deserved for being so ugly.

Tyler took a step then another but didn't dare look back. The mask man was for sure behind him. For sure. A warm breeze tickled his nose, the blue sky shining from a square hole atop the ladder. It was a long way up, and his side burned, but his daddy could be up there.

A voice echoed from above, and Tyler inched back.

Kev blocked the sun, peeking down with a smile. "You good, little man?" he asked.

Tyler hurried to the bed as Kev climbed down the ladder. The mask man continued to stare, and this time Tyler glared back. "You're gonna get it now, mister."

"Who you talking to?" Kev asked, glancing around.

"Him." Tyler pointed to the corner, and Kev swung his shotgun forward. Tyler shrank down, waiting for a loud blast, and got a chuckle.

"That's just a radiation suit, buddy."

When his uncle grabbed the mask man off the shelf, Tyler saw it wasn't a man at all. Just a silly costume.

"Is it for trick or treatin'?"

"Umm…" Kev dropped the costume to the ground, kicking it under the shelf. "Yeah, sure." He lowered the gun, sitting on the bed. "How ya feeling, your stomach, side?"

"It hurts! I wanna go home. Where's my daddy?"

"Relax, man, you'll pop a stitch. I just talked to your daddy. He'll be home soon."

"He ran away, didn't he?"

"What!"

"One night, I heard daddy and uncle Otis talking about how my mama ran away. I left the house without permission and got hurt. That must be why Daddy ran away."

"Your dad would never run off. And your mama didn't run away either, she just…got a little lost after she woke up from her princess sleep."

"Kevin Pritchett," a woman's voice hollered from the hole in the ceiling.

"Oh shit!" Kev jumped off the bed, and his gun clattered to the ground.

"Who's that?" Tyler whispered.

"That's *my* mama," Kev said, smoothing back his hair.

"You have a mama!"

"Yeah. Be cool, little man."

Since Tyler wasn't exactly sure what be cool meant, he copied Kev and crossed his arms.

"What in tarnation is going on 'round here. I was winning big on the riverboat." The woman climbed down the ladder, took one look at Tyler, and stopped short. "What is this?" she said with one of them fake smiles grown-ups liked to use so much.

"This is Tyler," Kev said, pointing at the bed.

"I know who he is. Why is he here, in this dirty hole in the ground?"

Kev looked at Tyler, shrugged, then veered his fake smile to his mama. "It's a long story, and I'm sorry I fucked up your vacation but—"

"Language."

"But," Kev said, loudly. "I need you to check the kid's stitches, and he's been complaining about pain."

"Where's his pa?"

"Good question," Tyler said in a huff.

"Dammit, Mama. Can you just—"

"Yeah, yeah." The woman knelt down, squinting as she stared at Tyler. "Well, I'll be. You look just like your mama."

Tyler moved closer to the edge of the bed. "You know my mama?"

"Sure do. I'm Miss June, the school nurse at Hazard Elementary. Your mama would come in my office every week with cuts and bruises. She was a scraper."

"That's my mama, all right." Tyler grinned. He couldn't even imagine what his mama would look like without a bruise somewhere on her face. It's how she looked when he first met her, how she looked in all the pictures.

"What you got going on under all that gauze, sweetie?"

"I had my spleen takin' out," Tyler said, pride locking his spine stiff despite the pain.

Miss June curved toward Kev. She grumbled, and he cowered down. Mama's were rough.

"Why ain't he in the hospital?"

"He got out early," Kev said, winking at Tyler. "The doctors forgot to give me his medicines."

"Yeah, right. Do I even want to know where Desmond is, or how you got the kid out of the hospital?"

"Desmond." Tyler snickered.

"Probably not," Kev muttered.

Tyler tapped Miss June on the shoulder, gaining her full attention. "We went out the window!"

Miss June's face turned beet red, and Tyler bit back a giggle. He leaned close to the woman, placing his hand on her arm. "It's okay, I'm not kidnapped. My daddy and my mama know where I am."

"Sasha's back!" Miss June shot to her feet to better glare at Kev. "I'm gonna get my medical kit, make Tyler a bowl of Vicodin rice pudding, then you can tell me what's going on." All the wrinkles on her forehead smoothed out as she turned back to smile at Tyler. "I'll be right back, sweetie."

Kev waited until his mother climbed up the ladder, then pulled off his bandana and threw it to the ground. "Fuck!"

Tyler burst out laughing until the burn in his side turned his chuckles to groans.

Chapter Twenty-Three

Sasha

Sasha stood in front of Fat Tonys. The neon light cast a soft glow over the sidewalk. It used to soothe her mind, but today that red shimmer set her insides ablaze. Her toe dug into the plush carpet. That was as far as she could get to the front door. Not only were a table full of self-proclaimed tough-guys waiting for her within, but Dez would see the life she left him for. The glimmer that infested every surface, the women who loved to paw at her, the men who treated her as an equal. He'd see it all.

"It's not too late to bolt," Otis said, stepping beside Sasha.

Any second Dez would climb from the car behind her. She'd rather walk forward, even if it meant to her death, then look back at him.

"I got three guns," she said, glancing at Otis. "If we don't like what they say, we'll kill 'em all."

"I'm down for that."

Sasha nodded, pushing her feet onward. Walking

in with guns blazing did sound like a good plan, much easier then yapping around a table. Things needed to get done. Dante was out there, just waiting to be gutted. This bullshit was a waste of time.

The doors opened, and Sasha strolled inside. She could tell her boys had walked in behind her, because the hostess's jaw damn near hit the floor. These poor women, subjected to gluttonous city folk. Their brains got stupid when they saw a real man, let alone four.

"Sasha!" the hostess chirped after her man-shock wore off. She grabbed her clipboard, then trotted forward to latch onto Sasha's waist. "Your entire party is here." The woman's hands started to wander, and her lips brushed Sasha's ear. "Do you want me to go over names with you?"

"No. I think I remember this time." Sasha slid her hand down the curve of the woman's back, gripping onto her ass. "Thanks, babe." A twinge of guilt slithered beneath her skin as she walked away. She did not want to do that, but it was expected. Inside these walls, she was a Sasha the men behind her had never seen before, the real one.

Her steps slowed by the bar, and she glanced back at Vinny and Cash but not Dez, just his feet. "You guys wait at the bar. Look tough."

"There's only four of them," Vinny said, dipping his head to the long table up the small steps. "And your buddy."

Dez grumbled, pushing his way to the bar. He was all set with the intimidation bit, got Sasha pretty scared that a freak-out loomed on the horizon.

"Try to keep him cool," she whispered to Vinny, turning toward the table and the eyes glaring their way. Her shoulder pressed against Otis as they headed for the stairs. She could almost feel the nervous energy radiating off his body in waves. All she wanted to do was protect Otis and kill Dante. Which one she craved more, she didn't know, and it scared her worse than the assholes at the table.

"Othello," Enzo said, standing to shaking Otis's hand. With a half-grin and a light dip of his head, Enzo gestured to the wide chair at the head of the table. Not that Otis needed instruction. The man had spent his childhood in this restaurant.

Sasha got a handshake too on her stroll past Enzo. It was unusual. Plus, the timing, with Dez's accusation, totally sucked ass. She took her seat beside Otis, the other men stationed at the far end of the table. It wasn't her first time sitting next to the Don, but it seemed…different now, like true power.

"I'm sure you all know Othello Lazzari," Sasha said, leaning back in her chair to allow better access to the glock in her pocket. "But in keeping with Tony's tradition, which is his love for traditions…" she lit a cigarette, since the chuckles would flow for at least another three seconds, "I'll make some quick introductions."

The new capo, who was still struggling to make a name for himself, sat up straight. This guy was practically begging to be introduced first. It made Sasha want to forget his ass altogether, but the point of this meeting was to make everyone happy. Next time, though, she'd fuck with him to no end.

"Vito Pavoni, Capo of The Bronx." That put a smile on his lips. She never thought one sentence could earn a lifetime of loyalty. Everything she'd ever done had been executed ass backward.

Sasha turned to the round man beside Enzo. Dude had more jewelry on than Elizabeth Taylor, and it did him no justice. The bands of gold cut into his fat, creating rolls in places where they shouldn't exist. "Big Joe Santori, Staten Island."

"I was good friends with your son, Joey," Otis said, finally relaxing enough to light a joint.

"Yes! He's running a small crew on my side of town, anxious to see you again."

Before chatter of old times could kick on, Sasha gestured to the only man at the table who could give Dez a run for his muscles. "Frank Garfanzo, Brooklyn."

"No shit!" Otis said, passing Sasha the joint. "Frankie Two Legs is running Brooklyn." He grinned, tapping Sasha on the arm. "They call him that 'cause when he goes to collect, he breaks both legs. So they get the message."

"It's great to see you again, Othello." Frank got up to shake Otis's hand, smiling like he just touched a rock star. "Or, should I say, Boss."

"Hell yeah, say boss." Otis chuckled, slapping Frank on the arm.

Sasha held up the joint, hoping to lure Otis back into his seat. Of course it worked. The last man, whose leer had been locked on Otis since the moment they walked in, cleared his throat. Sasha tried not to look at the man. If she caught his venomous glare on Otis one more time, she'd have to put him down where he sat. "That's Rudy Valentino, Manhattan."

"Valentino, huh." Otis leaned back and everyone at the table froze. "I'm glad our families were able to mend fences."

"A marriage will do that," Rudy all but sneered.

"It will," Otis said in a cool tone, which clashed with his harsh eyes.

"Otis and I," Sasha said, slamming her elbows onto the table, "as the new bosses of this family, appoint Enzo the capo of Queens."

"Is that Queen's new crew?" Frank asked, gesturing to the bar.

Sasha looked across the room, shrinking back when she caught Dez's icy glare. "Yeah." It would take a fuck-load of sweet talking to convince Dez to stay and a shit-ton of blowjobs, but she was down for the challenge. "We got two more guys coming in."

"Now that the pleasantries are out of the way," Otis said, leaning on the table, "let's get down to business."

The way Otis leered, how the deep tones of his voice demanded the table's attention, sent chills through Sasha. There was no doubt that man was a Lazzari to the core.

Big Joe slid a piece of paper down the table, his grin as wide as his belly. "I talked to all my contacts, came up with this."

Enzo scanned the scribbles before passing it to Sasha.

"It's all the businesses owned by the Mancini family," Big Joe said. "Most of them are in our boroughs, right under our noses."

"Not in mine," Rudy sneered, downing his cup of wine.

"There's four in Manhattan," Sasha said, her voice bordering on a growl. She looked up from the paper, narrowing her eyes at Rudy. Enzo slid his hand under the table, the men beside Rudy scooted away, and Sasha grinned. That guy was done here. Manhattan would need a new capo, but first she'd make him clean up her messes.

"Those Mancini fuckers are set-up in all our boroughs," she said, passing the paper to Otis.

"All right," Otis said, scanning the list before handing it to Frank. "We're gonna hit 'em all, at the same time. Tonight."

Whether they liked the idea or not, each man at the table nodded. In every attempt to be slick, Sasha covered her mouth to hide her smirk. She used to be one of those nodding heads. Back then, it felt important like she was part of something larger, something profound. To be on the other side, tasting the sweet rush of power, was euphoric. She had no idea it would be so satisfying, so addictive.

Otis gestured for the list then lifted his empty glass. "Let's get this hashed out. It has to run smooth." The paper slid in front of him, and a waitress appeared with a bottle of whiskey and a smile.

***

Dez

Dez leaned against the bar. He tapped the glass in his hand as he stared across the room. Sasha was one lucky bitch. If he hadn't spent the last five years dealing with a child, he'd never have the patience for her ass.

Even though his glare stuck to the only table full of people in this ghostly restaurant of extravagance, he wasn't looking at Sasha. He was watching the scuzzballs. One can never trust an Italian mobster. That's the first thing television taught him.

The sway of a woman's hips trapped in her tiny black dress snagged his gaze, but only for a moment. He had to be on the ball. *His* woman sat far from reach, amongst soulless murderers. Sure, she was probably the biggest soulless murderer of them all, but she was his soulless murderer.

"This ain't like the meetings you guys used to have, huh?" Cash asked, ogling a woman who strolled up the stairs with a bottle of whiskey.

"No, it's not," Dez grumbled, downing his shot.

Vinny winked at the woman on her way back behind the bar. "We really fucked up not having big tittie waitresses leaning over our shoulders."

"We could have had that," Dez said, lighting a cigarette, "but Sasha would've fucked them all."

"Really, dude?" Vinny groaned.

"You saw that shit when we walked in here."

"Be happy the place is closed. I was in here with her the other night and—"

"I don't give a fuck," Dez said, a little too loud for such an empty room.

"What crawled up your ass?"

Vinny had a lot of nerve to ask that question, since it was his words that had riled Dez's mind. Sasha had it all here. The men up there respected her, accepted her. She had no reason to need him, no mother to please, no life to fake, yet she wanted him. He should be doing backflips. The woman who haunted his dreams loved him, and it made him the biggest piece of shit to walk the Earth. She was gay. Deep inside, she only wanted women, and he was a man.

Dez spun to face the bar, reaching under for a bottle. He hoped for a Kentucky whiskey, even a bourbon would do, but honestly he'd take peach schnapps right now. To his relief, the liquor was brown, so it must be good. He filled his cup, turning back to continue his bitch-boy watch duties.

Sasha hurried down the small steps, sneaking away from the men who were hovering over a piece of paper.

"Whatcha got here?" She took the glass from Dez's hand, her fingertips leaving a trail of sparks along his skin.

Dez looked at the bottle, squinted to make out the curvy script, but all he could come up with was, "Pear brandy?"

"It's fucking great!"

"Oh yeah." Dez took a swig from the bottle, since Sasha had emptied his cup. The sweet burn went down so smooth, crisp. If money had a taste, this would be it. "It *is* fucking great."

"Take it," Sasha said, slinking so close her chest rubbed against Dez. "We can finish it off later."

240

Dez took a step back, placing the bottle on the bar. "I'm splitting after this."

Vinny patted Cash on the arm, nodding to the lobby. "Come on."

Vinny and Cash shuffled away, but Dez didn't look. It was clear the glitz of city lights had hypnotized his brother. The ride home would be a solo run.

"For how long?" Her words barely made a peep, probably because she was muttering into her chest.

"I'm going home, Sasha. Otis needed me to do this one thing, and it's almost done."

"Well." Sasha slid her glass down the bar, shooting a small smile to the waitress who practically jumped to gain any type of recognition. "Otis might need you to do one more thing."

For all of two seconds, Dez fell into Sasha's dark eyes. If that stare didn't remind him of his child, who was hurt, scared, and waiting for him, he'd let it steer him straight to Hell.

Dez inched even farther back, away from Sasha's electric grasp. "Is this how it's gonna be? Every day is one more job?"

"No." Sasha grabbed Dez's hand, holding tight despite his light tugs. "If you want to go, we'll leave tonight. After I help Otis."

That fancy liquor had drugs in it, because Dez was hallucinating. Sasha's hand couldn't be clinging to his, trembling. No fucking way she just said what he thought she said.

Sasha dropped Dez's hand to glide her fingers up his chest. She wrapped her arms around his neck, her chest falling against his own. "I really want to stay here," she said, only inches from his lips. "But I can't do it without you and Tyler. I can't do shit without you two." She kissed him softly, and he couldn't help but squeeze her tight. "I want to go wherever you are."

Dez fought to control the quake of his knees. The unreliable status of his legs, plus the whirl in his mind, was fucking up any chance of enjoying Sasha's tits as they glided along his chest. If she was for real, he'd compromise. Any true relationship required sacrifice, and she'd given up enough.

The stupidest question lingered on the tip of Dez's tongue, and for the life of him he couldn't keep it in. "You want to be with me?"

"Fuck yeah!" Sasha said, without stopping to think twice.

A smile assaulted Dez's lips. He'd shove it back but Sasha's eyes lit up, and her body squirmed every time he grinned.

"Only me?" he asked, knowing that was pushing it.

"Only you."

Dez would search Sasha's eyes for the truth but that'd be impossible to do while kissing her, which was absolutely necessary at the moment.

"Sasha?"

Sasha turned away, breaking Dez's kiss, but didn't even try to part from his grasp.

"Who's your friend?" a round man asked as the others crowded down the stairs, stopping to stare.

"This is my husband." Sasha moved to the side, keeping one arm around Dez. "Desmond."

"Desmond," Dez snickered. "It's Dez," he said, shaking the man's hand.

"Husband!"

The guy gawked at Dez as if he were a miracle. In fact, all the men looked ecstatic. Seemed the city wasn't so different from the hills. The little men in their tall buildings were just mousier than the rest of the world.

"I had no idea," a young punk looking kid said, pushing his way through the small crowd to shake Dez's hand next.

"Then I guess our kid is gonna be a shocker," Dez said, and the men actually gasped.

"Sasha!" the round one said, clasping onto her shoulders and separating her from Dez. "Is there a Lazzari heir?"

The muscles behind Sasha's cheek flexed as her jaw clenched. Slowly, she nodded, and the man almost cheered.

"When this is all over," he said, looking between Sasha and Dez, "we're going to have one hell of a celebration. Welcome your husband and…"

"Son," Sasha said, with a sour look on her face.

"A son!" the man said, chuckling. "There are great things on the horizon for this family, I can feel it."

The man shook Dez's hand again on his way to the lobby. They all did, except for a short guy with beady rat eyes.

"Who's the little dude?" Dez whispered to Sasha.

"Rudy. He's gonna have to go. I don't like the way he looks at Otis."

"I'll help you take him out."

Sasha turned back to face Dez, sliding into his embrace as though she never left. "Does that mean we're staying?"

"Yea—"

Her kiss came in fast. He might've bit his lip a little, but then her tongue came in to caress it and all was forgiven.

"That's enough," Otis said, tugging at Sasha's shirt. "You can have him all night. Right now, I need my sergeant at arms."

Sasha groaned as Dez stepped away. Sergeant at arms. He didn't think anyone would ever call him that again.

Chapter Twenty-Four

Sasha

Sasha pushed her empty plate aside. The pound of spaghetti she just sucked down better digest itself quickly or she'd be waddling from a massage parlor as it burned around her.

Dez slammed his empty glass of whiskey on the table, drawing everyone's gaze. "Why can't I go with Sasha?"

"I need you with me," Otis said. "The building we're hitting is supposed to have an underground fight club in the basement. Sasha's just lighting up a massage parlor. It's small, easy."

"I'll keep her safe," Cash said, sitting up in his chair.

"I don't need anybody keeping me safe." The giant smile melted from Cash's face, and Sasha held back a snicker. "Thanks anyway."

Vinny shifted in his seat, stealing glances at Sasha. In the old days, he would have told them all to suck it and that he was going with her. That wouldn't be happening this time. The old days were gone. She slept right through them.

"Maybe me and Cash should take the fight club," Dez said, leaning on the table to give Otis the death-lock stare down. "We're the biggest."

"No," Enzo practically shouted, his face scrunched in confusion. "This isn't up for discussion. The Don gives orders, you all follow them."

Sasha turned away from Dez, who miraculously kept his fists to himself, and hurled Enzo a harsh glare.

"Except for you, Ms. Lazzari," Enzo sputtered, sinking down in his seat.

Damn straight except for her. She'd like to meet the man who had enough balls to bark orders in her face so she could slit his throat.

Otis sat back in his oversized chair, managing to look uncomfortable and tailor-made for the seat at the same time.

"Vinny and Enzo torch the warehouse," Otis said, staring directly at Dez, "Sasha and Cash will burn down the massage parlor." He reached under the table, pulling out a long green case. Plates rattled as the case clunked atop the table.

Otis opened the lid, and dim lights gleamed off a rocket launcher. "You're coming with me," he said, looking from the large weapon to Dez's now stunned face. "'Cause I don't know how to use this fucking thing."

A hint of a smile crossed Dez's lips as he stared into the case.

"It'll be quick, easy," Otis said, closing the lid

and snapping the latches shut. "One hour and we'll all be back here, smoking mad pot and fucking hot waitresses." He wagged his finger between Sasha and Dez as he sunk back into his chair. "Except you two, you're married."

Sasha shrugged. If they both fucked the hot waitress together, it shouldn't count as cheating. That would be something she'd have to ease Dez into. The fancy brandy behind the bar should help. She glanced at Dez. He had a leer in his eyes to match her dirty thoughts. It was shaping up to be one hell of a night: vengeance, a tiny massacre, the arms of the strongest man she'd ever met holding her tight.

A jitter took Sasha's foot into a steady tap. This show needed to get on the road so her amazing night of fantasy could begin. She glanced out the window, but the glow of city lights made it impossible to tell night from day.

"Is it time?" she asked.

"Yeah." Otis stood, grabbing the case off the table. "We all strike at ten on the dot, not a minute before."

Sasha climbed to her feet but didn't get very far. Dez stood so close, their chests brushed when she rose from her chair. There was no need for words. The look in his eyes spoke louder, meant more than any jumble of syllables his brain could produce.

Dez glided his hands around Sasha's waist and down her back. "Careful," he whispered, grabbing her ass.

His breath rushed over her lips, spreading tingles. All she had to do was lift her chin and his

247

kiss would quiet the frenzy beneath her skin, but she enjoyed this sensation too much.

"Never," she said. It was meant to be a joke, but the notion of caution rarely crossed her mind. She slid away, running her hand across Dez's chest. He'd have to wait for his kiss, which should give him incentive to come back alive.

***

A pink glow flooded the alleyway, the sizzle of neon lights bouncing off damp walls. Sasha tightened her hold on the plastic gas can in her grasp, staring down at Cash, who was on his knees. Cash's hands shook as he picked a lock on a steel door. The buzz of a flickering sign echoed in the cramped space, yet the clink erupting from Cash's hands seemed to boom over it.

"What the fuck, dude?" Sasha whispered, pulling a watch from her pocket. "It's 10:01."

"I got it." The door creaked open and Cash rose to his feet. "Sorry," he muttered, picking up his gas can.

"You take the top floor," Sasha said in a hush, inching inside the massage parlor. "I'll get the bottom."

Cash grabbed Sasha's arm, letting go before she could hurl a glare. "We should stay together."

"Don't be a fucking pussy." Sasha pulled her gun, keeping it close to her chest. "I wanna get this over with, quick." Into the dark she went, lugging a five-gallon jug of gas in one hand and a Colt .45 in the other. A dim light shined at the end of the hall, two women in kimono's strolling by. Sasha kept to the shadows, the only sound a slosh from the container in her grasp.

This building was full of women, slaves, like the ones she brought here so long ago. The deaths of those poor creatures weren't necessary. Sasha just needed the building in flames. A message to Dante, let him know she was coming.

Voices flowed as she neared the end of the hall. She placed the gas can down, looking back at Cash. The dude was steady, confidant. It was a goddamn surprise. She thought she was getting a dud.

"Clear out the women," Sasha whispered, leaning close to Cash, "cap the fucking men."

Cash nodded and Sasha cut around the corner, storming down an even tighter hall. She dodged paper lamps, swatting red tassels while creeping past closed doors. Just beyond the stairs, light shined from a curtain of beads. She peeked through, glimpsing an old oriental woman behind a tall wooden desk. The place could've been a Chinese restaurant with all the crap on the walls except for the young girls in lingerie who lounged around the room.

Sasha gestured for Cash to head upstairs then burst through the beads with her gun high. The old woman hobbled out from behind her desk, hands up. Gasps rang out as the girls huddled together, swallowed up by the old woman's weird sounding babbles.

"Out," Sasha barked, cocking back the hammer on her gun.

The old woman waved her hands about, shooing

the girls toward the front door. Foreign words continued to spew, mixing with the occasion "Fuck!" and "Shit!" until the thin glass door closed them out.

Sasha locked the deadbolt, doubling back for her gas can. She kicked open doors, splashing rooms while moving down the hall. Cash's heavy steps thumped from above, sending wisps of dust to float down.

"This fucking guy." Sasha tucked her gun into her waistband, brushing flakes of plaster off her head and shoulders. "Asshole," she muttered, kicking open the door in front of her. A fist greeted her in the doorway, slamming right into her nose. The hit flashed the world to red. Then came the sting, strong enough to blot out all sound.

Sasha staggered back, throwing a stream of gas out in front of her. A man shouted as she blinked a tear-filled haze from her eyes. The plastic handle slipped from her wet hand, and gas splashed her feet as the can tumbled to the floor. Sasha reached for her gun. Before her fingers could wrap around the butt, a wide hand latched onto her throat.

"You made a mess, little niece," some ugly bastard sneered in her face. He ripped the gun from her grasp, throwing it down the hall.

Her hands, feet, clothes were covered in gas, but she wasn't the only one. The asshole who was throttling her neck was even more drenched than she was. Just as her fingertips grazed the case of her zippo, the guy drove his knuckles into her stomach.

"Sasha, I lit the—" Cash stopped halfway down the stairs, staring over the rail at Sasha squirming under the Mancini fucker's clutch. "Oh shit!" He jumped over the railing, his boots crashing to the hardwood floor.

The crushing grip left Sasha's throat as the man charged Cash, tackling him to the ground. She dropped to her knees. Despite her deep breaths, air never came. The stench of gasoline devoured any trace of oxygen, coating her lungs in a prickly thickness.

Grunts and the slaps of fists pounding skin echoed down the hall, but Sasha's stare had become stuck to the ceiling beside the stairs. Beneath clouds of gray smoke, sharp flames peeked through. She tore her gaze from the inferno that raged above her, looking down the hall. The Mancini fucker snatched a gun from Cash's hand, then cracked it against Cash's cheek.

Cash dropped like a sack of bricks, and Sasha jumped to her feet. A gun was aimed at her chest, and an asshole grinned at her through rolls of smoke. He took a step, and Sasha flipped open the top of her zippo. Now it was her turn to smile. The guy ran forward and she lit the lighter, tossing it at his feet. Flames shot across the floor, climbing up his body and wrapping him in a shroud of blazing light.

Heat scorched Sasha's wrist, the smell of burnt hair wafting into her lungs. She looked at her arm as a wave of fire crawled up her shoulder.

"Fuck!" Sasha cried out, her shout falling under the howls of the man who was thrashing his fire-encased body against the walls. She ripped off her flannel, using it to beat the flames off her arm, leg, entire right side.

Cash ran through the blaze that roared within the cramped hallway, dodging the man's charred flailing arm.

"Shit," Cash yelled, practically dragging Sasha from the firestorm that encircled them, back down the dark hall they came from. With his big hand, he whacked her chest, arm, leg. He was probably trying to put out the fire riding along her body, but it felt more like a beating.

"I'm out," Sasha yelled, coughing on the thick smoke that still clogged her airways. Her arm ached, like needles dragging across sunburnt skin, but she ran toward the pink glow of the alleyway. The singed ends of her pants scraped like broken glass with every step. It was nothing, minor pain compared to what awaited her if she didn't escape the fire spreading along the walls beside her.

She burst out the back door, slamming against the alley's brick wall. A smile spread across her lips as she breathed in cool air that wasn't laced in thick smoke nor carrying the sting of gasoline.

"Are you okay?" Cash reached out, drew back, then took Sasha's lightly baked hand.

"I'm good," she said, slapping Cash on the shoulder. "Thanks, man. Let's get the fuck out of here."

They jogged from the alley, cutting onto the sidewalk.

"Freeze!" a deep voice yelled from behind them.

Sasha stopped short, her hand drifting to her side. There was no gun to grip in her waistband, but one cocked right behind her. The Mancinis got the jump on her. She'd be shot dead on this sidewalk, in front of gasping strangers, never to glimpse her son's goofy smile again.

Slowly, Sasha turned and a "Huh!" of true shock flew from her lips. Beyond the barrel pointed at her face, the fed who'd tossed her in a cell with a raging bulldyke hurled an evil leer.

"Pigman," Sasha said, holding her hands out at her sides. "You're a little far from your pen, aren't ya?" She eyed his back, sides. Swarms of federal agents weren't closing in. His heartless bitch partner didn't stomp forward with cuffs. The sidewalk remained clear, except for the crowd of dumbass people who gathered around to watch a slightly drunken man with a gun. This fed had gone AWOL, which made him fair game.

Although Sasha had no weapon and his was fully loaded, her legs pushed toward him.

"You're under arrest, for arson," he shouted in a weak, shaky tone. "Get the fuck on the ground."

Cash took a step toward the fed, and the blast of a gun cut through the night. The rumble bounced off buildings beside Sasha and sent a torrent of shivers down her spine. Cash fell to his knees. A flood of red drops seeped between his fingers, which clutched his chest.

"No!" Sasha yelled over the screams erupting from the ever-growing crowd. She dropped beside Cash, who fell to his back on the dirty sidewalk. A spray of blood burst from his mouth when he tried to speak, pelting Sasha's face.

"Cash!" She held her hands over his. "We'll get you patched up, brother." Her voice quaked harder than her shaky fingers. "Just hold on." Warm blood flowed along her palms, which slid as they pressed, until Cash's hands didn't tremble any longer. Garbles stopped scraping past his throat, ending with a long groan. He was gone. Sasha had to turn away, couldn't see more dead eyes of people she loved. Cash's stiff shoulders sagged, his arms flopping to his sides, and still Sasha couldn't look.

"Get down on the ground!" the man yelled over the screams of women.

"You killed him." Sasha veered her glare to the soon-to-be dead pig. Not even tears, which flowed from her eyes, could quench the rage that rose within her chest. "You're done, motherfucker."

"Help!" a woman yelled from somewhere in the distance. "This man has a gun!"

"He was coming at me," the fed shouted over his shoulder, keeping his gun on Sasha.

"He was unarmed," Sasha yelled, finally lifting her hands from Cash's sticky chest. The way the fed's eyes wavered, the quake of the gun against his palm, he was asking to get knocked the fuck out. Sasha was just about to jump up, hurl her knuckles at his face, when sirens screamed above the growing crowd's cries. Amazing, a fucking cop when you actually needed one.

It was crass, with her dead friend's blood soaking into her pants, but Sasha laughed. "I hope *you* enjoy getting raped in prison, Pigman motherfucker."

"Drop the gun," the policemen yelled as they ran up to surround the fed with guns drawn.

People scurried back, away from the crazed man

who screamed out a badge number while getting tackled to the ground, but Sasha just sat there. In a pool of blood, on the filthy city sidewalk, beside a burning building, she sat. Escape was totally possible. She could get up, slip into the crowd, and walk away. Cash would want her to go, but so would the asshole fed. Her fleeing would prove him innocent. Then he could say she had a bomb and they'd believe him. Now, she was the proof. There was also the added bonus of watching Pigman's face scrape against concrete as the police held him down, beside a used rubber.

A policeman knelt beside Sasha, taking her hand. "Don't worry, Ms. Lazzari. We were on break across the street, saw the whole thing. It went down just like you say it did."

Sasha looked up, beyond the officer holding her hand to another policeman who nodded. She recognized that man from the payoff route. These were two of the many pocket-police kept by *her* family.

"Thank you." Sasha allowed the man to help her off the ground, staying close to his side. The fed continued to shout, struggle, take hits with nightsticks as she was ushered from the scene. The two policemen snuck Sasha into the back of a cop car, jumped into the front, and drove away. She turned to stare out the back window. Bright orange flames consumed the building, bursting from every broken window and reaching for the dark sky. Their flicker cast a shadow over Cash's body, alone and so still on the sidewalk. She should've looked at his face before she left. It was probably peaceful, better than the visual of fright she saw right before he died. She'd never forgive herself for not looking.

Chapter Twenty-Five

Trees whirled by outside the window. It took Sasha quite a while to remember that there weren't any trees in the city.

"Where are you taking me?"

The men didn't answer or even bother to glance her way. Fucking rude. Two more jokers for her shit list, which might as well be a novel at this point.

"Hey!" Sasha banged her fist on the cage that separated her from the cops, but the pigs didn't so much as flinch.

"Relax. We're here," the guy, whose name she couldn't remember but face she'd never forget, said as he climbed from the car.

Sasha fumbled for the switchblade in her boot, but those cops were quick. They had her door open before she could hike up her burnt pant leg. She shoved, hurled elbows, but the police, whom she paid, pulled her into the humid night.

"Don't struggle, little girl."

That smooth voice snapped Sasha's spine straight, locking her arms stiff. "Dante," she said, her tone bordering on a snarl.

"I'm good," Sasha said, slowly lifting her hands. The police backed off, and she nodded. "I'll be sure to take care of you two later." She turned to face Dante, fighting back the urge to charge forward and gouge the man's eyes out. The dude actually looked happy to see her. He had to know she was there to kill him; he had to.

"Listen." Dante took a step, and Sasha inched away. "Come here," he growled in a low tone, dipping his head.

Sasha peeked over Dante's shoulder, counting at least six rifles aimed at her. The guns, and the pieces of inbred looking shits holding them, didn't scare her. It was the fear in Dante's eyes that sent chills. She stepped forward and Dante seized her by the arm, yanking her to his side.

"This shit ain't good, little girl," he whispered, taking small steps toward the pack of gun-wielding men in the small wooded clearing. "Sick shit happens in there."

First, Sasha eyed the men who moved in from all sides. Then her stare drifted to a large farmhouse peeking out from behind bushy pine trees. The place fit the bill for a typical horror flick house. She had no doubt sick shit went down in there. It was the home that reared her mother.

"They've had me here for two months," Dante said in a near whisper, keeping his tight hold on Sasha's arm. "I came back to regain my turf, but Tony wouldn't have me. He had you."

"So you ran to the Mancinis?"

"Yeah, but the old bat already knew about Ellen.

I've been a prisoner here this whole time."

"You didn't look like a prisoner at the warehouse," Sasha sneered, pulling her arm from Dante's grasp. "When you killed your brother."

"Fuck, Sasha. Didn't you see the stares I was giving you. I damn near screamed for help with my eyes."

"I didn't see no stares."

Dante stopped short, holding out his arm. Moonlight gleamed on the track marks that ran along his forearm, which led to puffy welts around his wrist.

"They keep me chained to a wall, shoot me up with smack...do fucked up shit."

One of the Mancini fuckers, who kindly escorted them to what looked like the Devil's vacation house, shoved Sasha then crashed the butt of his rifle against Dante's back.

"Walk," the man grumbled.

Dante took Sasha's hand, and she jerked it back.

"So what," she said as softly as one could while snapping, "you want me to feel sorry for you?"

"No. I want you to save me."

Sasha slowed her steps, but it did nothing to ease the whirl of her mind. It was the quiver in Dante's voice, the way he kept pawing at her in search of comfort. Her hate for the man warped into pity, and it drove her heart to pound.

"Fine!" Sasha stomped across the lawn, heading for the porch.

"Wait." Dante pulled Sasha to a stop just before the first step. "What are you gonna do?"

"Whatever that bitch wants me to. Then, once I

get us out of here, I can kill you myself for what you did to my mother."

"About that—"

The butt of a gun struck the base of Dante's neck, dropping him face down on the ground.

"That's enough talking," a man grumbled, jabbing Sasha with the barrel of his rifle. "Go."

Two men grabbed Dante, dragging him across the grass. For some insane reason, Sasha actually wanted to help him. His limp feet bounced as he was hauled behind the house, and she felt the urge to give chase.

"Was my pet naughty?" a woman's voice called out.

Sasha looked up the steps, into harsh eyes that could've been her mother's leer. Her arms almost opened for a hug. It had been so long since she glimpsed her mother's face, but this woman wasn't the legendary Ellen. Close, and yet so far.

"Come on inside, darlin'. There are many things we need to discuss."

***

Dez

Dez paced around the lobby of Fat Tonys, stormed out the door to stare down the sidewalk, then went back inside to pace some more. Sasha should've been back by now. Fuck, she should've been back thirty minutes ago. If he had any clue where 57th street was, he'd be there screaming out Sasha's name by now.

"It's cool, man," Vinny said, holding out a joint. "She probably stopped to…I don't know, do some shit."

"Yeah, right." Dez turned his back on the scent of kind bud, ignoring the solace its aroma promised to bring. He couldn't have dull senses. Not now, when there was possibly an entire city he had to slaughter.

"Otis and Enzo should be back soon," Vinny said, though the words brought no comfort.

"We should've went to look for her," Dez yelled, louder than he wanted to.

"We don't know this city." Vinny took another hit, squirming on a wide red sofa. "We would've gotten lost."

Tires screeched, car doors slammed, and Dez hurried to the front doors. One glimpse of Otis's stare, and Dez nearly crumbled.

"Where is she?" he shouted, clutching onto Otis's shirt the second the guy cleared the threshold.

"Come on," Otis said, his voice cracking. "Let's go sit down."

"Fuck that!" Dez pushed Otis against the wall, though not by choice. His body was no longer under his mind's control. "Where…is…Sasha?"

***

Sasha

Sasha sat at a small round table, staring at the woman across from her. Although her brain begged to look away, she managed to direct a hard glare at the old broad. It wasn't easy. The same steely leer that had plagued her childhood, the one she thought had been wiped out from this world, scoured her. A little more blonde instead of gray hair, less wrinkles, a trim of thirty pounds, and this old bat would be a living ghost of a long missed nightmare.

"You did a lot of damage tonight, darlin'," the woman said, sounding rather amused.

"I was just trying to get your attention." Sasha peeked around the room, counting guns. Ten, which was two more than the amount of men surrounding her. An extra shotgun sat mounted to the wall. It could be empty, broken, or just waiting for her to grab and unload. The other spare rifle rested at the old bat's side, propped against her chair. Sasha had maybe a one-percent chance of reaching either weapon before a bullet pierced her skull. Not the best of odds.

"My attention, or Dante's?"

Sasha steered her gaze back to the woman, who slid a shot of clear liquid in front of her.

"Your beef is with Dante," the woman said, downing her own shot. "I don't know why we're fighting."

"You hit me with a dump truck." Sasha leaned on the table, sliding her hand closer to the rifle. "My kid almost died."

"That was a mistake. Miscommunications are a bitch. My boys are strong," she waved her arm around the room, the bulky men standing nearby bubbling over with pride, "but they're not the sharpest tools."

The smiles faded from the men's faces. Their

shoulders slumped, and Sasha snickered. A few fake promises of loyalty, offers of stake in Lazzari enterprises, and she might walk her ass out of here. Hell, she might even get to carve up Dante to prove her allegiance. Then she could come back with that rocket launcher and fry all these twisted fuckers.

"My daughter held my hopes for the future of the Mancini family. That's why I allowed her to wander from my grasp. She got things done. Dante took Ellen from me, and he'll suffer for it. As long as I'm alive, he'll suffer."

Sasha shifted in her seat. She had said almost the same exact thing about Dante, many times, but it seemed so final when it flowed from this woman's mouth.

"Don't you miss family, darlin'? I know I miss having a girl around here to chat with."

"Family," Sasha sneered, slamming her shot. "I don't even know your name, lady."

"You can call me Mama."

The woman's glare turned cold, wicked, and the men standing around Sasha closed in. Shit was definitely getting weird. To put a cherry on top, whatever the fuck she just drank caused the room to spin and blur. This bitch didn't know who she was fucking with. Drugs were candy to Sasha, and it would take a hell of a lot more than one shot of any narcotic to lay her out.

"Stupid bitch," Sasha slurred, swaying in her chair. "My people will come for me."

"No, darlin'. Your people won't be coming for Sasha Lazzari. Sasha Lazzari died. Poor girl got herself shot in the face with a twelve-gauge. Those lovely policemen dropped her body in the alley, right before they snagged you up. The clothes, hair, right down to that trashy tattoo on your wrist all match. There wasn't much else left to identify her with, messy gunshot wound. All they'll have is…"

The man behind Sasha gripped onto her shoulders, pinned her down into the chair. One man yanked her head back, and another pried her mouth open. She thrashed her arms, kicked her feet. It was useless. A warm fuzz crept in to claim her body, turning her limbs to jelly. The woman hovered over Sasha, light glinting off a pair of pliers in her hand.

The dirt-covered fingers in Sasha's mouth forced her jaw open wider, and metal clinked against her teeth. With a tug and a ripping tear, blood replaced the taste of dirt and metal in Sasha's mouth.

"…this one tooth," the woman said, lifting the pliers to flash a flesh-coated molar.

Sasha gagged as a pool of coppery fluid amassed in her throat. The hands holding her down left her body and she leaned forward, hacking a wad of blood to the floor.

"What the fuck!" Sasha yelled. She cupped her cheek, but the throb of her mouth only grew. Her knees quaked as she tried to stand, and she fell back into the chair. "This psycho shit…" The barrel of a rifle blurred in and out of view. She reached out, swatting only air even though the gun looked so close. "Fucking…" Everything whirled, her mind, the room, every goddamn thought in her head.

"You'll fit in just fine here, Ellen," the woman said, smiling down at Sasha.

"My name is Sasha."

"Your mother was tough to break. I think it'll be harder for you, on account of your age. We'll see."

The old woman's words echoed in Sasha's ears, light fading to a dim glow. By some miracle, she was able to lift her hand and clasp the bitch's throat, but she didn't have the strength to squeeze.

"I'm gonna put you in your mother's old room, and you'll stay there until you're ready to be Ellen."

"Crazy bitch!" Sasha was yanked from the chair. In her mind, she had strangled that woman dead. Inside this haze, Dez carried her from the nightmarish house of psychos, except Dez wouldn't dig his nails into her arm, drag her feet along dirt-covered floors.

"What are you doing?" she sputtered, grasping at stone walls as her boots thumped down stairs.

"Be a good little sis, and Mama'll let you out," a man said, his voice so loud yet far at the same time. "It only took your mama eight years."

"Eight years?"

A squeak cut off Sasha's words. She swung her fists. At least in her mind she did. The tight grip on her arms turned crushing. The man lifted her feet off the floor, hurling her through the air. She slammed against hard ground. A puff of dirt shot up around her face, and sharp prickles spread throughout her body.

The crash of a metal door banging to a close jolted Sasha's shoulders. She peered up as a stream of blood trickled from her mouth. A thin beam of light shined beneath a solid steel door, hitting her right in the eyes. She pulled herself across the floor, closer to the sliver of light, cracking her head against jagged rock. The more her eyes adjusted, the faster her heart pounded. Stone walls surrounded her. She was trapped in a tiny cell with only darkness made blacker by the thinnest hint of light.

A cry escaped Sasha's lungs, and she scurried back. Her elbow whacked solid metal, its *ding* bouncing off the cramped walls. She looked behind her, at a thin metal cot. No mattress, no blanket, just rows of rusty springs. Her fight against whatever drugs she'd been fed had ended. Her limbs were now too numb to move. The fog that blurred her eyes had grown so thick she could no longer see beyond it. She laid her head in the dirt, letting a heavy weight take her eyelids down.

Chapter Twenty-Six

A steady pound ripped Sasha from a dreamless sleep. It took a few moments for her to realize the thunderous hammer was coming from inside her head. Grains of dirt dug beneath her nails as she pushed herself up. Her arms shook, threatening to give way, so she pushed them harder. Cool stone dug into her back as she sat against the wall. While lost to a drug-induced haze, someone had put a tray of food beside the locked door and a bucket in the corner.

"Fucking great," Sasha muttered, crawling across the floor.

The food tasted like shit and actually looked like shit, but the glass of water soothed her swollen mouth. She downed the entire cup. Hunks of flesh washed from the gaping hole in her jaw, following the water down her throat, but she couldn't stop drinking. She was so thirsty.

A thin flap slid open halfway down the steel door, flooding the tiny cell in white light.

"Morning, Ellen," that crazy cunt of a woman

said, all cheery and shit.

"Sasha! You stupid bitch." Her words came out in a jumble. A rainbow of colors, which weren't dancing in front of her eyes a minute ago, swirled on the walls.

"All right, darlin'. I'll check on you tomorrow then."

The flap slammed shut, its bang somehow growing louder as it echoed. Although the light was gone, the colors remained. A rolling shimmer traveled along the stone, from the floor that wobbled to the ceiling that swayed. No drug on this planet lasted this long. Flashes of memories pushed through the fog in Sasha's mind. She glimpsed Dez's smile, saw the old woman hiding behind her mother's stare, watched Dante flash the puss-filled sores on his arm.

Sasha dropped to her stomach, using the slice of light to inspect her arms. Smooth skin gleamed, brighter than it should. There weren't any marks, aside from a scatter of bruises and some charred flesh. They had done something to her. Something scrambled her brain, blurred the world, lulled her eyes to a close.

A rush of heat zoomed in, hitting like a fist. Sasha rolled onto her back, but the prickles of fire beneath her skin didn't fade. Little dots swirled above her. Red, blue, green, yellow, all the colors melded together, pulsing. It was strange, how the pulse of the dots synced with the throb inside her head.

Too fast, it all spun too fast. She retched, heaving, but she couldn't move. The only way to stop the whirl was to close her eyes. Even though she knew darkness would claim her, trap her in its icy clutches, she allowed her eyes to flutter to a close.

***

Trays of food came and went. There was no way to judge time without sunlight, no way to count days. Sasha tried to keep track of how many times the woman peered into the flap. That could signify days, each visit a new morning or night.

"Sand!" Sasha reached down, brushing dirt from between her toes. Wait. Someone took her boots. She moved her feet into the light, squinting to see through a blur. Little chunks of skin were torn from the tips of her toes, dried blood streaking her feet.

"Little fucker ate me." She groped the floor, kicking up dirt as she crawled around. Something crept in here while she slept and nibbled on her. She couldn't find the critter, but it must be trapped alongside her. Sleeping on the floor wouldn't be possible any longer unless she wanted to be eaten alive. Did she want that? It could be better. What was she doing here, in this tiny room of stone, metal, and dirt? Where was she?

The flap in the door slid open and those eyes peeked through. She knew those eyes. They were with her all her life, protecting, terrorizing.

"Good morning, Ellen," a soft voice said.

"Ellen? You're Ellen."

"No, darlin'. You're Ellen."

"I'm…" The name, her name, lingered on the

edge of memory. It had been so long since she'd spoken it, heard it called out. "Sasha!" That was right, that was who she was. "Sasha."

"Almost, darlin'. I'm happy with your progress. It reminds me of the time…"

The woman babbled on. Sasha couldn't follow the speed of those words, but she liked to hear them. The gentle tone filled the cold space around her with warmth. It was her only comfort. Comfort? No, this was a punishment.

"You're shooting me up," Sasha slurred, cutting off the woman's chatter.

"Heroin is a disgusting drug. I'd never pump that into my sweet girl's veins."

It was her, her mother, come to save her. "Mama!" Sasha gripped onto the thin flap, her fingers curling around the metal as she leaned in.

"That's right, Ellen. It's your mama."

"No." Sasha pulled her hands away. She wasn't Ellen. The eyes that glared at her through a slit in the door were Ellen. "No!" Sasha crashed her fists against the door, again and again until the flap slammed shut.

"No!" she screamed, kicking the door. "Let me out!" She pounded her hands, feet. Even though her skin was raw and sore, she pounded on the solid metal imprisoning her.

***

Vinny

Vinny adjusted the knot of his tie for the fifth

time, but it still looked wrong. Today wasn't the day to look like a slob. Hundreds of people would see him today, shake his hand, say shit that didn't make the world any less crazy.

That wasn't Sasha's body. All week the image of Sasha's blue tinged corpse lying on a metal slab in the city morgue haunted his mind. He knew every inch of that girl, every curve, every dimple, yet they all said it was Sasha. Doctors, the New York City Police Department, even the F.B.I. dipped their hands into this. They all said it was Sasha.

Vinny ripped the tie off his neck, throwing it to the floor.

"Uncle Vinny."

Tyler's meek voice pulled Vinny's stare from the mirror. He knelt down, and Tyler crept into his room. "What's up, little man?"

"Ms. Lydia's here to take me to the park. I wanted to say goodbye to Daddy, but he won't open the door."

A huff took Vinny back to his feet. Dez was really starting to piss him off. The man had hardly known Sasha. Dez wasn't the one who lost his best friend, his entire world. Vinny couldn't even grieve, hadn't been afforded the luxury to cry. How could he? His time had been spent helping Tyler get accustomed to this sterile penthouse, high above a dirty city. Thank God for Enzo's wife. If it weren't for Lydia distracting Tyler with her many children, the kid would've found out his mother was dead. That was something nobody could deal with yet.

"Just stay here, buddy. I'll go fetch your pa."

Vinny stomped out his room. His livid stare

271

reflected off the silver banister as he stormed down the hall. Dez's closed door neared, but Vinny didn't slow his rushed steps. Instead, he lifted his foot and kicked the door open.

Dez jumped up from the bed. The bottle of whiskey in his right hand sloshed, and the picture in his left hand fell to the floor.

"What the fuck!" Dez yelled, staggering to the center of the room.

"You're fucking drunk." Vinny curled his fingers into fists, fighting to keep them at his sides. "It's eight o'fucking clock in the morning."

"Yeah. I'm fucking drunk," Dez slurred, rocking in place. "How am I supposed to get through today, huh? Put her in the ground?"

"Daddy?"

Vinny followed the shaky voice to Tyler. The kid looked so small standing in the kicked-open doorway, so scared. It made Vinny want to hug the little guy and never let go.

Dez stumbled forward, grunting a bit, and Tyler gasped then ran away.

"Fuck!" Dez roared, throwing the near empty bottle in his hand against the wall. Glass shattered, raining down, and Dez dropped to the floor. "How am I gonna do this?" he sputtered, tears rolling down his cheeks. "It's only been a week."

"It'll get easier," Vinny said, kneeling beside Dez. "After today, we can go home."

"I don't have a home." Dez wobbled to his feet, backing away in a zigzag. "Just go, get the fuck out. Go fuck some skanks and feel better."

A broken man or not, Dez was about to get his

ass kicked all around this room. Vinny would, but someone had to go check on Tyler.

"Get dressed," Vinny barked, heading for the door. "And splash some water on your face." He stopped in the splintered doorway, turning with his pointed finger high. "If you disgrace Sasha's memory today, I'll slit your fucking throat. Then your kid *will* have no one."

Chapter Twenty-Seven

Sasha

A squeak erupted from the springs beneath Sasha, and she giggled. It had been so long since she heard sound besides the woman's soft voice. She missed that voice, those eyes, her mama. The voice hadn't come in a while. It should be here soon, flowing in to carry her away from the cold walls, whisk her into its warmth.

"Good morning, Ellen," Sasha muttered to herself, but it wasn't the same.

Sharp metal dug into her side, the springs slicing through her skin. She didn't move. Moving made the flesh shred.

Sasha ran her hand along the wall in front of her, which created a blur of fingertips. It was like she had five hands, but four were shadows that chased the first. Pretty, with the sparkles on the wall. How she loved when the sparkles lit the wall. The tip of her finger fell into a deep groove, stopping the wave of her many hands.

"What's this?" Her finger traced a deep line in the wall, which sat beside more lines. She sat up on the cot, her skin ripping from the rusty metal embedded in her side. The sting sent tingles, which brought a smile. It was like a hug, the pain, wrapping around every part of her. "Anything's better than nothing."

Warm streams trickled down her side, slapping the floor below. "Great. Now the rat will come back." That's fine, let the critter come. She had some words to exchange with that bastard.

She reached under her shirt, inspecting the damage. Not bad. This tear was only finger-wide. It'd mend in no time. "Time." She chuckled. She had all the time, and none at all.

"Ha!" A laugh shook her chest, sending out another wave of prickly pain. She slapped the wall, and her blood-tipped fingers painted a trail along the deep groove. "Interesting." Such a bright color, amid the gray. It set her mind ablaze. She lifted her shirt, pulling her cut apart. A thick stream of blood ran from her torn flesh and she gathered up as much color as she could, smearing it along the indents in the wall.

Over and over, she traced lines. The barbed metal of the cot sliced her knees as she moved, following the indents on the wall. The groove stopped, ending with rough stone, and she leaned back. "Is it art?" She climbed off the bed, backing to the door. The fuzz in her eyes slowly lifted as she squinted. Bit by bit words faded in, clearing for split-seconds before returning to a cloud of haze.

"A message!"

Now that she knew it was words, she could read them with her hands. She hurried back to the cot when the flap in the door slid open.

"Good morning, Ellen."

That airy voice stopped Sasha short. She dashed to the door, dropping to her knees. Just beyond her mother's eyes, she could see light. A world, with things and stuff beside stone walls that sometimes sparkled.

"Good morning...Mama."

"Very nice. You didn't drink your water."

Sasha looked at her tray, sitting untouched beside her.

"Be a good girl, drink your water."

It sounded like solid advice. She was very thirsty. She wrapped her fingers around the cool glass and emptied it in one gulp.

"Good. Now, would you like to hear about the time you burnt down a warehouse when you were ten?"

"Yes." She had no idea what her mother was saying. A numb wave had washed over her, drowning almost everything as it heated her skin. The only thing left was the hum of that voice. When it was near, the world seemed perfect. She closed her eyes, a smile lifting her cheeks as the voice carried her into a cloud of bliss.

***

Dez

Dez stood in the only field of grass he'd been

able to find in this city, a cemetery. The gentle hills of this place reminded him of home. That could be the reason he came here every day and stayed for hours. He looked at the pile of dirt at his feet. That mound of black earth, with its little place card, couldn't be what drew him here. There was nothing to hold in that dirt. He knew, had tried in a drunken stupor and failed.

A shadow fell over Sasha's grave, and Dez looked over his shoulder. Vinny walked beside him, crossing his arms.

"I knew I'd find you here."

Dez returned his stare to the little white place card which rain or tears had smeared. "I'm not drunk."

"I didn't say anything." Vinny shoved his hands into his pockets, glancing up the gentle slope behind him.

"What are you looking at?" Dez asked without bothering to lift his gaze.

"Tyler's in the car."

"You brought him here!" Dez pushed Vinny aside, looking at the lone black sedan parked atop the hill. "What the fuck, dude?"

"He's singing that song at his daycare today. He really wants you there."

"Fuck." Dez ran his hands through his hair, smoothing it back. "I know. I knew about that. I'll ride with you guys."

"Why do you keep coming here?" Vinny asked, turning away from Sasha's grave. "You're just torturing yourself."

"It's been over a month." Dez plucked the place

card from the ground, tossing it over his shoulder. "They should've put up a headstone by now."

"Otis wanted some special marble brought in from Italy." Vinny looked back at the car, then to his feet. "It should be ready in a week or so."

"Why don't I know any of this shit?"

"Because you miss all the meetings, and the dinners, and the stupid fucking memorials."

The level of spite in Vinny's voice struck Dez like a fist. He'd been too consumed by his own anguish to notice his little brother's pain.

"I'm sorry." Dez reached out and Vinny backed away. He couldn't blame the guy. A maniac on a rampage had been Dez's new role for weeks. "A lot of shit got dumped on your shoulders, my shit. I shouldn't have ducked out on you guys. It's pathetic…I'm sorry. I'm here from now on, brother."

Vinny's eyes teared up and Dez grabbed his brother, drawing him into a tight embrace. It might've been the first time he saw Vinny cry since Sasha died. Hell, it might've been the first time he'd ever really hugged his little brother.

"I'm good," Vinny said, pulling away to wipe his eyes. "We gotta go."

Dez stole one more glimpse at the earth that had begun to settle, then followed Vinny up the hill.

***

Sasha

A sharp nip tugged at Sasha's fingertips. Her

mother's voice left her a while ago, but she remained on the floor beside the closed flap. A pinch replaced the nipping on her fingers, jolting her shoulders. She swatted her hand and a squeak rang out, popping her eyes open.

"Critter!"

She fell to her hands and knees, chasing the sound of tiny claws tapping the ground. Her head hit the wall, a long thin tail slipping through her fingers.

"Damn! Almost had you, motherfucker."

Next time. She'd catch that critter bastard next time and break its neck for nibbling on her. A rush of heat shot into her toes as she rose from the floor. The wall in front of her pulsed in waves. Such a tranquil sight, the deep red streaks rolling back and forth, up and down. That color, it wasn't there before.

"The message!"

Words had been found, and she had painted them in blood. She knelt on her cot, its pointed ends of metal piercing her knees. Slowly, her finger ran along the carved groove in the wall, and she forced the static in her mind into silence.

"I…" She moved to the next set of lines, the cot's rusty springs sawing out chunks of her knees as she slid over. "A…M. Am." The last series of marks were so long, halfway through she'd forgotten the game. It was to read the message. Two, three times of trying and she finally reached the end while remembering the beginning.

"Ellen?"

The squeal of springs filled her ears as she

jumped off the cot. Her back hit the door, and she stared at the red lines on the wall. **"I am Ellen."**

So bright, the words burned against the stone, shining and shimmering in the darkness. *I am Ellen.*

"No!" She pounded the sides of her head as she slid down the door. She wasn't Ellen. Her name was different. She was sure of it. Even though she couldn't recall it at this moment, the word was different.

The message floated away from the wall, drifting closer to her. She closed her eyes, but the words were seared into her eyelids. *I am Ellen.* It wouldn't leave her sight and now, it echoed in her ears. Who was saying that? Who was Ellen?

Her hand clutched onto her throat, a low rumble vibrating her fingers. *She* was talking. *She* was saying it. "I am Ellen."

"No!" She slammed her forehead against the wall. A buzz shot through her head, masking the words that circled the room. She fell to her back. A warm streak ran down the bridge of her nose, pooling in her eye. Since she could no longer see beyond the red haze, she stopped fighting it and fell into it.

Chapter Twenty-Eight

The door creaked open and Sasha hopped off her cot, leaving a good amount of flesh to dangle on the springs behind. A flood of light filled the room, blinding her with its gleam. The door never opened. The flap, yes, but not the door.

Her eyes watered and she peeked between her fingers, squinting. She didn't know the old woman who walked into her cell, or the two men beside her. When the woman crept closer, though, she glimpsed that stare. Why was her mother's stare on this old woman's face?

"There's a little problem, Ellen."

Sasha knew that voice. It was the one constant in her life, the thing that kept her going in the dark. Today, the voice didn't bring waves of bliss. It sounded cross, which trembled every one of her bones.

"It's been two months now, Ellen, and you haven't gotten your period. A shitsack baby isn't part of my plans. I'm sorry sweet girl, but we're gonna have to take care of this."

"What?" Sasha scurried away, and the men grabbed her arms. "No!" she yelled as they forced her to the ground, onto her back in the dirt. One man held her shoulders down while the other sat atop her feet to stop their kicking.

"Close your eyes, Ellen. This'll be over quick," the woman said, raising a shotgun.

Sasha tried to squirm away, break free, but the butt of a gun sailed toward her stomach. The hit knocked all air from her lungs. She gasped for breath when two more strikes slammed against her stomach. Pain shot out like bolts of lightning, zapping her entire body with its razor-sharp teeth.

The grip on her arms and legs lifted and the door crashed shut, hurling her back into dark shadows. She pulled her knees to her chest. Every movement sent sharp waves of fire into her gut. Even her sobs burned, and tears were meant to cool hot cheeks. There was a baby, a baby inside her?

She slid her hand inside her pants, between her legs, coming up with a handful of blood. They killed her baby.

Her sobs turned to wails. She pulled her knees closer, hugging herself tighter. If only the walls would sparkle, lull her mind into a haze, but they stopped doing that the moment she smeared her blood over their shine. A warm rush flowed between her legs. She could feel it now. Her baby, seeping from her body. She had a baby, once, when she was another girl.

"Tyler," she muttered. The curves of his face were lost to her now, but his name could never be stripped from her mind. He must be out there, somewhere. There had to be an out there, beyond this cold room, away from the dark and dirt and blood. That's where her baby waited, Tyler.

***

Dez

Tyler tore through the living room, running up the stairs. Dez snickered as Vinny gave chase, tagging the little guy up with Nerf darts.

"That's why I love these big penthouse suites," Otis said, chuckling when Tyler's dart smacked Vinny square in the forehead. "Lots of room, lots of crazy."

"You only use your suite for nasty swinger parties," Dez said, lighting a joint, "and I hope there ain't no kids running around at those." After a few puffs, he held the joint out to Otis. "So, to what do I owe this honor? The Don of the Lazzari family, in my house," Dez said, laying the mockery on thick.

"Stop fucking around." Otis snatched the joint, making himself quite comfortable on the sofa.

"What? You've never stepped foot in this place, and we've been here for three months."

"I've been busy playing mob boss," Otis said between puffs. "This shit's hard. You'd know, if you bothered to help out."

"Fuck, man. I've been busy too." A little foam dart flew over the staircase, bouncing off the side of Dez's face.

"Sorry, Dad," Tyler yelled over the stomp of his running feet.

"This shit's hard," Dez said through a snicker, tossing the dart at Otis.

"When are you gonna come to the table? I need you, Dez."

"I can't go there, to that restaurant." Dez sat beside Otis, keeping his gaze on the plush carpet. Every muscle in his body trembled at the thought of walking through the wide glass doors of Fat Tonys, standing beside the bar, in the last place Sasha's lips touched his own. He turned away from Otis. Tears welled inside his eyes. He had to blink them back before anyone could see.

"Sasha would have wanted you to take her spot until Tyler was old enough to claim it."

"My son isn't gonna live this life. Tyler wants to be a rock star."

Otis chuckled. He rose from the couch, standing in front of Dez. "I won't pressure you. In fact, I'll never ask again. The seat will always be waiting for you." He handed Dez a smoking stub of a joint then slapped him on the shoulder.

Dez stared at the tunnel of gray smoke wafting in front of his face. Sasha would kick his fucking ass for being so weak. Otis needed him. What the fuck was he doing?

"It's not as bad as you think at Fat Tonys," Otis said from the doorway. "You can almost feel her energy there."

It was probably true. Sasha was most alive when she had an opportunity to be bad. It would explain why Vinny hung out there so much.

"I'll come down tonight, have a late dinner," Dez said, walking from the room to escape Otis's stupid grin.

***

Sasha

"Sasha."

Somebody was talking to someone else. It wasn't her business. "It's best to mind your own business 'round here," she mumbled, burying her cheek against the sharp metal cot.

"Hey! Little girl."

She sat up, her cry eclipsing the sound of metal springs ripping her skin. Damn, she'd stayed too long in one place. "When you stay too long, the skin becomes one with metal," she said, flicking clumps of her torn flesh off the cot's springs. "Not good."

"Sasha."

There was that voice again, calling to someone she knew, in a deep tone that boiled her blood.

"Who's Sasha?" She turned toward the door, catching a different set of eyes in the flap. These eyes were dark, wide with fear. Was it her? She couldn't be on both sides of the door, not at the same time.

"You're Sasha," he said, reaching his fingers through the thin slot.

She leapt off the cot, latching onto that hand before it could pull away. A gentle touch. It was like magic. She rubbed the rough fingers on her sore cheek, soaking in a warmth that had abandoned her so long ago.

"You have to stop drinking the water, Sasha."

285

"*I* am Sasha?" It had to be right. This man called her that, and she knew this man. Every word he spoke brought her closer to the cusp of a memory.

"That's right, little girl."

"Dante," she grunted. She hated him, but she loved him more than anyone else in this moment. His hand, caressing her cheek, was the best sensation she ever experienced.

"Yeah. I found you, little girl. Would've come sooner, but they just unchained me."

"Open the door." She lifted a shaky hand, banging on the solid surface.

"Shh. They don't know I'm down here. Don't drink the water. It's loaded with LSD."

She looked at her tall glass of crystal clear water. How could she not drink it? She was so thirsty.

"Here." Dante pushed a plastic baggie through the slot, drops of the water within spilling from its seam. "It's rainwater."

She poured the warm liquid in her mouth, gagging on bits of leaves.

"Empty out the glass in your shit bucket," Dante whispered. "I need you to be strong. We're busting out of here."

Sasha dumped the drug-laced water in the putrid bucket that was her toilet, hurrying back to the flap. "Let me out. I can be strong now."

"I don't have the key. When they come to bring your tray tonight, use this." Dante shoved a sharp piece of metal into Sasha's hand then backed away.

"No! Don't leave me," she cried out, reaching her fingers through the thin slit in the metal door.

Dante kissed Sasha's bloody fingertips then

pushed her hand back inside. "I'll be waiting for you, tonight. Don't drink the water." His eyes wavered, filling with regret before he slid the flap shut.

***

Sasha sat in the corner right beside the door. If rough edges of metal weren't digging into her palm, she'd never believe a devil had come for a visit. Her gaze stuck to the wall, and the faded words that kept her company. *I am Ellen.*

"You," she growled at the wall. "You are Ellen." She was Sasha.

Someone would come soon, dump her bucket, and replace her tray. The soothing voice she clung to which hid behind her mother's eyes didn't come with the second tray. At least, she didn't think it did. She didn't know how many trays equaled one day, or who brought them. A whirlwind of swirling shapes, colors that melded, had been all she knew. Until that voice drew her out.

"Good morning, Ellen," she sneered. No more. Never again will she hear that phrase, nor slip into a world of shadows.

Footsteps thumped in the distance, each heavy thud quaking her bones. She slumped down, gripping the metal tighter. Its barbed edge sliced her palm, blood ran down her wrist, but she didn't dare loosen her hold. The flap slid open, and her eyes snapped shut. Her glass was empty. Whoever peeked inside would think she was knocked out, but she wasn't.

The door creaked open, sending jitters into her skinless toes. She peeked through her tangled, crusty hair. A man knelt on one knee, placing down a tray, and Sasha lunged forward. She wrapped her arm around his head, and her nails sunk into his eye. Before he could yell, she jammed the pointed bit of metal into his neck. Blood sprayed her face as she tore. The metal gouged her hand, biting her skin, but she kept pushing, pulling, ripping.

Watery garbles fell under the squish of tearing flesh. The man dropped to his side, and Sasha's knees hit the floor. A gaping wound drew her stare. The shards of skin, flapping against veins as they pumped blood to the dirt, was more beautiful than art.

More footsteps thumped from beyond the open door. The open door! A gunshot rang out and Sasha jumped to her feet, running out of the dark cell. Light pierced her eyes, shooting straight to the back of her brain. She staggered down a narrow, stone passage. Flakes of rock showered to the ground as her sides bounced from one wall to another. She blinked back the sting of bright lights, stumbling toward a set of wooden stairs.

Her foot caught something hard and she tripped, landing on the bottom step. She glanced back as a shotgun clattered to the floor. A wide smile split her cracked lips and she grabbed the gun, wobbling up the stairs.

A barrage of gunshots rattled the wood beneath her bare feet, growing louder as she crept onto a dim landing and inched down a hallway. Each blast jolted her achy muscles. Her legs fought every step, but she kept going. She had to get out, away from that stifling room of darkness, far from the walls that swayed.

Sasha stumbled into a living room, landing at the edge of a shootout. A line of men stood in front of her, firing their guns across the room. Clouds of smoke rose from flashing barrels. She couldn't see what the men were shooting at, didn't know who these men were. The thunderous pops of gunfire filled her head, and gray fog crammed into the room. She couldn't think, beyond the fact that these people stood between her and the front door, so she raised the gun in her hands and pulled the trigger.

A man dropped to the floor at Sasha's feet. The deafening booms lessened, guns veered her way, and she fired off the last round. Pellets of buckshot scattered out. Two more men fell to the floor, but they weren't out. Their strong groans sent the promise they'd rise again, ready to blast her ass to shreds.

An old woman swung a handgun toward Sasha, pulling the trigger. The gun's flash blinded Sasha for a split second. Her shoulder rocked back as a bullet tore through her flesh, but she didn't feel it. Hot blood gushed down her arm, pellets of shotgun rounds flew past her face, but all she knew was the fiery scorch of rage that swelled inside her chest.

Sasha stepped toward the woman who'd stolen her mother's glare. Another bullet struck her left arm, flinging it back, yet she hobbled forward. She clutched onto the woman's neck with one hand, seizing the wrinkled wrist that clung to a revolver with the other.

"I…am…Sasha," she growled, forcing the gun in the woman's shaky hand away from her chest. Sasha squeezed the woman's neck, pushed the bitch's arm until the barrel was positioned under the woman's own chin. A bright flash erupted from the gun's barrel, clouding the world in white. Warm drops splashed Sasha's face, and the old woman dropped from her grasp.

Sasha staggered back from her dead mother's eyes, which rested on an old woman's blood-streaked face. Her feet tangled into a pile of limp arms, and she crashed to the floor. A steady buzz claimed her ears, and a red haze snuck up to drag her into its clutches. Gunfire still circled the room. She couldn't hear it but every bang seeped into her body, shuddering her bones. It wasn't over yet. She'd come too far, was too close, to just die on this floor.

Energy trickled in, though not enough for Sasha to peel her back from the floor. She groped the splintered wood beside her, splashing puddles and slapping skin. Cool metal soothed the burn of her palm, a trigger grazing her finger. She rolled onto her stomach, clutching onto the butt of a shotgun. A cry ripped from her chest as she pushed herself to her knees. The buzz in her ears faded just enough for the click of a bolt action to stream through. She looked up, beyond the barrel in her face, to an ugly man's sneer.

A loud blast made Sasha cringe. The man dropped to the floor beside her, his hate-filled stare now empty and stuck on her. A hand landed on Sasha's back, and she jumped to the side. Even though her right shoulder throbbed and her left arm burned, she lifted the long gun in her hands.

"Sasha! It's me."

The man in front of her looked familiar, like a beaten-down skinny version of Dante. He lowered the rifle in his hand, nodding. The eyes matched, but that could be deceiving. A horrid lesson she'd learned in the dark.

"Dante?"

"That's right, little girl."

It was him. She could feel the frenzy of hatred only his proximity could provide. Sasha lifted the gun higher, right to Dante's face. "I hate you," she sneered.

"I know, little girl. I know." Dante dropped the gun in his grip, holding his hand out in front of Sasha. "Let me take you to your people."

"My people?" A tremble took the gun down, its barrel banging to the floor.

"Yeah. Your trucker brothers."

"Vinny!" Although Sasha couldn't picture Vinny's face, she could almost feel his arms around her.

Dante took Sasha by the hand, helping her off the floor. She teetered on her feet, flinching when his arm slid around her waist.

"It's all right, Sasha. I won't hurt you."

She let her weight fall to Dante's side as they limped to the door. "That bitch killed my baby."

"Tyler?"

"No. I was pregnant."

Dante tightened his hold, moving faster toward the sparkle of stars beyond a crooked doorway.

291

Sasha stopped in the threshold, looking back. Her feet wouldn't carry her ass from this place, not until she was sure that crazy old bitch was dead.

The woman lay in a crumpled heap. Pink chunks oozed from the hole in the top of the woman's head, and her cruel face was now frozen in a silent scream of agony. It was a wonderful sight. Bodies were scattered across the floor. It gave Sasha the strength to walk away from the hellish house and into the sweet smelling night.

Chapter Twenty-Nine

Sasha rolled her head away from a car's window, sinking into a ripped vinyl seat. Lights zoomed by in streaks, blurring in swirls of color, but she could tell they were in the city. Blood dripped from the bullet holes in her shoulder and arm, running down her fingertips and soaking into her stiff pants. It was hard to tell which stains were old and which were new. Every stitch of tattered fabric carried some shade of red or brown.

"We're almost there," Dante said. He looked so small behind the large steering wheel of this station wagon. Somehow, the man had lost half his muscle mass. She loathed the thought of her body looking the same, but it probably did...or worse.

Every second of fresh air brought clarity to her mind, though she still couldn't process what had happened.

"How long has it been?" Sasha asked, trying to put the days that passed in order and failing.

"I'm not sure. Two, maybe three months."

"Months?" The word barely made a sound. It

might not have even slipped past her dry lips.

Brakes squealed, and the car rocked to a stop. Dante turned to face Sasha, wiping a tear from her blood-crusted cheek.

"We're here," he said, gesturing to her window. "Fat Tonys."

Sasha turned to catch a glimpse, but a red-tinged haze had claimed her vision.

"Can you get inside all right?"

Nothing would keep her ass from getting into that restaurant, not even the fact that she could barely see it. Sasha opened her door, steering her gaze back to Dante. "We still have a score to settle, you and I."

Dante snickered, leaning against his door. The way he looked at her, with such pride and love. It was a gaze she'd never seen aimed her way before, yet it did little to quench the fire his face ignited in her veins.

"I know," Dante said through a smile. "Give me a few months to recoup."

"Yeah. All right." Sasha climbed from the car, nearly dropping to her knees. People shuffled along the sidewalk, jumping aside as she limped by. Their gasps filled her ears, echoing. The blur of lights almost forced her eyes to shut, but she was so close. She reached out, swatting air, and the door opened. A man stood beside her, waving his arms and fussing about, but she kept going.

Once her foot hit the lobby and she glimpsed a curvy hostess, her body felt free to collapse to the floor. People hovered over her; hands brushed her forehead. She strained to get a glimpse of a familiar face, but darkness came quick to drag her under.

***

Dez

Jitters ran through Dez, and he squirmed in his padded chair. Otis was a fucking liar. The energy Fat Tonys emitted didn't belong to Sasha. It spawned from greed. A shine coated every surface. It was a fake glimmer, designed to dupe the average idiot into wanting more. The worse part, it actually worked. Every table below their private section was filled as well as the bar and probably the lobby. What a spectacle, one he had no desire to witness. To think, he left his kid with a sitter for this shit.

Dez tossed his napkin onto the table. Just as he leaned over to tell Otis he was out, a scream echoed from the lobby. Dez jumped to his feet. Before his chair could crash to the floor, he ran from the table.

A crowd of people gathered in the lobby, crying out as they shoved one another to get a better look.

"Back up," Dez yelled, pushing people aside. He looked down and his heart jumped into his throat, blocking off all air. His legs gave out, taking his big ass to the floor. It couldn't be. Sasha couldn't be lying in front of him, covered in dirt and bleeding from ripped shards on every inch of her skin. For a second, Dez thought she literally clawed her way out of her grave.

Dez reached out, tapping Sasha's arm. "Fuck!" She was real. People gathered closer around him, and panicked voices rose. Dez wrapped his fingers around the butt of his holstered gun. Everyone who stood anywhere near Sasha was getting shot. Before he could pull the revolver from its holster, Vinny and Otis shooed the crowd away.

"Oh my God!" Vinny cried out, dropping to his knees. He pulled Sasha's limp body onto his lap, holding tight. "I knew that wasn't her in the alley. Fucking told you guys!"

Dez couldn't move, speak, breathe. He had touched Sasha's hand and felt it. Somehow, someway, she came back to him. It looked like she might have fought her way through Hell to do it, but she came back to him.

"We got to get her into the back," Enzo said. He knelt down, sliding his hands under Sasha.

"No!" Vinny pulled Sasha closer, her bloody feet leaving a trail on the carpet. "I got her."

A numb sensation held Dez to the floor, even as Vinny carried the missing piece of his heart away. He should chase Sasha's mangled body, but he was afraid. Even though blood still stained the floor, he couldn't trust what his own eyes had saw.

Otis stepped beside Dez and he shot to his feet, latching onto the man's shirt.

"Was that her? Was it really Sasha?"

"Yeah," Otis muttered, the whites of his wide eyes dull compared to the complexion of his face.

"We have to get her to the hospital." Dez kept his hold on Otis, pulling the man as he followed the path of blood.

"I already called our doctor."

"Fuck that!" Dez stopped short, shaking Otis. "Did you see her? She needs the hospital!"

"Our doc is better than any hospital." Otis placed his hands on Dez's wrists, holding tight. "Trust me."

Dez released his grip on Otis, running into the backroom. He shoved Vinny aside, wrapping his arms around Sasha. A groan seeped from her lips. The sound sparked a chuckle he couldn't stop. It meant she was alive. He kissed her forehead, getting a mouthful of blood. A small fee to hold his wife in his arms again. The icy grip on his soul melted the longer he clung to Sasha, letting bits of warmth back in. He may never let her go. It was too risky.

A man pushed his way into the room, tugging on Dez's arm. "Son, I need to examine her."

The guy was lucky he had a black bag in his hand. If anyone other than a doctor had tried to pull Dez from Sasha, he might have broken some jaws. Dez stepped back, as far as his body would allow. Three feet, at the most.

"I'm going to need privacy," the man said, opening his large bag and pulling out one barbaric looking tool after another.

"Too fucking bad," Dez said, shrugging away from Vinny's clutch. "She doesn't leave my sight."

"You want her to die then?" the doc asked, laying a pouch of blood labeled *Sasha L.* on the desk beside him.

"Come on, Dez," Vinny said, pulling on Dez's arm.

Dez almost spun around and slugged Vinny. They actually thought he would leave Sasha, alone, with some strange Italian guy.

Vinny took Dez by the hand, softly. He could

nearly feel the desperation beaming from his brother's grasp. His gaze veered to Otis, then Enzo. They were all terrified to lose Sasha after just getting her back. Dez walked to the door, which was a miracle considering the quake of his legs. Despite his mind's protest, he looked back into the large office. The doctor had cut Sasha's filthy clothes off, struggling to find a place to start. There wasn't a single place on her beautiful body that hadn't been bruised, torn, ripped open.

A cry skipped Dez's heart as it rolled past his chest, lodging in his throat. Vinny gave him a little push, which got his feet in gear. His mind, however, would need a much bigger shove.

***

Sasha

Sasha rolled her head to the side, forcing her eyes to open. She had no idea where she was. It was bright, warm, soft. They were amazing sensations, ones she had long forgotten. This could be Heaven.

A hand clutched onto Sasha's arm, and she jerked away from the tight grip.

"Stop," a man's voice cried out.

The grip tightened and Sasha hurled her fist, pushing at the solid body over her. "No! Let me go."

"It's me. Dez!"

Sasha stopped tossing punches and looked up from the wide chest in front of her. Electric blue eyes cut through the haze, driving a misty fog from her mind. "Dez?" That face, with a smile to boot. Now that she was looking at it, she didn't know how she could've forgotten it. "*I* am Sasha."

"I know who you are," Dez said in a half-cry/half-chuckle.

Of course he knew. She had to remind herself, one last time.

"You must have ripped your stitches," he said, staring at the red stain spreading along her fresh white t-shirt.

Dez moved away and Sasha pulled his arm, bringing him back to her side. "Dez." She drew his arm closer, squeezing it to her chest. Not even his touch could stop the tears which had begun to flow down her cheeks. "They killed our baby."

"What?"

He caressed her forehead, dulling her mind's ache just a tad. "I was pregnant. They took it from me. I…I couldn't stop them from…" Sobs choked out her words. Not that she had any left.

"It's okay." Dez wrapped his arms around Sasha, sending a million red-hot needles to assault her entire body. The pain was almost too much to bear, but his hug was the shit dreams were made of, so she let it go on.

"I thought you were dead," Dez whispered. His arms shook, so violently they rattled Sasha's bones. She squeezed him tight. He must've given all his strength to her. It was only right to bounce some back.

"I saw your body," he said in a quaver. "Buried you."

"Fuck!" Sasha leaned back and Dez moved

299

away, but not very far. "This must be one hell of a surprise then."

Dez laughed, even though tears streamed from his eyes. "A fucking great one." He lifted the blanket, crawling into the bed beside Sasha. His big, safe arm slid around her waist. It was amazing, his ability to hold her so tight and so gently at the same time.

"Tell me who did this to you. I'll carve out their intestines and strangle them with it."

The visual alone was enough to bring a smile, which quickly faded as jagged memories rushed back in.

"They're all dead. All of them."

"The Mancinis?"

Sasha nodded. She couldn't spout out any more words, deal with the memory of being trapped in darkness any longer. Her body ached, and her brain throbbed. She didn't want to dredge it up, tell everyone how she broke inside a tiny cell.

"You don't have to talk about it," Dez whispered, holding tighter. "Ever."

Sasha sank against the strong body behind her. Horrors couldn't touch her while tucked inside these arms. Only when she left their embrace did the nightmares begin. If he'd hold her forever, in this place of soft pillows and fluffy blankets, she could be safe.

A heavy weight pulled on her eyelids, but she fought to keep them open. She wanted to savor this moment. The tingles that spawned from Dez's fingertips had to be remembered, just in case she awoke in a cold cell.

Chapter Thirty

Cries of terror lured Sasha into darkness. She slid her hands along damp, rocky walls as she stumbled down a tight hallway. The wails that echoed around her didn't belong here, in this passageway of dirt and stone walls. It was a child, sobbing and screaming for help. It was Tyler.

She slipped on puddles of blood as she ran, banging on locked metal doors. The weeping drifted farther away with every step she took. She couldn't find him. Her son was trapped inside one of these cells, sitting in a corner, his tiny body picked apart by rats.

"Tyler!" Sasha screamed.

There were a million doors in this hall that never ended. They wouldn't open, and she could no longer hear her child's cries. The dim lights above her flickered. Someone seized her arms, shaking the world into a blur.

"Tyler!" Sasha sat up, and the narrow passageway of crumbling stone faded to the gleam of white walls.

"It's okay."

Dez's voice sent a spike of panic into Sasha's heart. If he was with her, who was with Tyler? She grabbed onto Dez's shirt, pulling him close. "Tyler! I didn't check the other cells. He's down there! I left him down there." She pushed the blankets aside, scooting to the edge of the bed.

"No," Dez said. He tried to push Sasha back against the pillows, but she wiggled from his grip. Her feet hit soft carpet, and her legs gave out. She braced for hard floor, but landed in soft arms.

"Tyler's safe," Dez said, cradling her on the floor like a baby. "He's downstairs with Vinny, playing board games."

"Are you sure?" She clung to Dez, wrinkling his shirt with her crushing grip.

"Yeah."

His gaze carried such certainty. It allowed Sasha's fingers to unclench, letting her stiff muscles sag.

"You want me to get him?" Dez asked.

Sasha turned toward the door, catching her reflection in the wide window. That couldn't be her. The person in the glass, with clumps of blood tangled in their hair and a face-full of gashes, looked like a monster. "No! I'll scare the fuck out of him."

"I never told him, that you...died."

"How long has it been?"

"Three months, one week, and six days." Dez glided his hand along Sasha's cheek, light and gentle. "That's how long it's been since I held you in my arms, before yesterday."

"Three months?" It seemed much shorter, and longer, at the same time.

"You said something about a cell?"

Sasha shrank down. The layer of dried blood on her body pulled at her skin, dropping flakes to the white carpet. She looked at the bed, the sheets smeared in red. Everywhere she went she left a trail of death, ruining the sparkle of this lavish room.

"I have to get this blood off me." She reached for her hair, yanking her hand away at the feel of dried clumps. "It's everywhere, on everything."

"I'll run you a bath." Dez helped Sasha off the floor, guiding her toward the bed.

Although her legs wobbled and her feet burned, she didn't sit. She had already fucked up those clean white blankets enough.

"Are you hungry?" Dez called out from the bathroom, over the rush of running water. "There's some food on the nightstand."

Sasha looked at the sandwiches spread along a silver tray. Real food, with colors other than gray. Just as she touched a soft roll, images of shoving slop in her mouth beamed into her mind. She jolted back, curling her fingers into her crusty hair. "Stop." She banged her palms against her head, but the memories wouldn't stop streaming through her mind. "Stop!"

A gasp drew Sasha's gaze to Dez, frozen in the middle of the room. It looked like he'd totally forgotten a monster was standing beside his bed. Dude must be freaking out, and her crazy ass wasn't helping. Anything she said right now would come out as babbles of insanity, so she kept her mouth closed and her eyes low as she limped toward the bathroom.

"Let me help you." Dez rushed to Sasha's side and she pushed him away, closing the bathroom door on his tortured eyes.

The cuts on her face, chucks torn from her arms, were nothing compared to the damage her cot must've done to her body. Dez shouldn't have to see that. She'd probably lose him forever if he saw that.

While avoiding the mirror, window, and every other surface that seemed to reflect her image, Sasha stripped off her shirt.

***

Dez

Dez paced in front of the bathroom door. He couldn't stand to have Sasha out of his sight. It had been ten minutes since she shut herself in the bathroom, which was ten too many. A little peek. He just needed a little peek.

In near silence, he turned the knob. The door cracked open, and he looked inside. A tall tub nearly swallowed Sasha up. Her mauled arm hung over the gold-rimmed side, sending pink drops to splash the tile below. She didn't notice him. Her stare was stuck to the wall in front of her, body completely still in red-tinted water as her lips slowly moved. Dez shut the door, taking a deep breath. A wave of tears rose inside his eyes, pushing for release. What a despicable piece of shit he was.

He should be in there, washing the crap from her hair. Someone had to clean her, but someone had to clean the bed for her.

Dez ripped the sheet off the mattress, pulling cases off pillows. Any trace of gore should be gone before Sasha emerged. It would make her all better, to have everything fresh and clean. While fitting a new sheet on the bed, Dez spotted the wide red stain on the white carpet.

"Fuck!" He dropped to his knees, rubbing at the bright mark with a soiled pillowcase. The mess only spread, growing brighter the harder he scrubbed. "No, no."

A light knock rattled the bedroom door as it opened. Vinny poked his head inside, looked straight at the empty bed, then barged inside.

"Everything all right?"

"No." Dez looked up from the stain on the rug and a tear escaped, gliding down his cheek. He lifted his hand to wipe his face, stopping at the sight of blood. "She's fucked up, man," Dez sputtered, staring at Sasha's blood on his hands. "I've never seen her so broken. She's just sitting in the tub, in her own filth, talking to herself. I don't know what to do, say."

Vinny knelt down, patting Dez on the back.

"You go in there," Dez blurted, pointing at the bathroom.

"What?" Vinny said, leaning back.

"She needs help. Every time I see the cuts on her body, I get so angry. It's scaring her, shutting her down."

"I, uh…" Vinny rose to his feet, staring at the

305

bathroom door. "You want *me* to go in there?"

Dez nodded, unable to hide his pleading eyes. He didn't give a fuck anymore. He'd share Sasha with his brother if it meant getting her back to the real Sasha.

Vinny inched around the bloodstain on the carpet and headed for the bathroom. A light knock, the creak of a door's hinges, and his brother crept into the room where the ghost of his wife sat. Dez gathered up the dirty linens, eyeing the stain on his way to the hall. That fucking blotch was getting a gallon of bleach.

***

Vinny

Vinny walked with heavy steps, hoping to announce his presence. It wasn't working. Sasha didn't look away from the wall she'd been staring at. He stepped beside the tub, cringing. The amount of fleshy chunks floating in the dark red water was enough to twist his stomach, and he'd seen some fucked up shit.

While kneeling beside the tub, Vinny placed his hand on Sasha's shoulder. She jumped to the side, splashing bloody water to the floor.

"Vinny," Sasha said breathlessly.

She lifted her hand from the water. Large hunks of flesh were missing from her fingertips, bones showing in places. When her scabbed fingers ran along his cheek, he had to force his body not to cringe.

"I remember your face," she said, with the slightest hint of a smile on her swollen lips.

"I remember your face too." Vinny poked Sasha on the nose, which got him a semi-smirk. He yearned to bombard her with hugs and kisses, but she'd probably gotten enough of that pansy shit from Dez.

"Let's get you cleaned up," he said, pulling the plug from the drain.

"Okay."

Vinny kicked off his shoes and took off his shirt.

"What are you doing?" Sasha asked, clinging to the tub's edge as the murky water drained away.

"There's no way I can do this from out here. Your hair's a wreck." He turned on the showerhead before dropping his pants.

"But Dez."

"Fuck Dez. The amount of time he's spent with you isn't even enough to fill a page. We've been best friends since we were nine." Vinny held out his hand, and Sasha's palm slid in it. Although her every limb trembled, she stood tall with her chin high.

Vinny only stole glances at Sasha's mutilated body. The shreds of dangling flesh on her knees, that giant bruise on her stomach, all the wide gashes running along her sides were barely noticeable. At least, that's what he wanted her to think. Hence the poker face.

"I knew that wasn't you in the alley." Vinny climbed into the tub, closing its curtain around them. "I've studied every curve of your ass, could spot it in the dark."

The roughness of Sasha's skin as it brushed against him incited the urge to flee, but he held steady. She fell against him, resting her head on his chest. It took a second, but he wrapped his arms around her torn flesh.

"God, I missed you," Sasha said, squeezing Vinny with shaky hands.

Words could never express the depths of anguish he'd experienced in her absence. He was used to missing her, but this time had been different.

Sasha pulled back from Vinny's embrace. Her gaze drifted down to his giant hard-on, then up into his eyes.

"I'm sorry," he said, looking away from her cheeky stare. "I can't help it."

"Yeah."

That smirk on her lips was too cute. He'd kiss her, if he weren't scared shitless of breaking her like a china plate. Softly, Vinny backed Sasha under the flow of water. Bits of brain and pieces of skull fell to his feet, clogging the drain. It took half a bottle of shampoo, but he finally got her hair passable for clean.

"I'm gonna need one hell of a comb to fix this mess," Vinny said, wringing out her long, tangled hair.

"Just cut it all off," she muttered, shivering despite the warm water showering down on her.

"Fuck that! I'll get it straightened out good and proper."

The strength in Sasha's grip faded and her hands slid off Vinny's chest, flopping against her sides.

"Should I—"

"I'm good," Sasha said, pushing her legs to stand taller.

He should scoop her up, carry her off to some secret place where no one could find them. A tropical island. They'd lie on soft white sand, soak in the sun's rays as warm water rushed in to tickle their toes. Fuck yeah. All that shit was going to happen. The moment she was strong enough to put up a fight, that's when he'd sweep her away.

***

Dez

Dez stood over the kitchen sink, scrubbing the blood off his hands. Dish soap didn't clean for shit. A pink tinge still stained his fingertips, painted his nails. He grabbed a Brilo pad, scouring his skin with steel wool. Over his grunts, and the rush of water, he heard nothing. No clank of toys echoed from the living room, giggles weren't flowing over the television's blast. That usually meant Tyler was doing something really fucking bad.

Dez shut the faucet, turning to find Otis beside him.

"Fuck!" Dez yelled, jumping back.

"Sorry, man," Otis said, leaning against the counter. "I thought you heard me come in. Tyler hollered for ya."

"The water was running." Dez snatched a dishtowel from the rack, drying his hands.

"What happened here?" Otis asked, gesturing to the pinkish splatters on the counter.

"Nothing." Dez wiped the countertop, chucking the towel in a corner. "She…popped some stitches."

"Who, Daddy?"

Dez looked over Otis's shoulder as Tyler walked into the kitchen, holding a guitar almost twice his size.

"Whatcha got there, little man?"

"Uncle Otis brought it for me. Isn't it freakin awesome! There's a video. I'm gonna go practice."

"Language," Dez shouted as Tyler trotted off. Otis chuckled, earning a harsh glare. "A guitar?"

"You said he wanted to be a rock star." Otis fished a joint from his front pocket, lighting it up. "So, how's our girl doing?"

"She's not up for visitors."

"I *am* going up there."

Otis held out the joint, but Dez didn't take it. That man had to be fucking crazy if he thought a poorly rolled joint would get him up those stairs.

"Suit yourself," Otis said, heading for the stairs.

"No!" Dez grabbed Otis by the arm, yanking him to a stop. "You can't go up there now. Vinny's up there."

Otis shoved Dez away, narrowing his eyes. "Doing what?"

"Giving her a bath."

"Shouldn't you be doing that?"

"Don't fucking start with me," Dez roared, wincing at his own bark. He peeked over his shoulder, making sure Tyler was still plopped in front of the TV, before leaning close to Otis. "I thought it would help her, to be…alone with him."

"I get that more than you do." Otis draped his

arm around Dez, holding out the joint. "Look, I'm going up there. You can smoke this joint, get a little buzzed, and stew about it, or you can sit here like an asshole bone-straight."

Dez snatched the joint and squirmed away from Otis's grasp.

"Good man," Otis said, slapping Dez on the back.

A long stream of smoke flew from Dez's mouth as he watched Otis climb the stairs. Everyone was running to Sasha's side and here he was, looking for reasons to avoid her. Which reminded him, he needed to fetch clean blankets.

Chapter Thirty-One

Sasha

Sasha sat on a small couch, curled inside an oversized robe, and watched Vinny dress. It was surreal, a glimpse into a life she could've had. This city should be just another stop. Vinny's antics should be her world, an open road her home. All that could've been, would've been.

What-ifs were for dreamers, and her dreams were filled with horrors. It wouldn't have mattered what path she stumbled down. She would've found a way to fuck shit up.

A knock shook the bedroom door, and Sasha flinched. She searched the room for a weapon, any weapon, but all she found were crystal ashtrays and vases of flowers.

"It's all right," Vinny said, walking to the door. "Nobody's getting by me, girl." He opened the door and Otis pushed by him, strolling inside. "Well, except for him."

"Give us a minute," Otis said to Vinny, dipping

his head to the open door.

Vinny snorted, crossed his arms, then looked at Sasha. His dramatic display was pretty adorable, for a dude. Sasha nodded, and Vinny rocked in place before storming into the hall.

"Those Archer boys are something else," Otis said, shutting the door.

"I don't know where I was."

Otis froze in the middle of the room, shaking his head. "That's not—"

"There's no reason to go there anyway. You'll only find corpses."

"I just came to check on you, kiddo." Otis sat beside Sasha, and his hand landed on her leg.

She flinched so hard, it knocked a cry from her lungs and he jerked his hand back. Although rationally she knew she was completely safe with Otis, her stupid body wouldn't let go of the dark.

"Sorry," Otis said, inching away. "I—"

"You're trying to tell me you're not dying to find out every single thing that happened to me? Who did...this?" Sasha opened her robe and Otis gasped, covering his mouth. Her eyes hadn't experienced the burden of viewing her own body yet. Based on the expressions Vinny failed to hide in the shower and the shock that gripped Otis, it must be ghastly.

"Don't you want to know?" Sasha was almost begging for his permission to let it all out. No one had asked. They didn't want to know, become saddled with her heavy load.

Otis closed Sasha's robe, his trembling hands cupping her cheeks. "Of course I want to know, but—"

"They locked me in a dark cell." Sasha clutched onto Otis's shirt, as if that could transfer her pain into his body. "They kept me dosed on LSD, told me *I* was Ellen."

It all came out. Every detail she could remember tumbled from her mouth. The rats that ate her in the dark, the metal cot that ripped away her skin, how she allowed her mind to break in the shadows. Otis didn't say a word. He just held her tight, kissed her forehead when the shivers turned to quakes. Once the entire nightmare left her brain to hang in the air, she waited. Any second now, a magic switch should click and everything would get better. Any fucking second now.

Sasha leaned back, looking Otis in the eyes. There was nothing in his stare that could piece together her shattered soul, make her whole again.

"I usually know exactly what to do, but goddamn Sasha, you really stumped me this time."

A chuckle lifted a fraction of her pain, and she wiped the tears from her eyes. "You can start with a joint."

Otis smiled, reaching into his pocket. "I got ya, girl."

***

Dez

"I'm going up there," Dez said, heading for the stairs.

"Why?" Vinny asked, hurrying to block his path. "You don't trust Otis?"

"He's probably up there grilling her for info, breaking her down."

"Otis would never hurt Sasha. She's a lot stronger than you think. You just don't know her as well as we do."

"I forgot," Dez lifted his arms at his sides, backing away, "you're the Sasha expert."

Vinny snickered, shaking his head. "I'm sorry, Dez, but as soon as she's better I'm stealing her back from you."

"Excuse me!"

Tyler looked over from the couch, and Dez forced his fists to unclench. Beating his brother's face, here, right now, would only destroy the scraps of love Sasha held for him. He knew it. The smirk on Vinny's face told him that asshole knew it too, which had to be the motive behind this baiting session.

Dez took a step toward Vinny, and Vinny crossed his arms all smug-like, pretty much asking for a punch. Rage surged but Dez choked it down, attempting a soft glare. "If we start fighting over her, we'll both lose her."

"I won't share Sasha, not anymore."

"Ha! Awesome." Dez plopped his ass at the kitchen table, lighting a cigarette. He had absolutely nothing to worry about. Sasha hated being smothered and loved the ladies. Any dude who wouldn't share her was doomed. He'd learned that the hard way. "Do your thing, asshole. You'll chase her away faster than a coyote empties a henhouse. You're the one who doesn't know her very well. She can't be owned, not by a man."

Vinny's jaw dropped but cocky words failed to flow. Only a bastard would be happy to see his little brother look so crushed, which must make Dez a bastard because he was ecstatic.

Dez's bedroom door creaked open, and Otis walked out. The man looked like he just left a room full of ghosts, with his pale complexion and the way he raced down the stairs. Dez jumped up from his chair, damn near chasing Otis as he made a beeline for the front door.

"Hey!" Dez called out, knocking Otis's hand from the doorknob. "What happened?"

Otis rubbed his brow, but his wide eyes only grew wider. "She's gonna be fine. Just treat her like normal. The more you spark the fires inside her, the faster it'll burn that shit from her brain."

"So what, I should go up there and start a fight with her?" Dez asked, hating himself for actually liking the idea. He'd do it. He'd do anything to glimpse that flare in her eyes.

"You don't have to be a dick," Otis said, opening the door. "Just don't be a pussy."

Dez leaned back as Otis stormed into the hall, slamming the door behind him. "I ain't no fucking pussy," he muttered, and Vinny shrugged.

***

Sasha

Sasha crept toward the mirror. The bandages on her feet rustled the carpet, blocking the soft fibers from tickling her toes. She'd stolen glances but hadn't full-on gawked at herself, until now. Her face wasn't as bad as she expected. It only looked like someone took hedge clippers to her cheek and not a chainsaw, which is what it felt like. Although her mind screamed no, her eyes wanted to see more.

She reached for the knot of her robe when the door creaked open behind her. In the mirror's edge, she glimpsed a little head poke inside then a big goofy smile.

"Tyler." Sasha spun from the mirror, and Tyler crept into the room.

"Mama? Is that you?"

"Yeah, baby." Sasha rushed forward and Tyler scurried back, crashing against the wall. The fright in the boy's eyes rooted her in place. A shredded face on a ghost mom was definitely the worst thing a person could see, this she knew.

While slipping her bandaged fingers inside the sleeves of her robe, she knelt down. "Can I hug you?"

Tyler ran into Sasha's arms, nearly toppling her to the ground. His tiny body pressed against her own, and the horrors wiped from her mind. "My baby." She pulled Tyler onto her lap, the warmth of his very essence overshadowing any pain his weight caused.

"Have you been scrapin'?" Tyler asked, running his little finger along a wide gash on Sasha's cheek. "You look like you been scrapin'."

Sasha tore her lips from Tyler's head long enough to say, "Scrapin'?"

"I went to a huge farm." Tyler pulled back from Sasha's tight hug, holding a serious glare. "Uncle

Kev put me in a big hole in the ground with a mask man, but there was a TV so it wasn't all bad. I met uncle Kev's mama and she knew you, said you was a scraper."

A long chuckle rolled from Sasha's chest, taking about ten pounds of hurt with it. "Sounds like you had one hell of an adventure."

"Yeah. Is that what happened to you too?"

It could've been. Every horrid memory, for her entire life, fell under a cloak of warm fuzz the instant Tyler's body snuggled into her arms. All her thoughts went to him. She needed to know him, wanted to hear the crazy shit he babbled on about.

"Yeah, little dude. That's exactly what happened to me."

Sasha planted her lips atop Tyler's head, and that's where they stayed the entire time as he rambled on about some guitar.

The End

Epilogue

Sasha walked into the Pink Kitty, and the half-naked hostess hurried forward to shove those big tits in her face. A fifty to the cleavage got Sasha a tongue down the throat and an escort to her favorite stool at the end of the bar. For the past week, this strip club had been her sanctuary. It was the only place where large men who could knock her ass out and toss her in a cell if they so wished didn't surround her. There was no threat in here. Just beautiful women, fragile creatures circling a pole. She could drop every one of these bitches with ease, which brought on a sense of security. It almost let her believe she was Sasha Lazzari.

"Back again," the brunette who liked hairspray a bit too much whispered in Sasha's ear. "You here for me?"

Actually, Sasha had come for the blonde twirling around the pole, but this one would do. "I sure am, sunshine."

The chick giggled. City girls always giggled at her accent. She cringed at theirs. A hand landed on

Sasha's thigh and she flinched, almost scaring the stripper off.

"Your man, or your daddy?" the chick asked, sitting on the stool beside Sasha.

"What?"

"Someone worked you over. A girl only lets her man or her daddy hurt her that much."

That sounded about right. Add a devious mother to the mix and this stripper would be right on the money. Big surprise.

"Maybe I did this to myself."

"No, you didn't." The woman snickered, eyeing the scabs that peeked above Sasha's low hanging tank top. "I have a little something that'll help with the...jumpiness. You want to take me to the champagne room?"

"Sure."

After shelling out five hundred bucks, Sasha followed a curvy ass up the stairs to a private room of couches. The chick pushed Sasha on a loveseat, hopped in her lap, then pulled a small paper pouch from her boot. While riding Sasha slow, she scooped a pile of white powder into her long pinky nail.

"No coke for me," Sasha said. "I've got enough trouble sleeping."

"It's not coke. It's china, H."

"Heroin?" Sasha asked, slanting back.

"Yeah."

Sasha shook her head, pushing the chick's hand away. "I don't shoot."

"You don't have to shoot, just take a little toot," she said through a smirk, snorting the powder up her nose. The second she inhaled, her body went loose and her thin bikini top came off.

"What does it do to you?" Sasha asked, leaning into the hard nipples that rubbed against her chest.

"It makes me forget my daddy kept me locked in a closet for ten years to rape me whenever he wanted."

That was pretty fucking hardcore. If that junk could make this girl forget all that and let her feel a hint of the ecstasy her face displayed, it might be worth a try. After all, how much harm could one hit do?

Acknowledgements

Blood and Tears is a difficult story to get through, much like most lives, which is why I'd like to acknowledge anyone who has ever suffered from abuse. Abuse victims carry their trauma with them every second of every day, strengthening their reflexes yet weakening their souls. To everyone who has suffered the injustices of hate, please know you are strong, beautiful, and a survivor.

About the Author

Jamie Zakian lives in South Jersey with a rowdy bunch of dudes, also known as family. A YA/NA writer, her head is often in the clouds while her ears are covered in headphones. On the rare occasions when not writing, she enjoys blazing new trails on her 4wd quad or honing her archery skills. She's a card carrying member of the Word Nerd Association, which means she's probably stalking every Twitter writing competition and offering query critiques so keep an eye out.

Twitter:
https://twitter.com/demoness333

Website:
http://www.jamiezakian.com/